THE
SHIPBUILDER
OF BELLFAIRIE

Also by M. Rickert

NOVELS

The Memory Garden (as Mary Rickert)

COLLECTIONS

Map of Dreams
Holiday
You Have Never Been Here (as Mary Rickert)

NOVELETTES AND NOVELLAS

Cold Fires
Map of Dreams
Journey Into the Kingdom
The Mothers of Voorhisville (as Mary Rickert)
The Little Witch

The Shipbuilder of Bellfairie

M. RICKERT

UNDERTOW
PUBLICATIONS

THE SHIPBUILDER OF BELLFAIRIE

Undertow Publications. Pickering, ON Canada

✦

For Bill, because you brought me balloons when my first
story was published, tissues and new pajamas when my first
(still unpublished) novel was rejected, and told me I needed
to send this one out into the world.

✦

Advance Praise for *The Shipbuilder of Bellfairie*

"Awash in sea rain, ghosts and the stories they trail, the sound of submerged bells from offshore (or their echo, or their memory), Bellfairie and its denizens are M. Rickert creations through and through—meaning magical, mournful, mysterious, profoundly human."

— Glen Hirshberg, Author of *The Motherless Children* Trilogy

"*The Shipbuilder of Bellfairie* is a dark, dream-like, psychologically astute novel about the outsider as threat and victim, about the power of crowds, and the betrayal of innocence, replete with uncanny secrets, signs, and symbols that echo and reverberate, intimations of an unseen, sublunary world."

— Douglas Glover, Author of *Elle*, and *Savage Love*

"Fans of M. Rickert's singular blend of the mundane and the monstrous will be drawn deep into the briny, haunted world of Bellfairie."

— Sofia Samatar, Author of *A Stranger in Olondria*, and *Tender*

"*The Shipbuilder of Bellfairie* by M. Rickert is a powerful evocation of an imaginary place, both magical and mundane; the tribulations of a good hearted hapless giant; and a compelling mystery. Dark and humorous and deep."

— Jeffrey Ford, Author of *Big Dark Hole*

THE
SHIPBUILDER
OF BELLFAIRIE

The true poem is the poet's mind;
the true ship is the ship-builder.
In the man, could we lay him open,
we should see the reason for the
last flourish and tendril of his work.
   – Ralph Waldo Emerson

What emptiness do you gaze upon!
Do you not feel a thrill passing through the air
with the notes of the far-away song
floating from the other shore?
   – Rabindranath Tagore

· 1 ·

The people of Bellfairie still speak of that last morning in the diner, how everyone was struck motionless with egg on their lips and coffee on their tongues, unprepared to offer solace to the giant sitting in their midst with his hands cupped over his face. And what was that noise? That strange sound, as though he held a baby bird in his palms that cried for its mother?

Weeping, they finally realized. Who could imagine? A grown man weeping like that?

They tried to make amends that very evening, arriving at his house with casseroles and beer kegs, but somehow it had not been enough. Who knows why? They expressed regret and asked forgiveness yet awoke, with hangovers, to the dismal news of his death wondering if, in their resolve for justice, they had contributed to a store of despair that could not be survived.

Later, after it was reported he'd left behind disturbing arti-facts like that bizarre sculpture made of bones, every house-hold received a letter in the mail with the word 'sorry' scrawled several times in black ink above his signature. They buried his apology under the coffee grounds and other garbage. The fact that Coral's wedding—planned well in advance—coincided with his funeral, was mere coincidence, and there had been so much sorrow by that point, who can blame them for choosing joy instead?

Some say if you walk on the bluff in the early morning,

when the fog hovers there, you will hear a baby cry. Others argue there is no infant ghost, only him, sentenced to call from the depths for all eternity as penance for what he did. The rest claim it is nothing so mysterious, just the ordinary shriek of hungry seagulls.

· 2 ·

H is name was Quark, and the worst thing he ever did was nothing at all. When the call about the Old Man came, it pulsated through the years, not in the pleasant manner of a star, but in the persistent, grievous one of a migraine. And why not? Why wouldn't he compare his entire life to the headache he experienced driving that familiar aorta of desolation to Bellfairie?

"Missing? What do you mean he's missing?" Quark asked, pressing the phone close to his ear as if the late hour had affected his hearing. "Is this a joke?"

But of course it wasn't. Sheriff Healy wasn't the joking sort.

"A confession?" Quark asked. "Do you mean an apology?"

He peered through the Ford's bug-splattered window into the gray dawn, but all he could remember—after the question—was the buzzing as if, through some strange night magic, he heard the reverberation of his existence, that dark persistent screed.

It was true the Old Man could be cruel, once tying an apron to the boy's pants, knotting yellow flowered fabric on the loop meant for a belt. Quark, who enjoyed the feel of material draped behind him, began spinning, his arms raised towards the ceiling, fingers spread and head tilted back like someone nearly drowned who, just in the nick of time, broke surface.

"What are ya? Some kinda fag?" the Old Man taunted.

13

Hunched over the steering wheel, Quark peered through the dark until it was broken by a snakelike fissure of dawn, reminding him of the rain that violent night so long ago, windows lashed until they were streaked with silver like iridescent worms. He recalled an oily smell, the waxy scent of crayons scattered across the table where he sat clutching the purple in his fist. The Old Man, who had been weaving through the house as though stranded on a rough sea, suddenly paused to set the plate down on top of Quark's drawing. Fried fish, lapped near the edge, as if seeking escape.

Quark, the man, recalled the boy's hesitation; crayon held tight before it was dropped. How old was he? Seven? Eight?

Maybe he was eight that night he abandoned his fanciful bird on the wooden plank table etched by knives. Time was lost after that first bite and the one he remembered next, bone drawn between his teeth then carefully placed on his plate— not tossed, but assembled—when he became aware he was being watched. He feared that to comment on the attention would destroy it. Instead, he sucked the last flakes of oily flesh, and set the translucent sliver neatly amongst the rest.

"What ya got there, boy?"

"Catfish," he said, proud.

"Thought it was a ship," the Old Man growled, turning away.

"That's what it is." Quark rearranged his sculpture. "These are waves, see?"

"Yah said 'catfish' din' ya?"

"It's the name of my ship."

"Are you a liar too?" The Old Man swept his hand across the table, scattering bones, sending papers aloft, crayons tumbling.

Quark gripped the steering wheel, no longer that boy who fell asleep brushing fingers over his scarred flesh, marveling at the pain of transformation, awakening the next morning, to stare out the small window, scanning the sky for birds before tiptoeing barefoot down creaking stairs, across the wooden floor littered with debris into the kitchen where he lit the oil lamp that awakened winged shadows. So young, he had to stand on a chair to reach the faucet and the stove where he stirred coffee grounds in water to boil while the stars outside the small round window disappeared into dawn. When he leaned over to turn off the burner, the heat brushed against his stomach, reminding him of his pet cat gone missing. She used to lie on his belly and keep him warm.

He cracked an egg into the bowl. Fished out the bits. Beat yolk and white with a fork. Measured it out with a teaspoon—unsure of the amount—then pulled the chair back to the sink where he filled two mugs before turning them over, watching the hot water spiral down the drain. He spilled some of the coffee as he poured it through the filter, which he quickly mopped up with a dish towel. It created a reddish-brown stain he didn't like, so he thrust it into the trash.

The Old Man was sitting in his chair, staring out the big front window when Quark approached with trembling mugs, unsure how to proceed. "Take it," he said, surprised when the command worked.

He set his own mug on the small table, cautious not to disturb the clutter of pencils, pens, maps and sextant, especially alert to the leather-bound journal in which the Old Man was writing his shipbuilding book, rarely seen since the time Quark had been caught brushing his fingers across the cover.

He returned to the kitchen for the chair he dragged (tearing papers and breaking bones) to position beside the Old Man. Together they stared at the oak trees clustered around the house, sentinels Quark once believed guarded against danger. He raised the cup to his lips, flinched against the heat, and sipped. It was his first taste of coffee. Bitter, he didn't like it, and that seemed right.

· 3 ·

Even though he knew well how the road banked around the bluff, distracting drivers, Quark was enchanted by the initial appearance of sun-washed buildings nestled amongst boulders before beginning his descent. When Bellfairie reappeared, the pristine palette of turquoise and white was replaced by murky water dotted with spinach-hued clots and buildings so long in disrepair only a few chips of color remained: a streak of mustard yellow, a smear of green, half a wall painted salmon ruined by abandonment.

He sighed as he entered the narrow, labyrinthine streets lined by dismal houses with withered plants in clay pots perched on sagging porches or cracked concrete stairs as if awaiting revival. Miniature domiciles, meant to provide shelter for birds, dangled from rusty hooks crookedly affixed to broken fences. Weathered bird feeders, hung from poles in almost every barren yard, were filled with seeds and suet. Perseverance, in almost any circumstance an attribute, fed off Bellfairie like a tumor. If the bleak atmosphere wasn't proof enough of such malignancy, surely that slender figure, traipsing down the side of the road, was. Quark slowed to reach across the passenger seat and roll down his window.

Dressed all in black, Henry Yarly had taken this walk every morning Quark could remember. A devil worshipper, some said, who sacrificed the missing cats of Bellfairie—the lost pets of his childhood—though the Old Man spit when Quark once posited this theory.

"My ass. Devil worshipper, my ass. Don't you kids know? Saying Henry Yarly is a devil worshipper's like calling your elbow a dick. You can tell your friends I said."

Without looking to see who slowed beside him, Yarly raised his hand, ring and pinky finger half bent, thumb angled in, a cross between Boy Scout salute and benediction.

"Hello. How are you, Mr. Yarly?"

Quark checked the road ahead as he eased into neutral. When he turned back, the man was grinning, affable as an egg.

"Is it you? Is it really you?"

Quark scratched the back of his neck.

"It's good you came," Yarly said in an uncertain tone. "Don't mind the scuttlebutt, okay son? You ain't dead and Thayer ain't either, am I right?"

Confused, Quark nodded. Why he was bothering to behave falsely, he had no idea, though he recognized a trait that always seemed pronounced in Bellfairie, the need to guard against revelation.

"Where you off to?"

"I thought I would stop at Nell's before proceeding with my day."

"Yah, you don't know, do you? She sold it after her son was kilt in the war. Cut his head right off."

"Wayne?"

"Right off. You can watch it on the computer, if you want. Why anyone would, I have no idea."

For a while Wayne had been Quark's friend, a skinny blond boy who grew into a handsome lad possessed of an easy attitude. Bellfairie fell into despair when he was reported missing, all those years ago, the summer they were twelve. Quark, who hadn't played with him for a long time by then, sat on the rocks and wept, which might have been fodder for mockery had not everyone been similarly affected. When Wayne triumphantly returned, reportedly sailing home in an old bathtub with oars he'd stolen from his father's woodshop, they had a celebration where he sat as head of the long table, his golden curls a halo in the candlelight, the Bellfairian bounty set before him—bruised oysters in half shells, mussels and clams stacked in wooden bowls with wedges of lime and lemon, platters of roasted corn and red potatoes dripping in butter—regaling them with the story of how, swept far out to sea, he heard the voice of the dead and was not afraid, at which point everyone paused to cross themselves. Where had he really gone, Quark asked, years later when they worked at the restaurant together, momentarily anointed by Wayne's smile before he turned away without answering.

"Didn't mean to shake you up, son. You two would be round the same age, am I right?"

Quark swatted the air, as if it didn't matter.

"Nell tried to keep it going but she was all adrift, burnt the fries, lost the payroll, one thing after the other like that, so she called it quits. She and Seamus still live up on the hill, and he still does his woodwork. Some inlanders bought it and called it a...watchamugger? A Sue she place? You can guess how that went. After they left, Dory bought it. Don't worry about the sign. She just never got around to a new one. Menu the same as Nell's. They tell me. I don't have much occasion to go there, myself."

Quark couldn't say if the sudden exhaustion he felt was brought on by the shock of Wayne's death, the long ride through the night, the weight of not knowing where the Old Man was, or simply being back in Bellfairie with its over-whelming atmosphere of decay.

"I will eat breakfast before I talk to Sheriff Healy. Do you need a ride?" Quark grimaced when he realized his mistake.

Yarly shook his head no, as if responding to an ordinary question.

Quark considered an apology, but decided it was probably best not to make a big deal out of it. He raised his hand in a goodbye salute, and continued down Seaside Lane. *No other place like it*, he thought. Though admittedly, he had not traveled widely. Bellfairie's salty air nipped the tired muscles of his face, the ocean scent imbued, for as long as he could remember, with a stench like bilge water, the source of which he had never been able to identify.

Scent of ghosts, he thought and almost missed his turn down Avalon, going too fast for that dip in the road which, over the years, had only grown deeper. Naturally, nothing was done about it. To the citizens of Bellfairie a pothole was a matter of terrain, not a problem with a simple remedy but the inevitable erosion—impossible to combat—of life.

If Bellfairie had a main street, Avalon, where the buildings leaned away from the ocean's greedy maw, was it. Whenever Quark remembered it that way, he thought he must be exaggerating, but as he parked his truck he noted that the buildings clearly maintained a tilt. Even the flag jutted from its post office perch at a precariously low angle, its red and white fringed edge dangling above the ground. Only the bronze statue of the Birdman, aged to a blue-green patina, seemed unaffected by the pull inland, his arms stretched straight to the sky, talons spread wide to receive the seagulls that perched there and on the wings, ignoring Quark.

I should leave, he thought.

He reached to roll up the window, but stopped. Even with loose change right in the open, there was no need to worry about petty theft in Bellfairie, which was one of the town's few charms. His legs stiff from such a long ride, he eased out of the driver's seat and stood, rattling keys like a gambler with dice, taking in Bellfairie's dismal remains, library and post office (their shared crooked stairs splattered with white drippings of seagull scat) the old dime store with a For Sale sign taped to its dusty window, the Brass Lantern, out of which, he imagined, its last rum-soaked patron stumbled at about the same time Quark looked down on the village from that height where it seemed like a place someone might want to come back to.

Bellfairie was named after the doomed ship on which it was founded. Crashed on the rocks, she sank with her cargo of bells that still rang from the depths. The survivors decided to stay, using ship remnants for lumber. This, the Old Man said, made the sea angry. "She is unforgiving," he used to rant. "No one was meant to live."

The ground had a magnetic quality, that's what folks claimed. It brought ships to the rocky shore, held fog close, and pulled the moon so near that on some nights the whole town appeared inhabited by ghosts. Quark thought if he wasn't careful, he'd be stuck forever, standing by his truck, shaking keys like a death rattle. Hunched against the salty chill, he headed towards what used to be Nell's with its absurd sign, "Sushi Palace."

The bell above the door might have been the same that announced arrivals all those years ago when he worked there as a dishwasher. The booths were still rust-colored, but the tables were covered with red cloth, which he guessed were left over from Sushi's, as was the gold sea dragon hanging on the far wall where a fishnet had draped for so long. To his relief the old counter remained, a slab of teak said to have been used as a lifeboat by shipwreck survivors, lined with bar stools and topped with silver napkin dispensers at reasonable intervals. People in Bellfairie liked their personal space.

Quark was aware of an abrupt stillness settling on the place while he wiped his feet. Customers nudged each other, and jutted chins in his direction as he shuffled through the diner with his head lowered, a posture refined as soon as he was old enough to realize his size made others uncomfortable. He thought he heard someone whisper the old epithet, but quickly reassured himself it was imagined. After all, he was no longer taunted by boys.

Too late, already sliding onto the stool, he recognized the sheriff sitting one seat over. Not that Quark had anything to hide; he just wasn't prepared for serious conversation. The sheriff, absorbed in drinking his coffee, nodded and raised his finger to signal a passing waitress for more. She filled his cup and, without waiting for instructions, did the same for Quark, leaning close enough that he could easily read the nametag crookedly affixed to her uniform.

"What ya havin' this mornin'?" Dory asked, her tone pleasant, her face placid. *Well, a person must get used to sailing smoothly along if she is named after a boat,* Quark thought, chuckling, and she glanced at the sheriff.

Quark looked down, pleased to see the menu still featured the old classics. He tapped number five. Dory twisted her neck to see.

"Traditional or Belgium?"

Belgium? Belgium? He resisted an impulse to shake his head. "American."

"Belgium are the fat ones, kinda like cake. Traditional are thin and crisp."

He waved his hand, as if it didn't matter. "Traditional." Dory nodded and walked away, her gait plodding with a limp, which reminded him of a girl he once knew.

"Quark? It's Quark, isn't it?" the sheriff asked. "Good of you to come."

Taken aback, just as he had lifted his coffee cup, Quark caused a little spill. "You can't do anything right," he heard the Old Man grumble, though this was obviously imagined.

"You know how he can be to reason with. Like flogging a dead horse." The sheriff shook his head. "Kept sayin there was no need to bother ya. Kept sayin he was fine."

Quark tugged a reluctant napkin from the dispenser to wipe up the mess.

"Just wanted to keep him from harm. Nick Rogers...can you believe that name? Sounds like his folks were expecting him to be a comic book character, don't it? Anyhow it went to shit when Rogers got involved."

The sheriff stood and removed his wallet from his back pocket to extract a dollar bill he tucked beside his plate, cleaned of any evidence of the meal that had been there.

"Didn't think you'd make it, son." He slapped a heavy hand on Quark's shoulder. "But since you're here, you should probably come to the courthouse. Scheduled for nine. Don't expect much to come of it, but it'll be good for you to make an appearance."

Quark couldn't think of anything to say and, after a moment, the sheriff left, which was a relief. It wasn't long before the waitress returned with his order. He hadn't eaten a number five in years. The Old Man loved them too, Quark recalled, stabbing through the sauce to the American waffle beneath, cutting harshly, eager to taste the oysters in sherried cream, surprised when tears came to his eyes, happy no one noticed.

You could leave, he thought.

By the time Dory poured a refill, which was bitter and slightly burnt, just the way he liked it, Quark felt better. He glanced down the counter, looking for the discarded newspapers that used to litter the place, but all that remained of their once quintessential presence was something called *Bridal Bliss*.

"You don't recognize me, do ya?" the waitress asked.

He willed his lips into what he hoped was a convivial smile before he saw it, the perpetually distressed countenance of—

"Doris. Doris Lehart. Kindall now."

Quark struggled against an onslaught of memory, the face of the girl he'd known buried within the woman's flesh. "Tony?" he asked, certain he misunderstood. Even in Bellfairie such a union was not possible. "You married Tony?"

"That's right." She moved to give Quark a refill he blocked with his hand. "Thought I was seeing a ghost when you walked in."

He shivered.

Dory graced him with her crooked smile before moving on to attend to other customers, returning only long enough to slap his tab on the counter. He set two dollars beside his plate, double what he'd have left if he hadn't known her as Dolly Lehart with her collection of dirty stuffed animals she pulled in an old red wagon with a loose lug nut or, much later, as Whoredore. That's what they called her. He cut a sharp look and, all the way at the far end of the counter, in the midst of pouring, she turned to gaze at him. He added another dollar then, worried it was obvious he was trying to assuage his guilt, considered taking it back, thought better, and walked to the cash register where he waited to pay his bill.

A few words drifted from the gray-haired couple at a nearby table, the man intently drinking his coffee, the woman in her Bellfairie sweater leaning over a yolk-smeared plate. "Missing," she said, "probably dead." The man clicked his tongue which caused the woman to sit back so abruptly she knocked over a salt shaker. Right then the cash register rang. Quark turned to pay the girl who didn't look old enough to be out of school, but what did he know of such things?

"Are you on holiday?" he asked, handing her a ten.

She snorted, counting his change before answering. "That's right. It's all a holiday now. Fun times." When she closed the drawer he saw she was pregnant which, for some reason, made him blush. To make matters worse he tipped his imaginary hat at her and left Sushi Palace with the girl's smirk embedded in his mind. She had dark hair, pale skin, and deeply red lips. Like Snow White.

He spent the short drive from restaurant to his childhood home trying to remember the old fairy tale she reminded him of, but it kept getting mixed up in his mind, which created a disturbing montage, cartoon-like in its horror. *How did she die? She fell asleep, right? No, that doesn't make sense. She ate something first, didn't she? A pomegranate? But before all that, she was given a golden necklace, fashioned by dwarves in exchange for sleeping with them, right?*

The game of distraction served its purpose. When Quark turned onto the old drive he felt magically transported, memories lurking along the way undisturbed until he was confronted by evidence of the reason for his extended absence. White stones glinted and glared beneath the morning sun, unhindered by what remained of those once-great sentinels reduced to jagged stumps. Without trees the house looked naked and, even sheltered in his truck, Quark felt exposed.

He imagined snow falling from a metallic Bellfairie sky, flakes drifting to the ground, covering dirt, cracks, peeled paint and mismatched pots, all of Bellfairie smote by an icy benevolence, even that girl lying in her open coffin, hands folded over her great belly, metamorphosed into a pleasant slope of white, a gentle hill of sleeping beauty.

With a sigh, he spun the steering wheel, rumbling fifty feet down the drive before realizing he had a flat. He did not kick the tire or hurl stones as the Old Man would have. Instead, Quark shoved his hands into his pockets and hunched his shoulders against the chill for the short walk back into town, following the blue cobblestone road he used to believe was the revealed spine of a buried dragon, his head bowed as though the sky sank into his massive shoulders, his limbs molten, every step a lunge.

· 4 ·

H e didn't even remember his mother, but when the judge cited Thayer's murder confession (with all the gravitas of noting a shopping list) and named her as victim, Quark gasped as if sucker-punched, stunned until he realized—too late—everyone was standing. He rose under the bailiff's pointed glare, for a moment afraid he would be indicted in this mess, but the judge simply turned away, disappearing through a door behind her desk.

He had long suspected it, hadn't he? Ever since Thayer brought home that albatross with blood dripping from her breast, presenting it like something beautiful, Quark had feared the Old Man's brutality. Where would she have gone, so mysteriously vanished that there was no real explanation, only odd stories about her returning to the sea? What was it the Old Man used to say? "Your mother left puddles, not footprints."

Rogers (surprisingly toothy and freckled) left without acknowledging Quark's presence, but the other attorney approached him with her head tilted as if she needed to make the adjustment in order to accommodate his stature. Better at mimicry than innovation in any social interaction, Quark resisted the impulse to tilt his own head. When she extended her small hand, he concentrated not to squeeze too hard.

"I'm Coral. Glad you came."

"What did he do to her?" Quark asked, only realizing how

harsh he sounded as she leaned back, eyes wide. Familiar with the way strangers misread his appearance—his extraordinary height, protruding brow and aggressive chin—he relaxed into a slump. "The sheriff didn't say anything about murder."

"No. He wouldn't."

Quark felt as if he had been clenching something in his heart, something thorny and dark which, upon release, became effervescent. He'd misunderstood! Of course he had. The Old Man wasn't capable—

"Only Rogers," she said. "And I don't think even he really believes it. It's just ridiculous. Almost everyone knows Thayer suffers from dementia. You heard the judge. She was pissed, right? Quark? It's Quark, isn't it? I'm sure this is a great deal to process but you might want to check your attitude. A lot of people have been watching out for him for quite some time. Did you know he stayed with Sheriff Healy for a while?"

"I did not."

"I'm sorry, but I have to go. I have another appointment. I'm getting married. We should talk. Here's my card."

"You're getting married today?"

"Cake tasting. Call if you think of anything, okay?" She sidled, crab-like, between the pews. "I hope you aren't planning to shove off. I think he'll need you when he finally shows up."

Quark resisted the impulse to shake his head no. "Yes," he said, he would stay "at the old homestead."

She paused with her small hand on the massive door, rumored to have once been a decorative panel of the doomed ship captain's private chambers, elaborately carved with petrels, gulls, whimbrels and moonbirds.

"Everyone knows what happened. Everyone knows how she died. Everyone knows her body washed out to sea. My cousin, twice-removed, remembers Thayer walking the bluffs. She used to call him the crying man." Coral smiled before opening the door, momentarily flooding the room with that

Bellfairie air—briny, sweet and fetid, the scent of rotten eggs with clams in a bed of sea salt and fennel.

Behind the judge's chair hung a painting of pelicans, the largest striking her own breast with her beak. Quark hadn't thought about the old story in years, how the mother pierced her flesh to feed the starving young; meant to convey the sacrifice of parental love. On Sunday someone would drape a cloth over the frame, and replace gavel with chalice, transforming the space from courthouse to chapel. He thought of dropping to his knees but couldn't figure out what he'd do next. Clearly the notion was reflective of his exhaustion. He flicked the lights off on his way out the door which, in Bellfairie fashion, he left unlocked.

Though Quark found the idea of going back to the house for a nap appealing, he walked in the opposite direction, surprised to discover how much he enjoyed the pull in his quadriceps that the sharp incline engendered, determined not to believe he'd missed Bellfairie or fallen for the attorney's false compassion. Where was all that concern when he had been a tormented child, so afraid he took shelter in branches and graveyard, behind boulders on the shore, amongst the birds and dead and drowned? Where was the zeal for justice then?

Quark longed for the clarity of his work: the small bones awaiting excavation, the delicate balance of preservation and decay, his quiet room filled with shadows beyond the orb of light that guided knife and needle. He had struggled to find his way in the world far from Bellfairie, and never once regretted leaving. Was he now expected to search for the Old Man? Why? What was he supposed to do with him, once found?

· 5 ·

"Y ou haven't been around, son. I'm just sayin'. Nobody blames ya. What you need to understand is, it's not like anybody believes him. Except Rogers who's too green to be taken seriously. Especially once you showed up. I mean, it's obvious."

Quark shifted against the confines of the small chair, the windows were inexplicably closed and the atmosphere stifling. "I'd like to see it." He felt he shouldn't have to explain. After all, this was his own father they were talking about, this was his life.

The sheriff sighed as he lifted his feet off the desk to thumb through a stack of papers. When he didn't find what he was looking for he turned to rifle through the file folders on the cluttered shelf, mumbling about "this damn mess."

Quark couldn't fathom working in such disorder. *What else is lost*, he wondered.

"Ok. Here it is. I suppose you know he was my guest. Stayed in the room off the kitchen. One morning I wake up and he's gone. Left this on the bed. You can understand the situation I was in. I had to read it, but are you sure you wanna?"

Quark took the paper. *Imagine, that such a flimsy thing could cause so much trouble!*

Healy, apparently unable to neglect an opportunity for investigation any more than Quark could pass by a small animal without considering its skeletal structure, leaned back to watch.

"I did not get much sleep last night," Quark said to explain his trembling hand.

Comes a time when a man can no longer avoid settling accounts. This is my confession. My ma said I had unnatural eyes. Quark does too. His little dark eyes like roe. Even when he was no more than a nipper he looked at me like he knew what I'd done. Do you ever ask how a man goes out on a ship with six souls and returns alone? What is survival? In that dark time when rats jump ship, choices are made. You probably know what you will do. You will be a hero. Am I right? It is easy to believe you will be brave. I thought it of myself. I was a captain who would go down with the ship. I was a captain who would die saving everyone. Their screams never stop. They started that night and never end. I can't escape them. I would have died if not for that horse. I thought it was a nightmare until it swam close and I grabbed hold and climbed atop. Riding to hell. When I smelled the oranges I thought it was the scent of death. Yes, it is true, I found my wife there, but the sea never forgets.

Where is Quark? I look everywhere for that boy but he doesn't return. I know why. I fully confess I killed him with my fists. He used to glow like a lantern, always watching with his light. I killed his mother too, and loved her so. I killed that albatross for him. So he could be free. We are all cursed, don't you know? He told me I was the devil when I cut down his trees, and I laughed. What am I? I am a poor shipbuilder weak in the waterways. I spread broken glass on the drive to keep away the spirits but they come closer and the trick won't last. What have I done? What have these hands made?

So ends this passage.

Quark pretended he was still reading even as he felt his cheeks turn red, the telltale give-away of the flash of emotions he could not contain. For the first time he wondered if the Old

Man's precious shipbuilding book was nothing but incoherent ramblings. When Quark finally looked up it was into Healy's gaze direct as an old dog's, watching, waiting, patient and intense.

"I am not dead, am I? Clearly he was speaking...what's that word? Something like a lie? He didn't really kill me, obviously. He did spread broken glass over the road, however. I got a flat."

The sheriff leaned forward, hand extended to take the paper. "Well, you know that's a private drive. It's not municipal business."

"I'm not saying—" Quark caught himself. Took a deep breath. "I can't believe anyone is taking this seriously."

"Well, son, mostly I agree. Most everyone does. The judge agrees, which is a good thing all around. But now there is that issue, you know."

"What issue?"

Sheriff Healy frowned and leaned back, his eyes steady on Quark's face. "What do you remember about your mother?"

"Nothing."

"You must have some memories."

"I do not. How could I? I was a baby when she died."

"You were eight."

"I was—What?"

"Have it right here." The sheriff tapped the open folder on his desk.

Quark shook his head. "You've made a mistake."

Healy tapped the page. "Eight."

Quark felt his jaw drop.

"People tell me he was hard on you, son. Nobody blames you for staying away so long, but if there's anything you been too afraid to tell—"

"No." He shook his head. "No, no, no."

It took several beats before he regained control, and by then it was too late; the sheriff was appraising Quark like someone reconsidering a purchase.

"Well, all right, then," Healy said and cocked his fingers into a gun. "Just keep in mind. If you recall anything—even a small thing—you come tell me about it. You'd be surprised what I can do with a clue. I know how things used to be around here. I know about Bellfairie so-called justice. It's not like that anymore, all right? You come to me, if you remember something."

"I will be sure to notify you if I recall anything."

"In the meantime, don't give up the ship. Everyone's looking. He's probably just sleeping off a bender somewhere."

Quark found himself tipping his hat as he made a hasty exit. It was a cool day, the sort of chill that went to the bones. In the distance, he heard the metallic clang against mast that filled him with longing. He decided to leave. It wouldn't be as if he were abandoning the Old Man. Not really. No one was abandoned in Bellfairie. Everyone minded each other's business too much, even if no one had minded his. He shoved his hands into his pockets, awkwardly hunched into himself as he listened to the distant waves, only broken out of his reverie by the scent of chocolate that wafted from the air vents of the candy store. He stopped to study the window display of caramel apples decorated with nuts, marshmallows and rainbow-hued gummy worms. He was tired, his bones ached and how was it possible he'd forgotten his own mother?

"You really are some kind of freak," the Old Man said, more than once.

As tears rose to Quark's eyes he realized the terrible thing wasn't forgetting his mother, or even remembering the Old Man's taunts, the terrible thing was what the Old Man said only once—when he was drunk—but still.

"It don't matter what you are, boy. Don't you know I love you?"

A grown man can't cry in the middle of the street even in Bellfairie, unless at the scene of a car accident in which a loved one died, or some other irrefutably tragic occurrence. Quark dipped his head beneath the gray sky and turned down the nearest side street, immediately removed from the depressed shops and occasional baffled tourist. (No one came to Bellfairie on purpose, it was always a wrong turn in someone's life.) He walked with downcast eyes all the way back to the house where his truck remained parked on broken glass, lopsided with the deflated tire.

He stood for a long time, looking at the old homestead, but there was never any doubt, never any real doubt he would find that skeleton key beneath the rock, and enter the place he vowed never to return to. So tired, he collapsed onto the sagging couch without even pausing to remove his shoes or take in his surroundings before closing his eyes.

He would not say he was home, but that he had arrived, and he would not say he loved the Old Man, or that that the Old Man loved him, but that once he had said he did. It wasn't much, Quark knew. Probably wasn't even enough. But it's what he had. Not all his memories were bad.

· 6 ·

He dreamt the Old Man tapped him on the shoulder and said, "I'm drowning." It was a dream, not a portent, and even if it were, what did it portend? In the language of dreams everything could mean its opposite; a dream of rain foretold sunny circumstances on the horizon, a cat dream meant a dog would soon appear, and a dream of a wedding warned of a funeral unless it didn't. Dreams could be predictions, omens, mysterious clues to the shipwreck of the mind, or utter nonsense. Yet, as Quark laid there, his shoulder tingling, he wondered if the borders had been breached. Was that why he felt he was being watched? He jumped back—or what he could do while reclined—thrusting neck and shoulders into the old couch, gasping at the female figure in the corner before he recognized her for what she was, a dark-haired figurehead with bulging eyes carved from wood.

When Quark finally left Bellfairie, he rejected everything: the crooked streets that led to dead ends lined by abandoned store fronts, the rowdy sea, the language of moons, the God who spoke through weather, the old stories about shipwrecks, witches, bells, birds, and a cobblestone dragon. Still, he felt a tug of discomfort as he studied the figurehead's profile, certain there was something wrong about her presence inside the house, some curse associated with such dislocation.

He rubbed the back of his neck, assessing the surroundings he had been too tired to consider earlier. The Old Man's chair with the small, cluttered table beside it, still faced the picture window. The plank-wood table, scarred by slips of the knife, defined the dining room such as it was, beyond that was the kitchen, another little table in the corner. Between the head (tucked under the stairs) and kitchen was the Old Man's room, the door—in keeping with tradition—firmly shut.

Quark guessed he'd slept through an entire afternoon and night, evidence of an exhaustion not warranted by a single disrupted slumber. He often suffered insomnia, a trait he had inherited. Funny that the first good rest he had in weeks happened in the place of so much turmoil.

It occurred to him he could sit in the Old Man's chair. Once gold, it had aged into piss yellow, the armrest nubby. How many mornings had Thayer sat with the shipbuilding book in his lap, pencil poised, staring out the window?

A small, unidentified flutter drew Quark to peer through the early morning fog. He abandoned his seat to walk nearer to the glass. One can imagine so many things. She was only there for a moment, hovering above the shards, a woman he might have remembered. Or a Rorschach composed of mist and desire. What did it matter? What did any of it matter? She was gone.

· 7 ·

He stood at the threshold of the room cast in a tarnished light filtered through drawn drapes, the narrow bed covered with faded yellow spread. He needed something to wear. What had he been thinking to come without a change of clothes? He hadn't expected to stay more than a night. It had been impossible to believe his presence mattered. He felt a surge of terror when the floorboards squeaked as he entered the forbidden space, fearing the Old Man might come out of a dark corner roaring at the intrusion.

He considered opening the dingy curtains, but decided it would be wiser to leave no trace of trespass beyond the reasonable endeavor of looking for something to wear, searching through the closet cluttered with a tangled net, deflated ball, old boots, bulging boxes, the meager wardrobe of threadbare shirts, a rack from which hung belts made of knotted rope and—strangely—a tie. Nothing would fit correctly, of course. In spite of Thayer's domineering personality, he was a small man. When Quark opened the dresser drawers he briefly considered the dilemma of underwear, but that, he felt, was too much. He selected a pair of jeans, the kind the Old Man had always favored, baggy on him, snug on Quark, and a tattered T-shirt he suspected had once been white. He searched, in vain, for a button-down shirt with sleeves long enough to cover the scars that ensnared his arms like branches, finally settling on a flannel shirt he was unable to button, its cuffs dangling near his elbows. Once dressed, he peeked at his reflection in the spotted mirror but turned quickly away, as he usually did when confronted with his own image.

While he had tried to let go of all its nonsense after he left Bellfairie all those years ago, Quark discovered its superstitions clung to him like barnacles. He often found his rational mind in dispute with the myth-imbued reality he was raised in and, that morning, could not help but think he needed to talk to a witch. Wouldn't it all be so much easier if there was someone who knew the secret to unlocking his past and predicting the future? Wouldn't it be nice if all it took to find the missing was a charm of bone and feathers? And wasn't it actually wonderful that Bellfairie was home to someone who once upon a time had appeared to produce such magic?

Mrs. Winter had, in fact, been a frequent substitute at Our Lady of the Sea elementary school. In spite of her stature (small even to the children) she exuded a pronounced authority. When she presided, normal order was upended. Boys who usually wielded mean power were diminished under her gray gaze while Quark—transformed from fool to page—clapped chalk from erasers, retrieved things out of her reach, carried stacks of chairs to the basement for assembly. It wasn't that she was sweet to him. She wasn't sweet to anyone. Not even Nora Searers, who wore so many flowers in her curly hair she looked like a bouquet with legs (and was known to share her ample lunch with Doris Lehart) received anything more than the general courtesy Mrs. Winter delivered to all her students, apparently unaware of the trauma such equability caused.

She didn't follow lesson plans, much to the dismay of Mrs. Rallsorn whose difficult pregnancy caused frequent absences that year. (Though she always commented on how organized everything was upon her return, the chalkboard wiped until Quark could see the outline of his distressing reflection in it, trash cans emptied, papers neatly stacked, crayons sorted by color in bins at the back of the room, even the windows so thoroughly polished they had to hang charms to warn swallows away from the glass.)

Once, Mrs. Winter taught them how to cut paper snow-flakes, turning the classroom into a wonderland that—though reason told Quark wasn't possible—produced an actual snowfall to drift from some mysterious source beyond the fluorescent lights.

Another time she told them to close their eyes to make a secret wish, and that afternoon Quark walked the whole way home without harassment.

✦

But his favorite memory was when she instructed them to set aside their history books so she could tell their truestory, as she called it.

"I am sure you have all heard about the ancestor's war," she said.

Quark held very still. He knew better than to shake his head the way other children did.

"What are they teaching you?" Mrs. Winter asked.

"The shipwreck," said Doris. "That's all we know."

"The ship's wood was used for building," Nora added, "but the bells sank."

"And mussels," Quark blurted.

"Muscles?" Mrs. Winter asked.

"He means they ate mussels for their first Thanksgiving."

"And why was that?"

"Cause they taste friggin delicious," Tony said.

The children laughed but Mrs. Winter sighed. "Bobby, check the door. Make sure no one is coming."

An immediate hush settled over the room, broken by the sound of Bobby's chair scraping across the floor, and his footsteps as he walked to the door. "Ain't no one coming," he said.

"Good. Turn off the lights."

Bobby shuffled back to his desk and the children turned to Mrs. Winter with the sort of full attention other substitutes asked for but never received.

"The thing to understand," she said, "is that all life is about the stories we tell. Don't let anyone convince you otherwise. Remember, if they try, that is a story too. The story of doubt. Choose carefully the stories you believe. The next important thing to know is that wars never end. After the battles for the flesh, there is the battle for minds." When she pointed to her own head some children giggled.

"Don't be silly," she scolded.

"The story they tell you is that our ancestors were at war. They will say that our ancestors fought valiantly, and with honor. That part is true. It is also true that the enemy was as vicious and cruel as any ever known. They skinned alive those they captured and ate their flesh like common hunters."

"That's not true," Nora said.

"Child, it is. Our ancestors were driven from their homes and chased to the sea in the ship of bells."

"You saying our ancestors were sissies?"

"No Tony, I am not. There is no shame in escaping harm. Do you want to be skinned alive? I don't think so. But the sea changes even the most docile folk. Survival is never free. When the ship of bells was set upon by pirates, our ancestors fought with the blood skills learned from their enemies. We don't need to get into details. Our ancestors won, and became sovereign over two ships. The ship of bells sailed out but the other one returned to surprise the invaders. Those who returned, won their war, and those who sailed away lost their homes, their stories, everything."

"I don't think you should be talking like this," Bobby said.

"Yes, well, you would say that," Mrs. Winter sniped. "Do you want to hear this story or not?" she asked and, without waiting for a response went on to describe how, when she was child, a mysterious ship arrived in the waters off Bellfairie, its sails glimmering in the setting sun. The crew, dressed in white robes with sleeves that belled wide at their wrists and hoods caved so broadly around their faces only their extraordinary sharp noses could be seen, rowed to shore where they traded the blue stone they used as ballast for flour sacks filled with white sand, pots of beach bur and nettles, nets of starfish and oysters, baskets of cinnamon rolls, and tendrils of seaweed dotted with heart-shaped cockleshells. They communicated with long fingers that pointed out from the drape of their sleeves and, though they preferred their own company, seemed gentle creatures, gliding along the streets in spite of their large, wide feet.

"Like beams of light that dance on water before sunset," Mrs. Winter said.

Then, one night, she was awoken by a cacophony of noise, brays and yelps, and a clattering that sounded so much like the stacking of stones she initially thought there had been a catastrophe of some sort.

"I was surprised my sisters remained in their beds, and my parents still snored beneath their quilts. Only my kitten, new to the household, was awake when I tiptoed down the stairs, through the small rooms made blue by the moon."

She poured a small dish of cream for her pet before sneaking out the door to walk past the park and graveyard, up the winding path to the bluff that overlooked the folk gathered on the shore.

"They had stripped off their robes," she said. "They were covered in feathers, and their faces were beaked. I was so surprised I fell from that great height. I should be dead, you know, but several of them rose up—I realize this sounds impossible, but it happened to me so it is true—and one caught me in mid-air.

"Their wingspan was massive. Twelve feet, at least. They

flew out over the ocean and returned with squid and crabs and whatnot. One dropped several cuttlefish into my lap but when I just watched the little things, came back to eat them herself.

"I was so young I didn't even have enough sense to be frightened. When the sun began to rise, they donned their robes and prepared to row out to their ship. Through their gestures, I was made to understand I could leave with them.

"But I went home the same way I left, on my bare feet, surprised, and maybe even a little disappointed, that no one noticed my absence. I tiptoed up the stairs and crawled into bed, not aware of the bloody footprints I left in my wake.

"When I woke up that morning, my mother was standing beside my bed, asking if I was hurt. I told her what had happened. I showed her my feet, cut by the rocks. She bathed them in lavender and wrapped them in cloth. She said she was glad I had chosen home but, after that, whenever I tried to talk about the bird folk, she insisted I suffered from sleepwalking. That's the story she chose. My grandmother, however, walked with me on the bluff and told me the true story. Our ancestors were bird folk who fled their homeland, all those years ago, in that ship of bells, so traumatized by what led them to leave in the first place, they stayed where they crashed. Over time, they forgot their own power and their own story. Sometimes the bird folk come back, my grandmother explained, to see if there is anyone who remembers, who wants to go home again, though that happens less and less over the years.

"The true stories are in danger of being lost. Many no longer believe them. Life is like a mirror, I want you to understand. What you see is a reflection of yourself. Don't let anyone tell you that you can't fly away," she said, scanning the room to land her gaze on Quark. "You can."

"Remember now, be kind to all birds for they are your kin and to harm one is to be cursed."

Then she taught them how to fold origami birds they

took out into the playground and released to the sky. Quark still remembered the sound of rustling paper as they circled overhead before flying away and how, the next morning, after the storm, Bellfairie was littered with shredded paper.

None of it could be true, Quark knew. Still, he appreciated how—within the squall of all he could not recall, and the sad moments he did—he'd found this precious store of enchantment. Like the tale she told about the year so many men and boys were lost at sea that, for one generation, the population was composed mostly of women and children. ("Young ones, before that age when they start making real trouble.") He was not unsympathetic to the misery such loss had caused, yet liked to remember that story for the comfort it gave him. *What would it have been like to live then*, he wondered, *in a time ruled by women?*

Mrs. Winter had been able to make Quark, the boy, believe in a world beyond the one he was tormented in, for which he would be forever grateful. Yet Quark, the man, knew that the secret of her charm was simple whimsy. Still, if anyone had a question about ancestry or Bellfairie's past—in the time before computers and DNA-by-mail analysis—she had been the person to ask. He didn't believe Mrs. Winter, already old when he was a child, would still be alive, but thought it possible that, in Bellfairian fashion, her old house with the collection of newspaper clippings, might have been passed on to relatives. He dared to hope that Mrs. Winter, with her love of stories might have shared some about his family.

Though the path was circuitous, Bellfairie was small enough that it was reasonable to describe any location as on the way to any other. By the time Quark realized he had misjudged his appetite and should have eaten breakfast first, he was standing before Wintercairn, as it was called, the cheerful red clapboard house nestled snugly between park and graveyard, a tendril of smoke curling from its stone chimney, so hungry he almost made an escape after the initial knock. If he had left then, everything would have turned out differently—perhaps even well—but the wooden door opened (without the usual warning of locks undone and chains undrawn that accompanied such events elsewhere) and he was caught with his hand raised in a fist, flabbergasted by Coral, the attorney, standing before him in a long white dress.

He tried to smile. "I come in peace," he said.

She squinted, her head at a tilt. "Quark? What are you doing here? Wait. You're not obligated to tell me anything. Everyone knows memory is unreliable."

"I am sorry to disturb you. I didn't realize you live here. Mrs. Winter was my substitute teacher. She knew the history of Bellfairie so I thought—"

"Oh, you came to see Aunt Charlotte?"

"I know she can't still be alive, but—"

"Don't let her hear you say that. Quick, come in. I don't want anyone to see us."

Once his eyes adjusted to the change of light, Quark found the room, stuffed with books, an over-sized chair and a saggy red loveseat near the hearth (the small fire providing a great deal of heat) pleasantly ordinary. No singing plants, self-lighting candles, mysterious mirrors, or sorting hats. No bones or boiling cauldrons. No cobwebs or swooping bats. No children's fingers in glass jars, or generations of Bellfairie's missing pets, though a three-legged white cat did saunter across the oriental carpet, her narrow tail erect. The ceiling was quite low. He found he could reach up and, without even fully extending his arm, touch the wooden beam.

"Sorry. Old house, you know. People used to be shorter. How tall are you, anyway?"

"Six foot, ten inches. Last I looked." She did not seem to understand he had made a joke, so Quark forged on. "Is that your wedding dress?" Coral glanced down at the drape of white lace pooled around her bare feet, and he steadied himself against the sarcasm sure to follow. What a stupid question!

"I thought it would look better. Ever since I was little, my mother said I could wear it, but now I'm not so sure."

The sleeves draped over her hands causing her to look amputated, the waistline—which landed at her hips—added pounds, and the chest area puckered in a most unfortunate manner. Yet, the lace reminded Quark of pigeon featherings and the neckline, which gaped widely as though she had been swallowed by the garment, revealed an attractive clavicle.

"I know a little about sewing. For my work. It just needs a few adjustments. It will look very nice."

"You think? Are you a tailor?"

"Taxidermist," Quark said, eyeing the three-legged feline, his professional assessment awakened.

Coral bent over and scooped up the cat who glowered at him beneath a lowered brow. "I'll see if she can talk to you. We're pinning the dress, but—"

"Oh, I don't want to disturb anyone." He began to back towards the door. "Don't bother, I'll—"

"Quark. Stop. Just wait, I'll be right back."

He was very hungry. Famished, really. It had been a bad idea to undertake such a visit before breakfast. Could he leave without saying goodbye, he wondered as he watched her walk down the hallway, the white cat, tucked under her arm, switching its tail. *She looks like a good witch,* he thought, *even if ineffectual.* This was what happened in Bellfairie. Already he was being sucked into its crazy.

"Well. You finally returned. Still shaking your head against the world?"

"No, I…" Quark felt himself flush. *Stop shaking your head,* he thought and, after several more beats, did.

"I don't recall you being so tall."

He didn't know how to respond. He had long thought his memory of her elfish statue had been compromised by fancy. How old was she? She looked ancient.

"I suppose you're here about Thayer."

"Yes, I—"

"Heard he confessed to murdering half the town."

"Is this a bad time to talk?"

"Who said it was a bad time? Oh." She glanced over her shoulder. "They don't need me. They just include me to make me feel like I matter."

Quark wasn't sure how to respond.

"This is where you say, 'don't be silly, of course you matter.'"

He felt his face flush.

"That's what I always liked about you, even as a boy you were unusually sincere." She shook her finger at him. "No bullshit. I like that. Come on now, why are you here?"

He nodded. That was the question, wasn't it? *Why was he here?* "I remembered how you used to tell us the true stories about Bellfairie. I thought you might know something. A clue. To find him."

"Thayer?"

"Or if you know anything about my mother. I don't remember much. In general."

"Still? After all these years, you still don't remember Starling?"

Quark closed his eyes, but all that came to him was a distant melody, a flash of light and the subtle sound of wings in that initial moment of flight.

"What's the old saying? She was the sail of her father's ship. A darling child, the sweetest dimpled girl this town knew. Ever since she could safely watch for traffic she roamed the streets like a cat. She used to stop by for my ginger cake and cream. How that child loved cream! I used to call her Kitty! Oh, my darling girl." She dabbed the corner of her eye with a crooked finger. "Thayer was in mourning you know, after the tragedy, and never fully recovered."

"The shipwreck? He talked about that many times."

"Oh, I forgot about that one. So many tragedies, Quark. Well, obviously, your family is cursed."

"Cursed?"

"Stop. I can't tolerate this new fashion of repeating single words as a parlay in conversation. It's an insult to my intelligence. Are you listening or not?"

"I haven't eaten breakfast and—"

"Surely someone told you about the curse?"

"I don't believe in such things. Anymore."

"You don't believe? Anymore?" She turned her head to give him a sideways look. "Well, aren't you funny? He was cursed twice. It seems hard to accept that such a thing can happen, but the world is capable of multiplying grief just as surely as joy, alas. So we can only guess—and I would rather not—at the dark corners of his life. Your grandfather carried that corpse right through town as if he didn't mind what anyone thought. And who knows? Maybe he didn't. What difference does one more curse make to a man already suffering under another?"

"A corpse? What corpse are you referring to?"

"Why the albatross, of course."

"Oh, I thought you said my grandfather. That is why I was confused. I never met him."

"What? What's gotten into you? Why are you talking nonsense?"

Quark mustered all the benevolence he could access. After all, Mrs. Winter had been good to him when he was young and dearly needed it, surely he could return that kindness.

"Did he hit you in the head once too often? Is that it?"

"Who? What...I don't even—"

"Your grandfather. Thayer!"

"Excuse me, Mrs. Winter, but Thayer is my father."

"Come here. Come closer. Give me your hand. Look at me."

Quark, towering over the old woman, still felt like a child

looking down into her uncompromising gray eyes.

"You were my favorite boy. Not like those others. Like I said. Sincere."

She squeezed his hand. Quark was surprised how well he could distinguish the fragile bones beneath her thin flesh.

"Everyone knows he was changed by the tragedy. Broken. Made stranger. But I had no idea he never told you. Listen to me. Thayer is your grandfather."

He didn't realize he was trying to pull free until he felt her clasp tighten.

"Stop. Stop shaking your head. You're not going to have one of your fits, are you? All right. Good boy. Don't be angry. I'm sure he had his reasons for letting you believe otherwise all this time, or maybe he didn't, but here you are. Thayer is your grandfather and that's a fact."

"If he is not my father, why did he raise me? If he's not my father, who is?"

"Everyone loved Starling. She was popular with all the boys, but Thayer—"

"My grandfather?"

"Yes, Quark try to keep up. I know you've had a shock, but this is important. And who knows? I might not be here next time you return with questions. I'm not immortal, you know. In spite of what some folks say. Now, where was I? Oh, yes. He doted on her."

"On my mother?"

"Yes."

"Mrs. Winter are you saying that my...that he had an improper impulse toward—"

"No, that's not what I'm saying. I'm saying Thayer doted on his daughter, Starling, and there was nothing improper about it. Who would have guessed he would be such a good father? But he was."

Quark hated Bellfairie. The place was full of meanness, superstition, and God-fearing atheists. The sort who looked up at the sky to ask for help whenever there was trouble then spit in the wind for luck, the kind of people who'd make a kid feel special—cared for, even—while knowing secrets about that child's life, like how his father was really his grandfather and his mother…. "What changed him?"

"Maybe you should sit with your head between your knees."

He did sit, perched at the edge of the loveseat so low to the ground his knees obscured the view of Mrs. Winter who sat in the overstuffed chair across from him, her short legs extended into the room revealing the purple soles of her pointed shoes.

"Thayer never cared for your father, Quark. It's hard to imagine he would have cared for anyone. After his wife died… you do know about your grandmother, don't you?"

"I do not."

"How extraordinary! What a peculiar life you've had! Well, I'm afraid I don't have a lot to share. Your grandfather, Thayer—born and raised in Bellfairie—was always an outsider in his own way. It's just how your people are, Quark. You are all Isolatoes, as my old friend Melville would say. It stood to reason Thayer would marry a woman who couldn't talk to anyone else. She carried a basket atop her head to market and wore sheets she dyed in a big kettle in the backyard. He got shipwrecked and came back with her. I am quite old now, but even after all this time, I remember how handsome he was. Oh, you didn't know? Not movie star looks, not like that, and it is true he is on the short side, but he had so much presence. Those eyes! Well, time dimmed them, of course. But when I was young, we girls used to say if we were ever caught in a storm we'd want him to be looking for us because his eyes were like lanterns in the dark. Or I said it, at least. This was before his unfortunate experience, obviously.

"He was never much of a talker, himself. I was quite old before I realized I'd filled his silence with a deep discourse of things imagined. I fashioned a perfect companion out of his reticence. In truth, it's only in the past decade that I've gotten to know him, and you know how he is. All mixed up. He believes in the old ways and doesn't. Makes no sense but that explains a lot.

"Where was I? Oh, yes. Your grandmother. What did he call her? I can't remember. Maybe it will come back to me. Then again, maybe it won't. I suppose she was lonely. She did not speak our language. Never indicated any interest in learning it, from what I saw. You have not heard about this? How extraordinary!"

"How did they communicate?"

"Well, whatever they said to each other, from what I observed, seemed to involve a good deal of gazing and touching. I thought then that what I wanted was someone with whom I could share a secret language, though I changed my mind, of course, for the obvious reason.

"I spied on them, you know. Oh, don't look so shocked. I am sure you have done some spying, yourself. All quiet people do. They danced in the cove with the only music the waves. As soon as they started kissing, I left, of course. After the first kiss, at least.

"Forgive me. I seem to have gotten ahead of myself. Or behind, as it were. An old woman's memories have no sense of order, you know. Where was I? Oh, yes, the shipwreck. He washed up on shore, and the first thing he noticed was how sweet it smelled. Like—"

"Oranges."

"That's right. So you do know this story?"

"Only some of it," Quark said. "He talked about the screams. And the oranges, but not much else. Oh, and the horse."

"The horse? Well, I never heard anything about a horse. He said he awoke on the beach to the sound of birdsong. So many birds. He thought he was dead. He often said he should have stayed there. He wondered if things would have been different if he had. Well, obviously, right? One small change can make such a big difference. He thought it would have been better, but who knows? The choices we don't make remain unsullied by reality. When a ship was blown off course and dropped anchor for a night, he saw his chance. Homesick, he said.

"She died in childbirth. Your grandmother. That doesn't happen so much anymore, but it wasn't unusual back then. She took part of him with her when she left. It doesn't always go that way, but it did with them. Left behind just a shell, like a mollusk. Funny thing is, that's how they met. Your grandfather washed ashore where your grandmother was collecting seashells. Don't let time fool you. Whatever it gives, it takes away. But what can be done about it? What is the alternative? Wait. What are we talking about?"

"My mother?"

"Yes. Yes."

"He used to take that little newborn—your mother—and pace the cliffs, crying like a baby. Some folks worried he'd throw himself and her over. Don't look so distraught, Quark. Obviously he didn't.

"Instead, when Starling was about three years old, Thayer started planting acorns. He got them sent in the mail because, as you know, oaks don't generally grow around here. He dug the holes and let her drop the nuts into them. Half the time, when I saw her those days, she had dirt on her hands and face. He said he wanted to give her something that would last.

"Folks thought he let her go wild but I always believed he did things right. Some children, if you hold them too close, their spirit breaks, and it can take a lifetime to recover. Some never do. He was a very good father."

Quark had to remind himself to breathe. He'd come for his story, hadn't he? What was he so upset about? This was what he wanted, wasn't it?

"Are you all right? Would you like a cup of tea?"

Clearly, he should have eaten before undertaking his

investigation, but there he was, and it was futile to wish he wasn't.

"Please. Go on."

"Well, it shouldn't be much of a surprise that your father, your birth father I mean, was one of the lost. He was searching for stars. No. Wait. He was 'observing the stars,' that's how he said it. We used to think that was hilarious. Observing stars as if they were capable of going any place or doing anything interesting at all—"

"Well, actually—"

"Of course. But he made it sound like they might stop existing if he didn't keep watch. That's what I mean. He was arrogant, to be honest. He had no sense of how to behave with Thayer who, I suspect, wouldn't have been kind to any boy that courted Starling, but your father, with his strange occupation and his odd ways made a particularly easy target.

"They got married in the little forest she and Thayer planted. You might have called it a grove back then. It was spring, and the leaves were pink with a touch of silver as if fairy folk had painted them. Everyone agreed it was a special setting.

"I couldn't see what she saw in him, and neither could Thayer, but that's not really the point, is it? He was quite tall by the way, in case you ever wondered where you get your height.

"They found his body in the cove the very next summer, before you were born. There was some of that star-gazing equipment of his up top and evidence of a fall he fought against. Some say it was because of the curse, as if a man's fall was never caused by reaching too far. Some even tried to blame me for it. Oh, don't look so alarmed. I know what they call me, and I know what I am. Your mother wouldn't hear of it. Neither she nor Thayer. People are always finding ways to blame others for their troubles, as I'm sure you're aware. I have been saying for years we need to erect a fence up there but everyone says that would spoil the view and people would just go further down the coast to tumble into some other town's cove. Who knows? Maybe they're right. Oh, he gave you your name. That might be of some interest.

"I was baffled why anyone would name their child after a cheese, but I didn't want to be rude. I don't care so much about being polite anymore, but back then I did.

"Anyway, I had no interest in shaming him. I waited until we had some privacy to ask why he'd chosen it. First, to make him comfortable, I told him what I'd seen when I was a girl, about the bird folk. You remember don't you, Quark? Yes, I thought you might. You were an extraordinarily good listener back then. I shared how I had always expected Starling to continue her family tradition and name her children after birds. You know, like Robin, Dove and Crane. He listened quite intently, I must say, and I liked him a bit more for it. When I finally got to my point and asked about your name, he laughed. He had a surprising laugh, heartier than I expected from one so slender.

"Not cheese at all, he said. A star! A very special star. I wish I could remember everything. It was a fascinating conversation. Oh, listen to me, going on! Do you already know about your name?"

"I do not."

"How odd. I would have thought you'd be curious. You were quite curious, in your way, as a boy. Oh, I remember! It just popped in my head again like a wren in a bird house!

"To begin with, no one is even sure if a Quark exists. I rather like that, don't you? It speaks to the existential, I think. Now, this star, your star, is formed inside a larger star as it breaks down. Isn't that interesting? And that's it. The wren flew away again. Well, I'm sure you can research this further if you have any interest. The important thing for you to know is that it has nothing to do with cheese. In case you worried about that. Your father gave you a spectacular name. It's a name you can be proud of."

"And my mother?"

"Well, she tried. But she spent too much time staring at the sky. Too much time weeping. She fell asleep at inappropriate moments. She forgot to feed you once or twice, and lost track of you a few times. I don't know if you remember your experience in the heron's nest, but you were perfectly fine. Never mind what anyone says. They were not going to eat you. Herons can be quite protective."

"Excuse me?"

"It was only a few hours."

Quark couldn't think straight. His stomach hurt.

"So. That's how you came to be living with Thayer. It was meant to be temporary. Well, you know how mourning is. Grief eats up hours, and if a person isn't careful, entire years are consumed.

"The last time I saw Starling was her final afternoon on earth. Oh, how I wish I had foreseen what was to come! But it was an ordinary day, and I am an ordinary woman. No. That's not right. It was a beautiful day. Exquisite. The sort of day where one expects good things to happen.

"She said she was going to Thayer's place to pick you up for a walk. Her cheeks were rosy, her hair swept into saltwater curls. We didn't talk long. I remember thinking things were going to be all right for you two. I have always felt terrible for not preventing it. But how could I? I see so clearly now what happens next. Well, I don't need to say any more to you, I guess. The next morning she was dead."

Quark felt his hand slap against his chest, palm flat over his wild heart. Was it too much to ask that he have the life he believed in? It felt a violence, it really did.

"Quark? Are you all right? Does it still hurt?"

"I'm adequate, Mrs. Winter."

"Adequate?"

"I need to go."

"This is a shock. I'll make strawberry tea. I remember how much you like it."

"Thank you, but I need to go."

He stood, tipped his hat and turned on his heels to leave, but the old door was stuck. No matter how hard he pulled, it wouldn't give.

"Here, let me help," she said, just as it opened with a pop.

Quark heard her say his name, softly, but pretended he didn't. He focused on walking down the stairs, avoiding even a glance in the direction of his old playground where headstones tilted towards the bay as if the dead had been chipping away at their graves. Instead, he concentrated on the sunlit children in the park chasing balls and sailing toy boats.

Ever since that day when she told the story about the bird people, Quark had wondered why. Why didn't Mrs. Winter want to leave Bellfairie when he would have happily jumped off the bluff to join them? Then again, only he had been raised by Thayer, and maybe that made all the difference. Quark adjusted the brim of his hat low over his brow, too distraught to make eye contact with anyone. On the muddy bank, a gull paused in the midst of pecking at the remains of a fish, a rope of silver flesh dangling from its beak, watching him pass.

· 8 ·

Sushi's had, inexplicably, run out of oysters.

"There's a whole ocean right there," Quark said, pointing his knife in the general direction. He had not meant it as a threat, though he was old enough to know one should not go waving knives about.

He'd been initially pleased to find a booth available, heartened by the comforting aroma of coffee, bacon and eggs, but Dory wasn't there, and his waitress was the pregnant girl. Her lips were startling red, bright and lush as the island flowers Thayer often talked about though, in her case, the effect was hostile. After unwisely waving his knife about, she spun away, surprisingly graceful in spite of her girth, leaving him to stare out the window at the Birdman statue being scrubbed clean after another assault of vandalism (obscene words spray painted on its base) his focus redirected when he heard, then saw, the squad car scream to a stop in front of Sushi's.

He turned to assess the restaurant's interior, wondering what he'd missed while everyone else had paused in their meals to look at him. Quark suspected they hoped he'd use his size to thwart danger. When Healy entered the diner, however, all the faces—shot with a sudden sunbeam that pierced the windows—turned toward him, instead. Relieved, Quark sank into the booth with a plan to collapse into the amoeba shape he'd taken shelter in as a child and, so occupied, didn't notice the sheriff's approach.

"Quark. Can you hear me? Sit up and listen now. You

scared Phoebe."

He was confused, first wondering why Healy was worrying about something so minor, before comprehending. "I just wanted the number five. I didn't mean to frighten anyone."

The sheriff stared at Quark for longer than was comfortable before launching into a lecture. A person couldn't just wave a knife around, especially if that person had "such an imposing physique." Further, he needed to understand that the community was "on edge these days" with the rumors of a murderer in their midst.

At that point they were joined by the manager (designated as such by the pin neatly affixed above his shirt pocket) a man with narrow eyes and a precise haircut, who caressed his chin like a cartoon character.

"Quark? It's you, isn't it? Hard to miss, I'd say. Haven't changed at all. Except maybe got even bigger."

Quark tried to assume an amiable expression even as he read the name printed in small dark letters beneath the title on the tag.

"Tony?"

"You remember me, don't you?"

"Yes," Quark tried to sound as if it didn't matter. "Tony Kindall."

"Dory said you were back."

"Yes. I am here."

Though the tenor of Tony's laugh had changed from the cruel mirth of his youth, something of its jagged edge remained, and when he spoke, he did so without humor. "You scared Phoebe."

Worried any response would be wrong, Quark held still.

"I think this is just a misunderstanding," the sheriff said.

"Yeah, well now that I see who it is. Tell you what?" Tony raised his voice loud enough for the eavesdroppers. "I'm gonna let it go. I heard what's going on with your old man. I understand you feeling pissed. All I ask is you behave yourself, all right? We can't afford to lose wait staff. I think it would be best, all around, if you leave. I ain't saying you can't come back. Let's just let things cool down some. All right?"

Quark nodded.

"It's been a long time, ain't it? But, hey, once things settle down, you should come by the house for supper. Get the old gang together, huh?"

Healy's expression was disappointingly bland, apparently unable to discern the threats lurking behind everything Tony said. Quark nodded.

"Well, all right." Tony turned to the sheriff. "I'll explain to Phoebe. She's been kinda bitchy, actually. Dory says cause of hormones."

By the time Quark walked out of the diner, a small group of people had gathered to see what all the fuss was about. Wanting to reassure them all was well in Bellfairie, he tipped his hat in their direction which initiated a suspicious murmur. They behaved, he thought, as if he might be possessed of dangerous capabilities when, in reality, he was only a hungry orphan. Perhaps a silly term for a grown man, Quark thought it neatly described the desolation of his life. After all, there had never been someone waiting at the door with warm bread and jam, or candy in her pocket.

Or had there? For as soon as he mourned the lack he pictured a woman standing beneath the oaks, conjured—he assumed—like that morning's ghost, from longing.

Hunched against the misery of his life, Quark thrust his hands into the pockets of the ill-fitting pants, and turned down Market Street, which is how he came to be carrying two paper bags full of groceries up the broken glass drive, famished and stunned to see a woman standing by the door. He felt a momentary surge in his chest before recognizing Coral.

"Do you need help?"

"Thank you, but that is unnecessary. I can manage." His

right hand was particularly cramped. He wasn't sure he could make it up the steps without dropping a bag.

"Really, you should let me—"

"What are you doing here? Where's your car?"

"I needed a walk. You know, after all that cake. Sheriff Healy asked me to—"

"I haven't eaten yet." The bag began to slip, and he propped it up with his knee.

"Here, let me at least get the door."

Blinking against the change of light, Quark hurried inside to set one bag on the narrow counter and the other on the small table, before peeking around the kitchen doorway to see that Coral remained at the threshold to the house, a silhouette against the bright sky. Not sure what to do about her, he began unpacking the groceries. A loaf of sliced bread. A jar of peanut butter. Six russet potatoes.

"Quark? I have some news about Thayer. That's why I'm here."

"I haven't had breakfast," he called as a fly buzzed narrowly past his face. "Come in. Shut the door and come in."

He unpacked the tofu, carrots, onions, cauliflower, turnips and saltines but left the package of toilet paper in the bag rather than call attention to his bathroom needs.

"Good news. They found him. Thayer. Sheriff Healy's bringing him home."

"Here?"

She lifted a foot to frown at the sole of her flip-flop. "Can I sit down a minute? I think I might have stepped on glass."

Quark wasn't sure what was expected. After all, wasn't the chair obvious? He pulled it away from the table and waved his hand over the seat like a conjuring magician. She sat, but not before giving him a funny look he wasn't sure how to decipher.

"Turns out he was with Henry Yarly. You know Henry, right? Apparently he thinks he has to keep everyone's secrets.

Anyway, Healy, oh, Jesus Christ, no wonder." She lifted her hand, a sliver of glass held between thumb and finger. "I'm all right. You don't have to be...see, it barely broke skin."

Uncomfortable with her naked foot, Quark turned away. "Better check the other one," he said, setting aside three potatoes then adding another, in case she was hungry.

"I don't think that's necessary. I mean what are the chances?"

"He spread glass all over the road."

"What? Why?"

"Because of the ghost. She comes and stares at the house. My mother, I guess. He wants to keep her out. I don't know why."

"But that doesn't make..." she stopped in mid-sentence and slipped off her other flip-flop.

Quark offered a saucer, which she looked at quizzically until he said, "for the glass."

Later, after she was gone, he tossed out the shards, three glass slivers spotted with blood.

There was a brief period of consternation when Quark discovered neither salt nor pepper to be found but, rather than have a fit, he ate the unseasoned potato wedges at the plank table, staring across the room at the Old Man's empty chair, trying to comprehend his return.

After finishing his breakfast Quark stood to watch out the front window, noting how the driveway sparkled like a mirage or barely remembered dream. He would never get used to the absence of trees. He could never forgive it. Weary of the ravaged view, he decided to take his coffee to the backyard, stepping out of the kitchen into a strange world where a tall ship rose against the sky like a fairy tale.

He had no idea how long he remained there, staring at the ship in that stony yard, the late morning fog woven through her ribs, singing briefly in a breeze, the wood still finding her stretch. Not finished yet, but an accomplishment all the same.

Quark couldn't decide if he was impressed or dismayed. How long had it been going on, the Old Man building an ark? Surely it proved his mental capacity, didn't it? No one could build such a thing from the workings of a mind in chaos, could they?

Curls of shaved wood unsettled by the breeze tumbled past Quark's feet, across the yard, and beneath a long work bench protected by tarp. He paused beside the display of old instruments—adze and wedge, hammer, chisels, gouges, knives, and drills—like a man at a yard sale with a serious interest in tools as if that, and not the ship, was the material of greatest interest.

Only after he returned with his second cup of coffee did Quark dare confront her. He estimated she was a fifty-five-footer, composed of cedar, fir, and black locust, but mostly oak. Here were the branches he'd climbed, finding comfort in the shelter of leaves. Here were the trees he loved, the severing of their relationship based, not on the destruction he couldn't abide, but on a creation he had never imagined.

How does one recognize a clue, anyway, he thought, *out of all the flotsam of life?*

Quark drank his coffee and waited. Who knows how long he sat on the same flat rock he used to pretend was a table for magic tricks, considering the mysterious vessel, before he heard the unmistakable sound of tires on gravel, car doors slammed, a curse?

He found himself hurrying to the front of the house, like a man happy to greet his visitor, but felt a tug of reluctance when he saw Thayer meandering towards the door. Sheriff Healy, leaning against the squad car, nodded and Quark nodded in return. Unsure where to begin, he said "hey" three times, before the Old Man looked up from beneath unruly brows. The blue cast of his gaze, diluted by time, gave him a slightly haunted look which, combined with the wild hair, mustache, and beard made a crazed Santa or, as was appropriate, an old sea captain who swallowed anchor, as the saying went.

After fixing Quark with that long look (which filled him with guilt for the transgressions he'd made, invading the Old Man's closet, wearing his clothes, discovering the ship in the backyard, brushing his fingers along her hull), Thayer opened his arms wide, as though to measure half a fathom, or so Quark thought, before realizing it was the beckoning of a hug.

The Old Man still possessed surprising strength. Quark was relieved when finally released.

Only after Thayer shuffled into the house, did Healy step away from the car, fixing Quark with a steady gaze. "You're not leaving, right? He can't be alone. I told him he could stay with me but he wants to be here. With you."

Quark nodded as if this was all perfectly natural though he felt strange. What was the feeling? *Something like happiness. To be chosen.*

"I don't know how long I can remain. I have my work."

"What is it you do again?"

"Taxidermy." And, when the sheriff frowned, "I preserve animals so people and museums can keep them."

"Is that right? You make a living at that?"

Quark nodded.

"Well, I'll be damned. Do you do...pets?"

Quark knew that there were two kinds of people, those comforted by his work and those who weren't but, worried that even an innocent falsehood would be discerned by a man whose job it was to recognize lies, he nodded.

"Yeah?" Sheriff Healy shook his head. "Well, takes all kinds, don't it?"

Quark hated the way his hand enveloped the sheriff's and the momentary surge of strength his clasp incited. Other men were threatened by his size, though he never felt up to the competition. The end of almost every handshake was accompanied by a bemused look. It was to the sheriff's credit that his expression remained neutral even as he turned away.

Quark watched the squad car roll slowly down the drive.

Stopped at the crossroad, the signal light blinked far longer than necessary—there was no traffic to wait for—before making the turn.

Quark eyed his truck, still parked where he had left it, then opened the door and followed the Old Man into the house.

· 9 ·

Thayer sat at the plank table, an open bottle of rum by his elbow, two shot glasses poured. One of his eyes had grown rheumy while the other remained bright, *like a broken lighthouse*, Quark thought, surprised by the wave of sorrow he felt as he sat, pretending grave interest in the rum he gulped in one horrible swallow.

"C'mon, boy, down the hatch, heh?"

The Old Man scowled, and after his own glass had been dispensed several times began to argue with himself. He was the luckiest man who ever crossed the sea or the unluckiest who ever lived. He had nine lives or nine tragedies. He had been saved by a horse, swept overboard in a gale, lost his ship, terrorized by a ghost, ate bad mussels, kissed a witch, almost died from a tattoo, was nearly hit by lightning, lived.

"You know what happens when a bolt strikes you, don't you son?"

"Someone hit by lightning," Quark began, but the Old Man leaned across the table to deliver a rum-soaked response to his own query.

"A man hit by lightning talks to ghosts. He doesn't just see 'em. He talks to 'em like they ain't dead, or like he's one of 'em."

"You are the only person," Quark said (as though he were intimate with many) "who thinks not being hit by lightning was an unfortunate event."

"Well, what would you know about it?"

Quark peered into his glass, inhaling the scent of vanilla, cinnamon and clove. What did he know? Really, what did he know about anything? And why was he so frightened of an old man with trembling hands and wavering focus babbling about ghosts, witches and storms?

"The sea never did call your name, did it, boy?"

He learned early he was not made for it, suffering nausea even on the pier if the day was windy enough. Thayer paid others to bring Quark out until everyone knew all it took were a few whitecaps before his skin turned gray. No amount of orange slices could prevent the inevitable, apparently limitless vomiting. He became a joke, though even he understood it was not meant unkindly. People in Bellfairie often showed affection through humor. Unfortunately, he rode the teasing as well as the waves. He hadn't thought about the humiliation in years, but the woozy drunken feeling brought it all back.

"What is your intention with that ship?"

Quark knew, from experience, that it was best to walk away from the kind of dead calm his question raised, but he was a grown man, not a terrorized child.

Thayer leaned forward, elbows on the table. "Did I ever tell you what happened out there?"

"Out where?"

"I built her—"

Quark sighed.

"With my own hands I built the coffin I thought was my dream. It took me four years. Too long, you know. She was infected by the seasons, but when she was done everyone wanted to be a part of the voyage. Think of that, why don't you? I had to turn away crew. Those boys survived to become men with children and grandchildren. Why do you look at me like I'm a terror? What do you believe in anyway?"

"I—"

"Nothing. That's what. You believe in nothing."

"That is incorrect I—"

"We launched her with blood. We did it right and everyone cheered."

"Can we—"

"She broke apart."

"It wasn't—"

"One storm was all it took. She broke like a bitch. Eight of us when she went down. Eight. Only I survived. I went down with her. Popped up again like a god damn cork. That is my curse. I was young. I didn't know how to die." He squinted at Quark. "Why'd you stay away so long?"

"You know why."

"You still mad about damn trees?"

Quark looked at his hands and found them, in his inebriated state, shockingly large. *It's amazing,* he thought, *that I can do such delicate work with such monstrous hands.*

"You and your hysterics over trees! Did I tell you about their screams?"

"What? Trees don't scream."

"Try to follow along, boy, all right? We're talking about the wreck. I meant to die with them, but I went adrift. You know life is a curse, don't you? I taught you that, right? Their way was death. After a while one man's cries start to sound like another's until they sound inhuman. Like birds. Like your name, squawking gulls."

Quark had sat through recitations of the story so often that when he heard a seagull's call the first thing he thought was that someone was dying.

"Why do you have to talk about this now? It was a long time ago. There was nothing—"

"I swam in the dark until I was half-dead then I climbed aboard a horse. I smelled oranges and thought death was sweet. Why did you stay away?"

Quark rubbed his fingers across the gouge marks on the table. He had learned to whittle there, starting with wood before graduating to bone.

"What is your intention with that ship?" he asked again.

The Old Man's eyes narrowed, his expression sneering and cruel. "What is your intention?" He mimicked Quark's plaintive tone. "What do you think? I'm going back to sea, boy. And you're coming with me."

Quark turned to look out the big picture window at the bright blue sky cut by a lone gull. A moment later he heard its mournful cry.

· 10 ·

Returning to his childhood home reacquainted Quark
with the boy he'd been, awkward where it seemed he
should have been most comfortable, lonely amongst those who
knew him best. What was it Mrs. Winter said about his family?
Isolatoes? Yes, he was an Isolato, and that was all right.

What was this then? This restless feeling that kept him
awake, staring at the ceiling slanted close over his bed? He
wanted to push it away. Every time he drifted towards sleep
he awoke with a start, his breathing labored. How had he slept
beneath it all those years, like a boy in a casket propped open
for viewing? What a thought! What a morbid idea! Yet, what
was he to make of the great unmooring? His father was not his
father. His mother was gone. She had always been gone. But,
no, Quark had been eight years old before she left. Where was
she? Somewhere in his mind. But how to find her?

He felt a tug at the corner of his thoughts, a sensation
similar to that of a remembered taste, and found there, not his
mother but Cheryl, his childhood pet, peering around a dark
corner. She almost made him smile, though that was quickly
interrupted by Thayer's incredulity. "Cheryl?" he'd barked.
"Where'd ya get a name like that?"

Quark sighed. What was the use? Why was he even
trying? He rolled over, carefully planting his feet on the old
braided rug, his shoulders hunched, a habit established long
ago, when he went through his growth spurt and could no
longer sit straight up in bed or stand tall in his own room

without hitting his head.

There was a single small round window at the other end of the narrow space, his old bedside table beneath it. He wondered what had become of the desk that used to be positioned there, though it had never been anything special. When he was young he had liked to pretend his room was a captain's quarters, the window, a porthole, which dispensed a milky light he initially mistook for dawn.

Stepping off the rug, Quark recoiled against the cold floor. *Why, summer is almost over,* he thought, walking through the glow to peer out the window at the vessel below, mysterious as a ghost ship and—like all skeletons—strangely beautiful.

He leaned closer to the porthole to be sure. Yes, the Old Man was balanced against the moon, hammering. Thayer had been drunk when Quark went to bed, and had to be drunk still. It wasn't safe for him to perch there, the hammered hand raised.

He could fall, and this would all be over.

Careful to keep his head bowed, Quark walked across the room and down the creaking stairs where the moon cast a bluish sheen over the half-empty bottle and two shot glasses. He paused for a moment to appreciate the beguiling effect before proceeding through the kitchen, out the back door, into the stony yard.

"You are going to catch cold," he hollered. "You could get pneumonia."

Thayer stopped mid-swing. Illumined by the moon, he was made incandescent, his hair—like the wild fright of a cartoon character—almost ghostly. "You worried I'm going to die?" he bellowed.

"Come in. The neighbors—"

"The neighbors? What's got into you? Everyone's worried about my head and you're talking about neighbors? What neighbors? We don't got neighbors and never did."

"Sound carries. That's what I'm saying."

Thayer responded by resuming his work. Quark kicked an acorn with his bare foot. He watched until he was sure that, in spite of reasonable expectations, the Old Man was stable— at least physically—before going back inside where he found socks, shoes, a sweater draped across the couch; surprised to discover that beneath the anger, resentment, disappointment and sheer bafflement there remained this desire to be needed.

Other than an occasional grunt of direction they didn't speak as they worked. It was crazy. Symptomatic, even. But, after a while, Quark had to admit he enjoyed the deep silence punctuated by rhythmic sound, the distant whisper of waves, the feel of moon glow on his skin. When Thayer pointed east and said, "She's bleeding. Time to go in now," Quark was sorry to see the pink slit of morning. Together they walked back to the house where it felt good to fall into his boyhood bed, to sleep deeply, untroubled by dreams or unanswered questions, his body aching. When, hours later, he was briefly awoken by the cry of a seagull, Quark wondered why he had never noticed before how much it sounded like his name—as if someone might want him—or how soothing it was to hear the distant bells tolling from the wreck.

· 11 ·

Judging by the pool of light spilled through the small window, Quark guessed he slept late, which made sense after spending much of the night on that ship. *No, that couldn't be right.* He shook his head against the persistence of dreams, the way they sometimes stuck like cobwebs. The dull ache in his temple, however, provided dismal proof that the previous evening's drinking actually transpired, which gave rise to the conclusion that building a ship in the backyard might have occurred as well.

Alas, such heightened awareness did not prevent Quark from butting his head on the low ceiling. He lay back down until moved to the deed again (without the damage) by the overwhelming heat he recalled as a force of expulsion during his childhood, driven out to play his solitary games in the shade beneath the oaks. The little attic room (for that's what it was, wasn't it, just an attic) had been a sauna in summer, and so cold in winter he sometimes wore mittens to bed, the window often glazed with ice, though he almost smiled to recall the shiver of anticipation he used to feel, that delightful sensation in his toes all the way up his legs through the length of his spine to the top of his head, when he heard the jingle of bells that signified the horned beast's arrival on Christmas eve.

Had he always gone down the stairs to use the bathroom tucked in the corner there? He must have, of course, both then and since his return, though he only had the vaguest memory of doing so, signifying he had been—until that point—

somewhat of a sleepwalker. Hunched beneath the dangling light bulb as he pissed into the rust-stained toilet, Quark considered his options. He had to choose whether to stay or go. It shouldn't have been a difficult decision. He owed nothing to the foolish ship building project, or its captain.

Rejecting the bar of grease-splotched soap, he opened the mirrored medicine cabinet, hoping to find a package of Dial or Irish Spring. The old names came to him with a vague pleasant olfactory accompaniment cut-short when confronted by the feminine evidence. A small glass bottle (nearly empty, labeled Rain) an opened box of tampons, a comb he lifted for inspection—as though it were some strange tribal artifact—long dark hair wrapped in the tines, a few strands (apparently preserved for decades) loosened by his investigation. He tried to tuck them back and, after one quick tap to ascertain the comb was securely positioned, closed the cabinet. Resigned to using the unappealing bar of soap perched on the basin, Quark rubbed his palms until they were covered in a hive of bubbles.

The towel hanging by the sink was also grease-streaked. He dried his hands on the pants he slept in, causing the clumsy sensation of swatting himself as he surveyed the dismal bathroom he'd been too distracted to assess earlier, clearly in need of major cleaning, a matter he decided to consider more thoroughly after his morning coffee, stepping out of the cramped, gloomy space into the room filled with light.

The picture window framed a bright morning, a blue sky above the long broken glass drive that sparkled towards the horizon. He might have appreciated the view had not the truck, with its deflated tire, reminded him of his entrapment. Why was it that whenever he left Bellfairie, swearing never to return, he always did? Why was it that, once arrived, he found it so difficult to depart? He knew locals would say it was the curse of a town built from the wrecked ship, the curse of the bells, the curse of a vengeful sea, the curse of the moon, the curse—apparently—of his family, which he did not believe

in; though recalling Mrs. Winter's casual reference to it sent a
shiver down his spine.

He padded across the wood floor, surprised to discover
no sign of the Old Man's morning ritual. No pans on the stove
or in the sink, no mug ringed with coffee, no evidence at all
that Thayer had awoken. Odd, he had always been an early
riser.

It was then Quark felt the first ping, a small alarm, like
that of a bicycle bell (the kind he had as a child) swaddled
against his heart. He opened the back door, hoping to find
Thayer with his ridiculous enterprise but, while the ridiculous enterprise remained (and didn't it look, in all its peculiar-
ity, magnificent, rising from the yard?) the Old Man was not
there.

"Dad?" Quark choked out the word, startled by its arrival,
so tremulous it seemed to come from the boy he'd been. "Dad?"
he said again, louder, walking slowly across the kitchen floor,
past the plank table where the glasses and rum bottle formed
a tableau.

Old people sleep late, he reasoned, eyeing the closed
bedroom door, turning the glass knob with the careful execution of a thief. Sure enough, Thayer was lying in bed, glowing
in the gold light diffused through drawn curtains.

As he backed out, Quark wondered if he should make
coffee for two or just himself. The Old Man looked so
harmless, vulnerable even. What an imperfect father he had
been—or grandfather—at any rate all the parent Quark had
ever known.

He turned so suddenly he tripped over his own feet,
stumbling into the room making a ruckus to wake the dead,
though it didn't work. Thayer's chest remained unmoved, like
an old boat set on blocks for winter.

✦

Once, Quark taxidermied a little dog for a woman who had begged him to give her that solace. His resistance had not been motivated by moral compunction but practical considerations, apparently what seemed consoling in those first hours of grief became unbearable, and people rarely returned for their pets. He didn't fully understand it, but could not dispute the evidence of two hamsters, a gray cat, a miniature horse, and the parrot that occupied various perches of his office. He tried to develop some affection for them beyond vocational, but never did.

Mocha, however (a white-haired thing, much like a terrier but for the beagle ears) remained curled on its scotch-plaid bed at the front of the shop and, while the grief-stricken owner never did take the little dog home, she stopped by to visit—frequently at first, and then every six months or so—sitting on a straight back chair, her feet firmly planted on the ground beside her beloved. Sometimes she brought a book, sometimes her knitting. At first she made Quark uncomfortable, self-conscious and awkward in his own space, but eventually he forgot her presence as if she were just another glass-eyed creature, startling him when she leaned over to pat the little head at the end of the visit. Several times, in his solitary hours, Quark found himself talking to Mocha, and once even caught himself pondering cheerful bags of dog food in the supermarket like a regular pet owner.

It was only that morning, as he sat in the Old Man's chair, staring out the window, coffee mug in hand, that Quark realized how long it had been since the bereaved woman had visited. Had she died? Had she gotten another pet? Or had the quality of her grief changed? He peered over the mug's rim at the blue day, hoping to find something in the landscape that would tell him how to proceed. He couldn't put it off much longer. Just one cup of coffee, he bargained. He needed a plan before all the excitement began. Remembering the funerals of his youth with their confluence of sorrow and celebration, he

had no doubt it would be exciting; the fish pie and Humming-
bird cake, the mourners' faces imbued with light as though
grief conferred halos.

Eventually he set the mug on the plank table between the
shot glasses, and proceeded to the kitchen. The old lobster pot
hung from the hook he had fashioned, as a boy, from whale-
bone. The dish soap scent was pleasant, neither fruity nor
flowery. He shook his head when he realized he needn't adjust
the water's temperature for a dead man, and continued to shake
it as he admonished himself that he, at least—still alive—was
worthy of such caution, and never again need suffer burned
flesh. By the time the head shaking was finished, the pot was
overflowing into the sink. Quark turned the faucet off then
searched through several drawers of jumbled flatware, balls
of string and old tools before he found several neatly folded—
though tattered and stained—dish cloths.

He returned to the Old Man's room, struck by the change
in atmosphere. As if the sun were in sympathy with the circumstance, grey shadows had replaced the earlier gold. Quark
set the pot on the floor beside the bed, and opened the curtains.
Who knows how long he stood staring at the ship? Time took
a strange course that day. He finally turned from the window
to attend the corpse, pulling the blankets back and releasing
a sour odor. He dipped a cloth into the soapy water to begin
the task of washing the gnarled feet, working up the bowed
legs to the scrotum—that small purple sac upon which the
placid penis rested like the pistil of a denuded flower—to the
barreled gut and tattooed chest. He leaned over to pick up the
distant hand, so much smaller than he remembered, washing
between the fingers and up the arm to the wiry neck, the water
cool. When he picked up the left hand, Quark pondered how
it would never again make a fist, hold a hammer, build a ship,
swim through danger or cradle a mug of bitter coffee offered
with forgiveness.

He gently rubbed the cloth over the tattoo heart wrapped

in thorns which, as a boy, had been frightening to consider. How odd, that only death provided the intimacy he'd yearned for all his life. When there was nothing left to do, but confront the face, Quark gasped at the blue eyes, locked open, as though stunned.

"Were you frightened?" he heard himself whisper, bewildered by the possibility, remembering the seagull's cry that had awoken him, how it sounded so much like someone calling his name. Shocked by the depth of his inadequacies, Quark wept into his hands, getting soap in his eyes. When he ran to the bathroom to cup cold water over them, his vision was so obscured he thought he saw Thayer standing in the dark corner, glowering at the incompetence.

✦

Quark closed the eyelids, but they popped right open again. After this happened several times, he went upstairs to his old room to search though his pockets for coins and, while there, get dressed, remembering to stay ducked low so as not to hit his head on the ceiling. For that brief period of time, sheltered in his boyhood space, the day seemed ordinary. It felt surreal to return downstairs to the Old Man's chair still facing the window, as if he'd only just risen from it when, in truth, he remained lying on the bed, his eyes open wide as if, he too, was surprised by that morning's events.

After some consideration, Quark rejected the idea of trimming the beard. He had never seen it any other way than wild. He chose clothes from the simple wardrobe. Trousers with knotted rope for a belt, the button-down shirt, tucked. No tie or pocket kerchief. No nonsense. *What to do about shoes and socks?* Overwhelmed by the absurdity of dressing a corpse, Quark nearly suffered an existential crisis over the issue, wavering so thoroughly he began to feel seasick.

The Old Man owned two pairs of socks, each with holes

in them which, for some reason, brought tears to Quark's eyes, though he didn't indulge. He would grieve later. There was too much to take care of for him to fall apart. The last thing he did, before going into the kitchen to make the necessary calls, was lightly press his fingers on each lid, drawing them down like a magician casting a spell, placing the quarters there, adjusting the coins so George Washington faced the ship but, when he returned, discovered the coins fallen to the pillow, clods of dirt around the bed.

"Time for you to go now," Quark said, glaring, slit-eyed, at the body in repose. He drew the eyes closed again, less gently this time, firmly pressing the quarters onto the lids. He might have said more, often wished he had, if not for the sound of gravel crunching beneath tires that thrust him into a sudden state of panic. It was too soon, wasn't it? There was so much they never said to each other.

"Quark? Quark? You in here, son?"

At the sound of the sheriff calling from the front of the house Quark did the only thing he could think of that might settle what remained unfinished. He leaned over to press his lips against the Old Man's forehead, a cold exchange like kissing a rock.

"Came right away," the sheriff said, squeezing his fingers deeply into Quark's shoulder. "So he cut the painter, did he?"

Disconcerted—Quark hadn't heard the old saying in a long while—he turned just in time to see Healy startle back, eyes wide.

Quark felt a momentarily thrill, barely able to formulate the notion that the Old Man had, in fact, risen, before realizing it was only the ship—perfectly framed by the window—that had drawn the sheriff's attention.

"Jesus. What is that?"

He didn't know what to say. He felt like he'd woken up to a different world than the one he'd fallen asleep in. The ship was an enchantment he turned away from to appraise the old enchanter, himself, laying in repose, coins beside his head, eyes opened wide, hands neatly folded across his belly, the vague suggestion of a smile at the corner of lips Quark would have sworn had been, only moments earlier, locked in a frown.

· 12 ·

Lost travelers who came upon Bellfairie nearly always felt they discovered the proverbial jewel until, upon close inspection, it was determined to be so seriously imbued with superstition and entropy that any charm was dissipated. In the matter of embalmment, however, Bellfairie's tradition of forgoing it entirely had persisted so long as to have become quite modern. Quark was pleased when the funeral director, Maude (heavily tattooed, pierced, and reassuring in her efficiency) told him the Old Man's body would be refrigerated until burial. "Or a viewing. If you want a viewing, we are here to assist you."

But when Quark said he would call with his decision, a shadow passed across her face, and he wondered if he had fallen into a type, like those people who never returned for their embalmed pets. Was there a whole population of refrigerated corpses awaiting resolution? He couldn't worry about it. He had enough going on in his own life without having to consider the abandoned dead. News traveled fast in Bellfairie, and the plank table, cleared of rum and its accoutrements, was laden with cakes and bread, casseroles and pies which, in spite of his grief, Quark found enticing. When his stomach growled, he tipped his hat at the funeral director in an attempt at distraction but she had already turned away to oversee the bagged corpse, on some kind of palette, being carried through the suddenly hushed assembly.

When his stomach growled again, Quark thought how it was like an uncooperative member of a silent cabal, a notion he found so amusing he let out a small snort, which incited a few smirks, though they were not meant unkindly. Bellfairians knew better than to cry over a corpse, less they wake the hounds of hell that would tear the soul apart.

Quark bowed his head occupying himself by trying to identify the foil-covered pie's aroma. Was it bumbleberry, apple, cherry or peach? He did not look up, even at the disturbing sound of something (the palette? the body?) jam against the doorway, followed by Maude's scold, "To the right, move to the right."

Having discovered how successfully the bowed posture served as deterrent against the uncomfortable exchanges he had suffered through most of the morning, Quark continued to stare at the wood floor, searching for the whorl he remembered from his youth that looked like a howling man, listening to the hushed voices in whispered conference. ("Should we go? Should we just leave? You know how he is. Come on, don't crowd him.") Even as his neck began to ache, Quark remained bowed until he was finally alone, at which point he immediately pivoted into the kitchen to find the rum, drinking right from the bottle, pleased how it warmed him as if he needed revival. When he sat at the plank table, utensils in hand, he thought he must be dreaming. Never had he seen so much food set before him, not even on holidays, which were simple affairs though, to the Old Man's credit, he had tried; one birthday presenting Quark with a fishing pole as though it were made of gold. It became a favorite possession for Quark, who much preferred playing magician to the gruesome business of hooking fish, after he realized it made a perfect wand. The pleasant memory was accompanied by distressing ones Quark scolded himself against indulging in. *Think of something happy*, he thought. Every year they had a special dinner of Christmas lobster. What Quark remembered most about that feast was his fascination with the crustacean's construction, contrasted by the vicious way the Old Man tore into the exoskeleton, breaking bone with abandon.

Well, enough of that, Quark thought as he lifted the aluminum foil from the pie plate he'd been eyeing since its arrival. Hit with the intoxicating scent of apple and cinnamon, he decided there was no reason to investigate further. The closest he'd been to homemade pie since he'd left Bellfairie had been in diners that advertised theirs as such, and he wasn't sure he could trust the claim. Nonetheless, he'd had some delicious slices—once, in a fit of gluttony, ordering six in a single sitting—but, as near as he could recall, this was his first verifiable homemade pie in years. He used a spoon to eat it right out of the dish, eager to scoop up the sweet liquid.

A devoted Pescatarian, Quark was not unfamiliar with the dismay of limited dietary choices, but after a careful search he determined that the lasagna was, indeed, vegetarian and though cold, better than any he'd ever eaten. He intended to finish his feast with a brownie. Overcome by his unexpected fortune, he neglected to check for offending elements. Finding walnuts in the first bite, he spit the remnant into a paper napkin plucked from a nearby stack. It had a Christmas holly border with small red bells and snowmen. Though full, Quark preferred to end on a delicious taste. He returned to the pie, which he finished, so satisfied, he might have reasonably sat there to digest.

Instead, bringing the bottle with him, he began wandering through the house, reminded of something—he couldn't figure out what—until he recalled the way the Old Man used to careen drunkenly about. At that sobering thought, Quark stumbled into Thayer's room where, beneath the lopsided cairn of stacked stones, blanket and sheets still held the shape of their last resident. Clearing the way with a swipe of hand, Quark fell across the bed, nose smashed into the pillow scented of rum, smoke and soap. The effect was comforting until it began to suffocate so he turned his face to watch the abandoned ship floating in a sea of tears.

· 13 ·

$\mathcal{A}$woken by a gentle nudge, Quark thought for a confused moment, that Mocha was looking for a human hand to feed her. Recognizing the notion as absurd as soon as it was formulated, he shook his head against the hallucination, which was a mistake. The rum pounded his temples. He eased out of bed, even in such a compromised state enjoying the vast distance to the ceiling before, suddenly nauseous, stumbling into the small bathroom where his retching reminded him of his childhood.

He didn't recall seeing mouthwash earlier but hadn't been looking for any, either. He reached for the medicine cabinet, startled by darkness where his reflection should have been, then pulled the black material off the mirror with a sigh, disappointed, as always, by his face, the terrible mask he'd worn his entire life, an inheritance he was only beginning to comprehend. What a relief to open the cabinet and escape the abomination.

How empty it was. How clean the glass shelves stacked one over the other like vertebra. He brushed a finger across each narrow plane, searching for a strand of hair or an oily drop of perfume, anything to verify his memory of what had been there.

"It's like you have a hole in your head," the Old Man taunted, more than once.

"No one remembers every moment," Quark said in defense of the boy who took things so literally he worried for years (years!) that he really did have a hole in his head like a gunshot victim, or a freak. He'd been just a child, after all, not schooled in biology.

Feels like I'm disappearing, he thought as he stepped out of the bathroom. He knew that the explanation for the dark cloth over the mirror was the well-intentioned preparation before a wake. Someone had obviously tended to the matter while he had been distracted. The room projected an unfamiliar antiseptic brightness which did little to dispel the gloom projected by the figurehead guarding the corner, her face draped in black lace.

He didn't have a hole in his head and never had. He did have a headache, though. A big one. *Coffee,* he thought, *with a splash of rum.* Isn't that what one drank to cure hangovers?

He searched, with increased desperation, finally locating the bottle on the floor beside the bed. Though nearly empty, he discovered that, by holding it under the tap and adding water to the dregs, he was able to produce a golden liquid too diluted to promise much medicinal value. Nonetheless, he poured it into his mug.

With a sigh, Quark sat at the plank table, dismayed that the neglected feast already emitted a slightly sour odor. Some of it should have been refrigerated. He knew he was expected to share the offerings with everyone after the funeral but suddenly decided there wouldn't be one. No laying out of the body, no procession of the curious coming through the house to drape cloth or gather tears in tiny bottles. He would serve no one, accommodate no one's grief but his own. Pleased with his decision, Quark was surprised to find himself weeping again. Why? Why mourn the death of the very man whose deeds frequently incited tears at that same table? Why mourn at all? Wasn't this the final abandonment he had always longed for?

· 14 ·

Bellfairians have a proverb, "Grief is a ship without a captain." This was said so many times that Quark passed through annoyance at the repetition to a state of poetic fascination. *Grief.* The word stuck in his throat like a small fishbone.

What is grief, he wondered, surprised how the weight of sorrow was relieved by the buoyancy of rum. How could it be that he, raised in the despair of alcohol, would find solace there? It made no sense unless grief was something more substantial than emotional residue.

"Like a dybbuk?" Felix (of Felix's Emporium) asked. "Is that what you're talking about, son?"

"I do not understand what lesbians have to do with it."

"Not lesbians," Felix snorted. "Dybbuk. You know, like a ghost inside you."

"A ghost inside me?"

Felix nodded. "Happened to Yarly, after his wife's accident, you know. You're too young to remember but after she died he never got another car. Won't go in one, either. That's when he started walking everywhere. Happened to Thayer, too, is what folks say."

"It did? They do?"

"Yep. Well, that's what they say. I'm too young to remember, myself. They say he used to go up the bluff and wail like the sound of a woman in labor. She died giving birth, yah? They say he wanted to fly away, though we both know that's nonsense, don't we, son? And then, of course, he had some good years until, well, your mother…that one put him over the edge. They say."

Quark nodded; dully relieved to have learned his history from Mrs. Winter before hearing the confused version from Felix.

"Well, what can I tell you? Grief is a ship without a captain. You're at sea now, son."

Quark careened out of the Emporium, his hand fisted around the newly purchased bottle. Was it possible, he wondered, as he weaved down the fog-dark road, that he had a ghost inside him? Was his new thirst driven by the Old Man's cravings?

"Grief!" he shouted.

"Frankenquark!"

For a moment he thought it was a call from his past. Anything seemed possible in the murky world of Bellfairie, even a path through time shaped more like cochlea than spine.

"Hey, Frankenquark!" The voice called again, followed by a rain of stones.

Not the past at all then, but a new generation of torment-ers. They stood on the other side of the road, boys who had inherited their fathers' cruel sense of play. One, wearing a red jacket, stood out amongst the rest. Quark began to veer towards him when Henry Yarly stepped out of the dark, shouting that they should be ashamed of themselves for treating a man in mourning so cruelly.

"Take it easy now. Hold steady there, son," he said, taking Quark by the elbow.

"Are you a ghost?" Quark asked and watched, in confu-sion, as his guide both shook his head and shrugged as if the answer was both "no" and "maybe."

"Steady," Yarly said. "You're the captain now."

"What?"

"Remember? Life is a ship. You all right? Just follow the sparkling road here, to your house. Go to bed. Everything will look better in the morning or at least brighter."

"The captain is dead!" Quark cried, walking up the glimmering drive. He felt like he had fallen, in some topsy-turvy fashion, and was traversing the Milky Way. "The captain is dead!" he cried again, maneuvering through the populace that milled about his yard. Apparently unable to accept there would be no funeral, they came anyway, bearing casseroles and bread, inexplicably carrying hammers and wearing tool belts, greeting him with the same regard he'd seen the Old Man receive—one eye on the bottle and one looking past his shoulder—as if, in mourning, Quark had become someone whose consolation rested in the disregard of others.

The racket they made encased the house at all hours, spurring his need for escape. He found himself waking in unusual places, once on a bench surrounded by a colony of gulls paused in the midst of grub-hunting to stare at him accusingly. Several times he awoke, his body sore, staring up at the Birdman statue's enormous wings. One night he found himself on the hard ground, peering through foliage as if blossomed there—a parentless being—blinking at the stars, wondering which one he'd been named after, and why? He reached for the bottle and, not finding it, clambered to a wavering stand. Trying to get his bearing, he studied the Quark-shaped impression he'd left in the middle of Mrs. Neller's rosemary patch, and leaned over—in itself, a precarious act—to lift a broken stem, but it collapsed as soon as he released it.

Too often he was awoken by the tormenters, though they seemed to have a talent for dispersing before his eyes were fully open, their taunts ringing in his ears.

"Frankenquark. Hey, Frankenquark," they called in singsong voices reminiscent of their fathers. "Are you stewed, again?"

On those rare occasions when he blinked his eyes open

to discover he was in his own house, he took to excavating the closet, cupboards and drawers, searching for the Old Man's shipbuilding book. *It couldn't have just disappeared,* he thought, *like a living thing.* He remembered how soft the leather felt when he dared brush his finger across the cover, his investigation interrupted by Thayer who, shockingly, did not scold, but picked up the book and said, "You are too young for this. Building a ship is like building a life. You can have it when I die. Maybe then you'll understand."

In brief lucid periods, Quark attempted to restore order out of the mess he'd made. Several times he swept everything into one of the plastic bins Coral had left for that purpose.

"Take them, Quark. They're yours to keep. Maybe it will help you get organized. I understand. Everyone does. After all, grief is a ship without a captain. We all know how close you two were."

Close? He wanted to disagree, but maybe they were right. After all, how much closer can two men be than that one is consumed by the other?

Finally, the morning came when, having awoken there, he walked the bluff, hoping to find some central reason for his life, so absorbed in his thoughts of legacy and inheritance, guilt and retribution, peace and despair that he was only broken out of his reverie by a seagull's cry, surprised to see the red jacket boy standing dangerously near to the cliff's edge, staring at his sneakers or studying the shore below. Not a boy, Quark clarified, a teenager, almost a man. How easy it would be to push him off the cliff.

Turn around, Quark thought, wondering if the crashing waves and tolling bells drowned out the sound of his footsteps. The boy's hair was cut neat around his ears and exposed the back of his freckled neck, which flinched as if sensing death's approach.

Death's approach! Quark recoiled against his own dark impulse, spun around and ran awkwardly down the hill through town, which smelled sweet and yeasty with the scent of that morning's cinnamon rolls. He was lumbering and out of breath when he arrived at the house, finally restored to its solitary state, no lingering Bellfairian to be found.

If not for the evidence of foil-wrapped and Tupperware-encased offerings stacked on the plank table and kitchen counter, Quark might have wondered if had imagined all the visitors traipsing through his life. He liked to think he had shed any remnants of Bellfairian superstition but found himself sitting in the Old Man's chair, staring out the window, looking for the fairies he had mistaken as hammer-wielding humans. What was the old saying? Oh, yes. "Don't eat the food they offer, or you will be trapped forever."

Quark began to shake, craving the poisonous cure. He ransacked much of the house, leaving crushed seashells and sand in his wake until finally locating the rum, oddly stored inside a terra cotta flower pot beside the front door. Grasped with a trembling hand, he brought it into the kitchen. Had he really entertained the idea of pushing that boy off the bluff, he wondered even as another voice insisted he was making a mistake. When he unscrewed the cap, that other voice (a dybbuk?) asserted that Quark, in mourning, had a right to unreasonable behavior. He began to pour the liquid down the drain but watched, in horror, as that same hand—apparently in dispute with itself—raised the bottle with a severe thrust towards his mouth, then threw it into the sink.

If contemplation of murder hadn't been enough to reassure himself that temperance was necessary, standing in the small kitchen, contemplating the arc of tongue necessary to procure a single drop of rum from a sliver of glass, was.

There followed a miserable period Quark was never able to fully reassemble. Lost in the debilitation of regaining sobriety, he discovered, was like being lost in the drunken hours, except that the latter state offered a pleasant stupor (as long as it was replenished) the prior state did not.

The pounding took permanent residence in his head, inescapable except during nightmares from which he awoke in his childhood bed, disoriented by finding himself facing the wall instead of the window, or sprawled on the couch (which held a distressing stench of urine) or kitchen floor, once curved in fetal position in the bathroom.

Undaunted, the visitors (fairies? demons?) returned with cakes, casseroles and pies.

"I'll leave it here, with the rest. No, no don't get up. You've had a shock. Grief is a ship without a captain. We know how you loved him."

Someone did the dishes and swept the floor—he never could recall who—while he sat in the old chair, staring out the window. Someone sang to him, or sang, at least, a song about roses buried beneath a shroud of snow.

At last the day came when he awoke in the Old Man's bed, encased between sheets that smelled vaguely of lavender, wearing a clean T-shirt and sweat pants. Disturbed to consider who had dressed him, Quark decided to believe he'd done it himself. He rubbed his hand over his chin, surprised to discover it clean-shaven, relieved to find no blood on his palm or pillowcase, which suggested he'd actually achieved equilibrium before taking the razor to his face. He judged, by the light diffused through drawn drapes, that it was early. Invigorated, he eased out of bed and padded, barefoot, into the kitchen where Tupperware and glass bowls were stacked beside the sink. He noted the remnants of masking tape, though the names had been smeared to illegible blots of ink. Had he really believed fairies brought their wicked enchantment to him in containers marked for safe return? He might have shaken his head had he not worried where that would lead. Instead, he continued his inspection, pleased to discover bread in the stocked refrigerator, coffee in the tin, salt and pepper shakers poised on the small table.

Driven by a desire for fresh air, even greater than his

appetite, Quark stepped into the backyard. For a moment he thought he'd been right after all—magic had occurred—before a swift glance offered evidence of human hands at work. He formulated an equation between the pounding he'd suffered through, the tool belt-wearing Bellfairians he'd dismissed as nonsensical, and the fully assembled ship. Stones and wood-chips poked the soles of his feet while he remained transfixed, inhaling the scent of cedar mixed with the floral note of oak, the vibrant aroma of fir.

She wasn't just enchanting because she had risen in his yard like some kind of ghost ship, but because, through com-pletion, she had become animated. Even the dark-haired figure at the bow, who Quark knew was carved from wood (her face pressed into the sky like a woman leaning towards freedom) stared at him with one cold eye, as if assessing.

How had he missed what had been so obvious? His visitors hadn't been there to entrap, but to offer this marve-lous, generous gift. Was it possible he had been wrong about Bellfairie? Was it possible he had been wrong about his life? Was it possible he had been wrong about everything?

That night Quark was awoken by a flicker of light, as though someone had lit a match beside the bed. Peering into the dark, he saw moments from his past. There he was, on the bluff, the fishing pole/magic wand raised to the sky. There he was, laughing with youthful glee so infectious the grown man found himself smiling too. There he was, staring out that round window filled with stars. And there he was, sheltered by the sturdy branches. All his life Quark had thought joy was some-thing that landed on a person like a butterfly that had never landed on him, but maybe it had been there all along and he would have seen it, had he only known where to look. There he was, carving in a circle of light like a boy with a halo while, nearby, someone hums and when the footsteps approach he doesn't even look up. How had he forgotten for so long? There was a time when he was not afraid.

· 15 ·

W*hat a mess life is,* Quark thought as he sorted. It was baffling that a man, who had so little, had so much! It occurred to him to walk away from all of it, clean out the refrigerator, turn off the lights and come back in the spring. He might have done so, had he not still hoped to find the ship-building book. It was promised to him, and he wanted it. In the meantime, trying to decide what to keep and what to give away was much more difficult than he had anticipated. Even the most mundane items, a spoon—a spoon!—caused a crisis. It was just a simple utensil, the one Thayer preferred for his chowder and stews, distinguishable from the others by its broad handle marked with wear. Several times Quark tossed it into the resale bin only to fish it out again.

Eventually, he decided to confront the freezer stuffed with newspaper-wrapped bundles, peeling back Sunday comics dated from his childhood to reveal mottled meat the color of a bruise, obviously long past edible. He didn't bother to look closely at the rest before throwing it into a heavy trash bag he stashed by the side of the house. Two days later, the odor was so bad he finally felt inspired to clear the glass, using a shovel to push stones and shards to the side of the long drive, then changed the flat and loaded the truck bed with garbage he took to the dump. Hungry after all that, Quark was tempted to stop at Sushi's, but worried that one such deviation might incite another; buying rum at the Emporium for instance. He drove straight back to the house.

Though the nights were cool, he took to sleeping with the windows open, trying to repair the overwhelming scent of decay that had begun to permeate the house. The briny ocean air did little to dismiss the fetid dark that never went away entirely, not even when he turned on the lights causing flies to rise from their private recesses. Even a bright morning sun couldn't dissipate the interior gloom, or ameliorate the stench.

Perhaps none of it was new; neither the stink, nor the dreariness. After all, one thing he clearly remembered from his childhood was an overwhelming desire for escape. How often he dreamt of leaving Bellfairie, the house, the Old Man, everything!

When Quark awoke one morning to the disturbing perfume of cherry vanilla scented tobacco he might have thought he'd imagined the death had he not washed the body, himself. He hoped he imagined the pipe's acrid odor that used to drift upstairs where he lay in his bed pretending he had a different family. He wondered if he had merely caught a whiff of historic smoke trapped, until then, in the folds of the drapes or beneath the Old Man's pillow.

Yet, when Quark pressed against the mattress to sit up, he was reminded of the discomfort such maneuvers had caused in his youth. He cautioned himself not to panic. There was no reason to attribute the pain to anything occult. After all, he'd been quite physically active since his arrival in Bellfairie. It had merely caught up with him, he thought as he stepped into a puddle.

When he was finished shaking his head, Quark continued to the bathroom. Careful of the dangling bulb that hovered above his scalp, he stripped off his bed shirt to inspect the small, finger shaped bruises—like little dark moons -- that had appeared overnight between the branches of his scarred skin. Cold, he donned the shirt, turned off the light, and stepped out of the bathroom into another puddle.

"What do you want from me?" he asked, both relieved and disappointed when no one answered.

After wiping up the puddles, Quark decided a man wasn't meant to remain housebound day-after-day, and could go mad trying. He needed to trust his own willpower to resist the temptations of the greater world. He reminded himself how, all those years ago, he had left Bellfairie to make his own life. People always thought he was strong—maybe even frightening—because of his size, but Quark knew his real strength was internal.

It felt strange to stroll by the mailbox at the end of the drive, as though doing something illicit, but by the time he walked past the Emporium, Quark had begun to feel like his old self again. He tipped his hat at the storefront window, unsure if Felix saw him, though the sheriff, cruising past at just that moment did, and pulled over to talk. They exchanged pleasantries about the weather, which was unusually mild for so late in the season. It seemed an amiable conversation until Healy inquired about the funeral arrangements.

"I am planning a burial at sea. It is what he wanted."

"I'm not sure you've left yourself enough time for that," the sheriff admonished, as though Quark had a hand in the arrangement of seasons. "Don't you have a job to get back to?"

"Fortunately, my work can wait." Quark surprised himself with his own wit though, judging by Healy's bland expression, he did not understand humor. "My clients are all dead."

"Is that right?"

"Not the humans. Of course. The animals."

The two men stared at each other until Quark tipped his hat and continued on his way, quite hungry by the time he took his place at Sushi's counter.

"Really?" Dory asked when she poured his coffee, as if in the middle of an exchange. "I thought you left weeks ago." She leaned so close her bosom nearly rested on the counter, and

Quark was suddenly reminded of the time he'd spied her half-naked, all those years ago, when he'd hid behind a boulder at the beach. Of all the memories he hoped to find, why did the ones he wished to forget resurface so persistently?

"I will be leaving soon. After the sea burial."

"Burial at sea? You sure you wanna get into all that?"

"I'm trying to do the right thing," he said.

"Well, of course you are."

He could not continue to look at her so he turned away, only to discover the pregnant waitress watching, her bright red lips in a smirk as if she knew all his secrets, which was impossible. She was a mere girl, nothing to be frightened of. Pretending not to care, Quark leaned on the counter, inadvertently knocking his coffee cup over with his elbow.

"Don't worry about it," Dory said, plucking a rag from her apron, pausing to smile at him though her gaze held a warning. Even as a child she'd worn an expression of duality, wariness and trust.

"I will leave after he has returned to the sea. It's what he wanted."

"Well, all right. Calm down. I'm just saying, what about cremation? You could sprinkle him, you know, in your yard, pour some off the bluff, take the rest with you and get out of here. Get back to your life."

"He always said he wanted to return to the ocean. That's where he's going."

She shrugged, as if it didn't matter. "Yeah, he used to come in here, those last few weeks, and order the sweet waffles, you know with strawberries and whipped cream. I remember him saying about going back to sea, though I didn't have any idea about that ship of his. It just goes to show, don't it? You think you know a person and it turns out you don't! I guess he thought he had time to finish it. Just goes to show."

Quark, whose memories of Thayer's appetite revolved around the bitter taste, decided to order his number five prepared sweet, as homage. Dory gave him a curious look, but he didn't feel compelled to explain his need to consume whatever he could of the man who raised him. Usually content to simply sip his coffee while waiting, that morning he leaned over to pick up an abandoned copy of *Bridal Bliss* which, he discovered, was mostly composed of advertisements. He was surprised by the options offered, twelve-tiered cakes, elaborate bouquets, bubbles, and doves "to be released as a symbol of your love," which he thought sounded nice.

Quark's mood was so improved by the time Dory slid his plate across the counter that he smiled though she moved on without response. Sadly, right from the first bite he found the new combination objectionable. Strawberries didn't make any sense with oysters, and the whipped cream was an unnecessary flamboyance. Even after he scraped away the offending elements, the waffle was ruined by association. Hunched over his plate, he wondered if the whole thing had been some kind of set-up, one last mean trick left by the Old Man.

· 16 ·

Dory told Quark that the small library, located snugly
between post office and tavern, had a public computer
from which he could access the regional newspaper. The Bellfairie Clapper, he had been dismayed to learn, was no longer
delivered as it had been when he was a child, tossed in the
general direction of the house at dawn. He wasn't a Luddite.
He had a computer for various bookkeeping issues with his
work. From time-to-time he enjoyed an evening of watching
old movies. Still, Quark was filled with longing as he remembered running barefoot to search for the bound paper, damp
with dew, to hand to the Old Man who always said, "Special
delivery, eh?" followed by the snap sound of the rubber bands
undone. Back then the morning sun glimmered through leaves
and the house shimmered green as though they lived under
water.

Even the librarian was different. Well, of course. Quark
was well aware he was not the only citizen who moved away,
his life not the only one touched by death. Still, he was sorry
he had never properly thanked Mrs. Eel who had been particularly kind to him when he had taken shelter there one brutal
day, his tormentors in pursuit.

The new librarian was young with short dark curls and
a penetrating gaze. He wondered if she was pretty. She was
clearly efficient and accommodating, setting him up with the
computer and explaining that he had half an hour if anyone
else was waiting. No one happened to be doing so, but she

wrote the time down on a pad of paper anyway, and he signed his name beside it.

The desk was small and the monitor rather large, but Quark liked how it was situated in a corner where he could spy both the librarian and the front door, yet no one could see his work unless they snuck up behind him. It wasn't that he had anything to hide. He just liked his privacy.

"For Burial at Sea," he typed. "Captain Thayer, the sole survivor of a shipwreck more than six decades ago." That should keep away those who believed in curses. Just put it right out there from the start. "Will pay top dollar."

Quark wasn't sure what "top dollar" might be but his situation had always been modest, and he'd been able, over the years, to set some money aside. He'd had a dream, "a small dream" as he called it, of buying the little house he currently rented. It wasn't easy to give that up but what else could be done? He had a responsibility he intended to execute with grace. He knew well what it was to be the recipient of unloved duty. He wanted to be a better man than the one who raised him.

All he needed was one person willing to take on the task of finding a crew for the ship's solemn voyage. And return, of course. He added, "Payment upon completion." He had just hit enter when he heard his name, startled to find Mrs. Winter peering at him, so close he could smell the lavender perfume he recalled from his childhood, which brought with it an unexpected time warp and what was she doing at his house, in whispered conference with Thayer?

"Quark? Are you all right? You're not having one of your fits, are you?"

He held his neck very still. "I am quite well. Thank you."

She snorted, causing the songbirds tucked in her hatband to quiver. "What's that you're doing?"

"I am searching for a captain. To take out my...Thayer's ship. For burial at sea."

"Oh, yes. I heard you were up to something."

"It's what he wants."

"Yes. He keeps insisting."

"Excuse me?"

Mrs. Winter sighed. Quark scanned the small room to see if anyone was disturbed by the confrontation, but the only other person present, the librarian, remained focused on her own computer, scowling at the screen.

"Don't you have a home you need to get back to, Quark? A job? People?"

"My work is very accommodating."

"What is it you do again?"

"Taxidermist, at your service." He tipped the brim of his hat.

"Is that right?"

Unsure how to extricate himself from her gaze, he nodded.

"Why don't you stop by again? I have that strawberry tea you like. There's always chocolate around the house. I don't know if you enjoy chocolate? My niece is a fiend for it."

"Thank you, Mrs. Winter. That would be nice," Quark said, and meant it, though he neither recalled the strawberry tea she referred to, nor enjoyed the way chocolate coated the inside of his mouth. "On what date and at what time should I arrive?"

"What an odd question." She shook her head so vigorously the bobbing birds appeared ready to take flight. "Come the next time it rains, of course."

"When it rains?"

"Remember? How you always visited during storms? Don't you remember?"

Quark had only one memory of a rainy day in his childhood and it did not feature Mrs. Winter. "Should I bring anything?" He'd seen people offer to do so in movies, and assumed it was the right thing to ask, but she stared at him with such scrutiny he wondered if he'd said something suspicious.

"Just bring yourself." She peered at him a moment longer and then, with an abrupt nod, turned away. He watched her walk to the foyer where she placed a gloved hand on the old door, which swung open without apparent effort. She stood there for a moment, as if unsure where to go next, the silhouette of a woman with birds on her head. Through a trick of the light—the shadow caused by the closing door, perhaps—it looked for a moment as if the blue songbird flew from her hat into the sky before she continued on her way.

He turned back to the computer, trying to recall what else he'd meant to research. It struck him as funny when he finally remembered and typed in his own name. Quark, he learned, was an elementary particle. He wasn't sure what that meant. It certainly didn't sound like the star Mrs. Winter had referred to. Well, what had he expected? She was an old woman with birds on her head, and bound to be confused.

No one had ever seen a Quark, which felt like a further diminishment unless—and here he suspected he reached for meaning—his father had offered the name out of some sort of fascination with the mystery of existence.

Further confusing things was the fact that Quarks (this rumored thing, this idea) did not exist in isolation but always clung to another. So far removed was he from such attachment, he laughed.

The librarian looked up from her work and said, "God bless you."

Quark was confused until he realized she'd mistaken his laughter for a sneeze. Embarrassed, he turned back to the computer. He decided to try again, and typed in "Quark star," pleased at the pictures that appeared, pretty crystalline circles of light. She'd been right, after all. He had been named after a star.

Or at least the idea of one. For, as it seemed to be with all things Quark (other than cheese) the star was also a hypothesis, formed either inside a neutron star or within the death of a massive one.

Something about that felt right, though he couldn't pinpoint why. Searching for an explanation, Quark was stunned to discover he also shared his name with a *Star Trek* character. He sat back with a gasp then checked to see if the librarian was angry at him for all the disruption, but she remained absorbed in tapping computer keys. He turned back to the screen to assess his own reflection superimposed over the creature's face. It was not an exact match, but there was enough alignment between their low-drawn brows, close set eyes, and stick-out ears that he wondered if the story of being named after the star was just something Mrs. Winter had made up to make him feel better.

This unpleasant rumination brought with it the torment of his childhood, the cruel taunt preserved through the years, re-employed during his current visit. They were children. He shouldn't let their squeaky-voiced barbs upset him.

It took a great deal of courage for Quark to walk over to the librarian's desk and wait for her to acknowledge his presence, which she did without looking up.

"You don't have to sign out. No one is waiting."

"Actually, I wonder if you could help me locate a particular book. If it is not too much trouble."

She looked up then, and he wondered what he had said wrong, before she smiled in a way he could not decipher. He hoped it meant she was happy.

"What title are you looking for?"

"Frankenstein," he whispered.

"Oh. We have that," she said as though it were a stunning development. "I can show you right where it is."

He followed her into the stacks where she brushed her finger with its bitten nail over the spines until it stopped on a thin red volume.

"Have you read it before?"

"I have not. I have meant to do so for quite some time."

"Well, you are in for a treat. It's one of my favorites."

He wondered if she was making fun of him, but she returned his stare with a direct gaze and a soft smile.

"I am going to read it now," he said.

"Here?"

"Not here. At the house."

"You have to check it out first."

He followed her back to the desk where she asked him questions about his address before handing him a card on which she had printed his name in neat black letters.

"I know it's old fashioned, but that's the way Bellfairie rolls."

He hesitated, unsure how to proceed. He didn't want to be brash. By the time he decided to tip his hat in gratitude, she had returned to her work. He took the book and left.

Back at the house Quark spent nearly an hour catching the flies that proliferated in his absence, slamming a cup over each one, gently sliding paper between rim and surface, turning the whole thing over with one hand while keeping the cover secure with the other. In this manner he made the difficult transition outdoors where he released each buzzing pest to the world.

Finally finished, he collapsed into the old chair, annoyed, at first, by the book's lengthy introduction though it soon became so fascinating the story, itself, seemed initially dull. Soon, however, he became absorbed in the tale of a quest to create life. He could relate. After all, his vocation was to give the appearance of animation to the dead. Sometimes, before he turned on the office lights in the morning, he felt the animals watching, and twice he thought he heard the rustling of feathers after he stepped out of the room, though he never found any proof to warrant his suspicion that death was not the impenetrable border others said it was.

He was so startled when he found the name (well into the

story) that he exclaimed, and then looked around the room, anticipating retribution. But he was alone. He read the passage again, and a third time out loud.

All those years! Most of his life, in fact, Quark had thought they were calling him a monster, but Frankenstein was a character to be admired, in spite of his sloppy work. A scientist! Clearly, the man should have shown more compassion to the victim of his research, but what person wasn't flawed?

Quark marked his place in the book with one of the Christmas holly napkins, pleased to return to his obligations with this new understanding. He spent several hours, as he sorted through the clutter, in an unfamiliar physical state that reminded him of the drunken one, though he remained sober. Rather than a blurred world, everything was bright.

Before beginning dinner preparations he stopped to sit and stare out the window at the long drive, trying to identify what he was feeling, other than drowsy, and began to suspect it was joy.

✦

He awoke to an enchantment of silver streaks darting through the sky.

Raindrops, he realized, falling so softly they might have been ghosts of a different storm.

"Run," a voice whispered. "As fast as you can, or you'll never get away from here."

Later, Quark would think the panic he felt was bizarre but, in the moment of experiencing it, he only knew the insistent need for escape. When he picked up his keys he clenched them so tightly that, once safely in his truck, he studied the impression in his palm as though reading it to unlock the mystery of his life. He thought he heard the whisper again as he turned the key in the ignition but when he paused to listen, there was only the sound of rain—falling hard by then—and a distant grumble of thunder.

The panic subsided as he rumbled down the long drive, becoming a mere remnant by the time he turned onto Seaside Lane, devoid of traffic, the shoreline wild with waves, his vision obscured by the swipe of windshield wipers. Quark was surprised that, from the safety of his truck, he found Bellfairie in the rain to be quite pleasant, the shabby buildings reflected in oily puddles like watercolors made with disappearing paint.

"Don't you recall how you always visited?" Mrs. Winter had asked. Why couldn't he remember? A sensation like a stone poked, not in his shoe but his brain, though he didn't have time to inspect it further, his reverie interrupted by the appearance of a hooded figure on the sidewalk.

For a moment he thought she was one of Mrs. Winter's bird folk but, as he slowed to get a better look, Quark saw a familiar face scowling beneath her hood. He drove a little further, put the truck in park and leaned across the seat to roll down the window. She turned to sneer at him, bright red lips a bloody slash in her snow-white skin.

"Oh, I recognize you. You work at the diner. Would you like a ride?"

"No," she said, without stopping.

He slowly eased the car forward but got too far ahead. Watching in his rearview mirror, he formulated a plan. "Get in," he would insist, but she crossed to the other side of the street.

Feeling guilty and somehow accused, Quark reached across the wet passenger seat to roll up the window, suddenly uncertain about his mission. What was he doing, anyway? Why didn't he just leave? Keep driving and never look back? He thought again of his desire to be a better person. He thought, also, about the missing ship building book. Probably nonsense, anyway. And yet, who was he? Who was the man who raised the orphan? Who was the man Quark had called father? Was it unreasonable to hope that the Old Man's book might provide answers?

What is my life? Quark wondered, turning off the ignition but remaining in the truck's cab to assess Wintercairn's undesirable location between park and cemetery where trees reached like claws above the dead. He held his breath as he ran to the house, careful not to slip when he lurched up the stairs. What was the old saying? Something about breathing near a graveyard. It was foolish, of course. Children played in the park all the time, and most of them lived long lives. He, himself, had enjoyed the graveyard as a boy. Nonetheless, he kept his lips locked, knocking with increased urgency until Mrs. Winter opened the door. Eyes wide, she reached for his wrist to pull him inside with a surprisingly tight grasp.

"Quark? Can you hear me?"

"Yes, I'm very well. You asked that I come the next time it rained."

"Have you eaten yet?"

He wondered if there was a correct answer, but trying to sort it out while dripping onto her fancy carpet seemed futile. He shook his head, closing his eyes against any distress his confession might cause.

"Is that your answer?"

He nodded.

"Well, try not to look like you're being led to an execution. No one's going to force you."

The last time Quark had been invited past the front room of anyone's house was as a child. The thought incited random blotches of memory, plastic soldiers climbing blanket hills, Wayne's mother saying, "Now what's he done?"

"You coming? Quark?"

The narrow hallway was lined with framed botanical prints and paintings of birds, some captured in a state of transformation between avian and human. He walked through the dining room with the ornate wallpaper—blowzy, bone-colored flowers against a backdrop of gold and red—into the kitchen where Mrs. Winter stood before the stove on a small footstool decoratively painted to look like a toad, stirring the contents of a large cast iron pot. No wonder people thought she was a witch. What if he had misunderstood all along and she wasn't good?

"Quark? You all right?"

He caught himself on the verge of shaking his head. "I am fine."

"Hope you like chowder. You're not one of those vegetarians, are you?"

"Pescatarian. Fish. No meat." He noticed the scowl this induced but paid it no mind. So this is how people live, he thought, the table set with bread and butter, the room filled with an appetizing aroma and no flies.

"Quark?"

"Yes?"

"Are you remembering? All the time you spent here?"

He felt bad that he wasn't.

"Well, don't worry about it. Come on now. Here you are."

Not wanting to ruin everything with a spill, he carried the bowl with both hands, eyeing the chowder for signs of a tempest, walking so slowly that Mrs. Winter had served herself and was seated before he arrived at the table, triumphant as a pilgrim.

"You really are very peculiar," she said. "I remember that about you."

Quark thought of the sea urchins he used to play with in the tide pools, the way they curled into themselves if he pointed too close to their vulnerable centers.

She didn't say grace, which was all right with him. The Old Man used to recite a short prayer before every meal: "Our Lady of the Sea, be good to us, the world is wide and our house is so small," but it had never made the food taste better, and it certainly hadn't stopped the pain.

A flash of lightning blazed the room, momentarily

suspending them in its violet web.

"Quite a storm," she said, her eyes focused on her spoon.

"See anyone out in it?"

"Just Snow White." Quark felt himself blush. "The one who works at the diner. She's with child. I don't know her name."

"Oh. Phoebe."

Mrs. Winter was so diminutive that she sat perched on a large cushion, like some kind of aged child at the table who, when she reached for the loaf of bread, appeared in danger of toppling over. Quark struggled with trying to decide if he should offer assistance or not. By the time he came to the conclusion that there would be no harm in a gentle nudge of the bread board in her direction, she had grasped it herself, leaning into her soup and causing a splotch of chowder to blossom over her heart.

"Phoebe reminds me of your mother."

Spoon poised at his lips, Quark hesitated. He pictured the girl, sullen and unkind, so different from the mother he hoped for. He shook his head against the image. Mrs. Winter paused in the midst of buttering her bread to watch. With great concentration he willed himself to stop. Once that was taken care of, he sipped the chowder, which was delicious, even if under-salted.

They ate (mostly in silence) Mrs. Winter would later say. Two people "Just appreciating our supper. Nothing strange about it at all. Some folks are talkers and some aren't. I would say he isn't a talker. For the most part."

Afterwards, they retired to the parlor where he stoked the fire. When he turned from the hearth he found her peering at him, as if confused how he'd come to be there.

"Don't you remember anything?" she asked.

"Not much." He turned to adjust the logs, trying to position them for a slow burn. It didn't take long, but by the time he achieved a promising flame, she had dozed off. Her skin had a porcelain cast to it, the same sheen as his favorite cup and saucer set on his work table back home, composed of ash and crushed animal bones.

What is beauty, he wondered. *What is love?*

When he stood to go, he had the idea of leaning down to kiss her forehead. He had never kissed a living person, and the compulsion frightened him. Instead, he tiptoed across the room, hoping to avoid initiating a squeak from the old floor. He mustered all his strength to open the door, careful to pull it closed softly behind as he stepped outside into a glistening world.

He drove home with the truck window rolled down—it was cold, but the damp air smelled like raw honey—thinking of all the things he'd wished he'd asked. By the time he parked in front of the house, he decided none of it mattered. So, he had questions. He had great gaps in his memory. Who didn't? Who could recall everything? In the end, what mattered? His past, with its gaping wounds, or the present in which he found himself called by name and fed by others? He went to sleep, untroubled by the buzzing flies or scent of pipe tobacco and, later, when awoken by the ghost, he simply rolled over.

· 17 ·

P hoebe was missing. Wherever Quark went—Emporium, grocery, and diner—the air fluttered with her name. Mrs. Winter left messages around town that she was looking for him. He returned from one errand to find a small plastic bird lying on its side on the top step to the house, like a calling card. Why? *What did she want*, he wondered, though he had his suspicions.

What difference did it make that he'd seen the girl the night she disappeared? They'd barely spoken. Rumor had it her boyfriend said she left in the midst of an argument about the baby. "She walked right out into the storm" was reported several times, in ominous tones.

Quark knew what others would say if they learned he'd spoken to her. He might have been confused about many aspects of life in Bellfairie (and elsewhere) but he'd watched enough police procedurals to feel certain he would be suspected of something terrible, which is why, when he heard the knock at his front door that afternoon, he did not rush to answer—hopeful of another lasagna to appease his mourning—but crouched beneath the kitchen table. Mrs. Winter was not the sort to mind protocol, however. She let herself in. He thought he heard her call for Thayer, but so what if she did? It took a while to remember who was dead, Quark reasoned. After all, he had once mistaken the sound of a barking dog for Mocha even as the little fellow rested in taxidermy-state and, just the other morning, had caught himself setting aside two mugs for coffee with the Old Man.

"Are you hiding from me?"

"What a pleasant surprise," he said, pretending to pick some infinitesimal thing up from the floor.

"Put the kettle on. We need to talk. I have been looking everywhere. Did no one tell you?"

She unpinned her hat with its depleted flock, draped her coat over the chair and heaved herself to sit, tapping her fingers as she watched him try to scrub a dusty film from the kettle.

"Stop. Just fill it up and set it on the burner. Who cares if the outside is clean or not?"

Quark had come to enjoy being in that house without experiencing judgment, but it seemed petulant to continue. He placed the kettle on the burner then turned to properly greet his visitor. "Welcome," he said, "How can I assist you?"

"Don't be coy. You are well aware why I'm here."

He opened the cupboard to search, without optimism, for tea, pleasantly surprised when he located a small box tucked in a dark corner. Worried she would criticize again, he surreptitiously wiped the dust off with the hem of his shirt.

"You need to tell Healy what you saw."

"I didn't see anything. Everybody knows she was out there. That's all I know too."

Mrs. Winter's expression was such a mirror of the girl's that night—the straight slash of lips beneath narrowed eyes—that Quark experienced a fleeting sensation of seeing what the young woman might have looked like had she aged. It reminded him of what Felix said about a dybbuk, the dead that come to rest in a living body.

"Mrs. Winter, I..." Quark began, but was interrupted by the kettle's whistle. He set the mugs in the sink for a careful pour. Boiling water was quite painful, he knew.

When she said, "honey" he thought it was meant as an endearment, and was moved, if only for a moment, before she added, "I would take honey if you had any."

"Sorry."

"Black tea needs a little something. You used to have yours with so much sugar your mother called it liquid candy."

"She did? I did?"

"Sit down, Quark. You make me nervous, hulking like that."

"Hulking?"

"You've no real sense of your size, do you?"

Quark, long aware of how people misjudged him based on his physique, had struggled much of his life to correct such misperception. He was disappointed Mrs. Winter didn't know that about him. He set his mug on the table near her hat then retrieved a chair from the plank table to squeeze into the tight kitchen space. He hoped a little discomfort might hurry her mission to conclusion. He knew this was mean and felt bad about it.

"Now. What were you going to say? Before the tea kettle interrupted?"

"I'm afraid I forgot."

She paused in mid-dunk to stare at him. "Remember when you were a boy, how you liked to break stones?"

As though memory itself was a stone her words had broken, Quark suddenly recalled the hammer, the chisel, the unremarkable gray shell of a glittering world.

"This is important. I want you to understand. I know Thayer wasn't easy to live with, but you mustn't doubt he loved you. He tried to do the right things to keep you safe. His struggle was not with you, but for you. Sometimes things look one way on the outside, but that is not what it really is. On the inside, I mean. How he was."

Quark did not like to argue and wouldn't have known where to begin, anyway.

"Do you understand what I'm saying?"

Rather than risk confrontation, he nodded.

Mrs. Winter sighed. "Well, for now let's stay focused on

the girl. When did you first see her?"

"Phoebe?"

"I'm trying to help. I hope you realize."

Quark tossed the tea bag, which reminded him of a skinned bird's craw, towards the sink. Never a good shot, it landed on the floor with a plop. Ashamed, he glanced at Mrs. Winter, so absorbed in her own dunking ritual she didn't appear to notice his failure.

"The first time I saw her was at the diner."

"Go on."

"She was working and I paid her."

"On the way to my house?"

"On the day of my return. When I first arrived. I was quite early so I went to the diner."

"Well, what does that have to do with anything?"

That was his point. Nothing he could share had to do with anything that mattered. Hoping to offer something of value, he said, "She looked like Snow White."

"Yes. I remember. You called her that. You said you saw her on the way to my house. That's what I'm interested in."

Quark relayed how he'd seen the girl struggling against the wind and rain, asked if she wanted a ride, her blunt response.

"That's it?"

He sipped his tea, which was pleasantly bitter. It wasn't coffee, but it wasn't terrible.

Mrs. Winter, who had begun tapping her fingers again, stopped. "Are you sure? You're certain she was alive when you last saw her, Quark? This is important."

"Yes. Of course."

"I have seen some spirits, myself," she said, her expression stern, as if daring him to disagree. "Not everyone can, you know. See them. I remember when you were a boy how your mother walked beside you."

"She did?"

"And?" she asked. "Has he hung around?"

"Who?"

"Why, Thayer, of course. Don't play games with me, Quark. I am far too old for such nonsense."

He felt unwilling to share the personal details of his life. It wasn't much, but it was his.

"I am not sure why you ask."

When Mrs. Winter's brows lowered he was reminded of an old cat he'd worked on—a particularly grumpy looking tabby, loved by her owner, an elderly gentleman who thanked Quark so profusely for his work he briefly felt as if he'd brought the feline back to life when, in truth, he'd accomplished so much less.

"It's not really something to smile about, you know."

"I never…I didn't mean…" How difficult it was to explain himself. He'd had little need of trying for most of his life. He was not prepared for the enormity of the task.

"She is only fifteen years old."

He would have guessed older. A fly buzzed into the kitchen and swirled above them.

"This is important. I have to know if she was alive when you saw her last."

"Yes."

"Are you certain? How can you be sure?"

He pondered this for a moment. "She was wet!"

"I'm afraid I—"

"Ghosts don't get wet," he said, holding his body so still he even held his breath.

She frowned, tapping the table until, with an abrupt nod, she stopped to sip her tea.

Quark exhaled, louder than he intended, judging by the way Mrs. Winter paused to peer at him over the mug's rim.

He hadn't meant to lie, exactly. He had no way of being certain about the origin of those mysterious puddles that had been showing up in the house. Should he tell her? Would she stop liking him?

Mrs. Winter set her mug down with resolve. Quark thought she was preparing to scold him but, instead, she lifted the teabag out by its string, rolled it into a small ball and, with a sly grin, tossed the wet sac over her shoulder.

Quark wasn't sure what to make of such behavior until she winked and cackled loudly. Laughing with someone, he discovered, was very nice. He'd seen others do it, both in real life and in movies, and had always wondered what it felt like. After the laughter stopped they sat in silence, which he found quite pleasant until she set her mug down with abrupt resolve. "You have to tell Healy." She reached for her hat. "It's the right thing to do. It proves what I've said about you all along." She stood to slip into her coat. "Who knows? Maybe Phoebe will show up the way Thayer did. Everyone gets overwrought so quickly these days. Remember that boy? What was his name? The one who supposedly sailed away in an old bathtub?"

"Wayne?"

"Yes. That's right. Wayne."

"What about him?"

"Oh. Just how upset everyone was. How sure they were he'd been kidnapped by our cat killer or something like that while, in truth, he spent most of the time sitting in my kitchen, eating blueberries."

"What?"

"You weren't the only boy who needed a reprieve."

The last button closed, she cocked her head, the birds trembling in the tilt. "Get your hat. I'll give you a ride."

Quark didn't believe she would take no for an answer so he donned his hat and double-checked that the burner was off. He considered guiding her by the elbow as they walked across the muddy drive but worried how to go about doing so and, before he could figure it all out, she was perched on a pillow in the driver's seat. Scrunched uncomfortably on the passenger's side looking through the twin peaks of his knees, they didn't speak further until exchanging goodbyes in front of the sheriff's office, which was fine with Quark. He liked to sit in silence and watch Bellfairie through the glass as though it were encased in one of those globes, the kind that shakes snow from the ground to the sky and he, unaffected by the turbulence.

✦

"So, you say she crossed the street to get away from you?" the sheriff asked.

"She crossed the street, but I was not threatening her in any manner."

Healy's pen, a manic little instrument ever since Quark announced he'd come to talk about the missing girl, hovered above the page. "Well now, no one said anything about a threat."

Quark wasn't sure what to make of the comment. Was he expected to respond? Why did the sheriff keep his office so hot, anyway?

"You all right, son?"

He nodded. He was fine. Just doing his civic duty. Trying to help.

"Thirsty? Want a coke? Water? Chocolate soda?"

Quark hadn't had a chocolate soda in years. He suddenly realized he'd missed them very much, but had no desire to prolong the exchange. "Not at this time. Thank you," he said, which for some reason caused Healy to scrawl across the page as if he knew it was a lie.

"Anything else you want to say?"

"There is nothing else."

"You sure?"

"Yes." Quark nodded for emphasis. How had he forgotten the existence of chocolate soda? The question brought to mind the more difficult material he'd set aside for a while, all the things he didn't remember about his mother, for instance. "Can I go?"

"You're free to leave at any time."

He didn't understand why, but learning he did not need to stay compelled him to remain seated, in spite of his hunger. If only Mrs. Winter hadn't insisted on this foolish confession he'd already be at Sushi's eating his beloved number five. "I am sure she'll show up soon."

"Yeah? What makes you think so?" Healy paused in his note taking to watch Quark answer.

He tried to shrug, though it felt awkward, like a puppet on strings worked by parties in dispute. Certain of his own innocence, he nonetheless felt guilty, as if he'd done something to that girl with those lips red as a wound. He was not surprised by the sensation. After all, he'd felt guilty for simply offering her a ride. In this way, he suddenly realized, he was like the Old Man, always seeking absolution.

"You look like you just remembered something."

"No, I…" Quark shook his head. "May I go?"

"Already said. Nothing's keeping you."

"Yes, well, thank you for your time."

Forgetting the chair was on wheels, he planted his feet firmly on the floor causing himself to roll away from the sheriff whose usually stoic expression revealed a small light of amusement, or perhaps derision. Quark had developed, over his lifetime, a practice of feigning ignorance when placed under scrutiny. Frequently the best avenue for escaping uncomfortable situations, he had learned long ago, was to pretend they weren't happening. He left the chair where it landed several feet from the desk—as if that had been his intention all along—tipped his hat, and was almost to the door before Healy spoke.

"You were one of the last people to see her. Anything you noticed might be of assistance. Even some small thing. I know you are a good person. I know that's why you came here today."

Quark was struck immobile by doubt. Was he a good person? He wasn't sure he was. The girl had looked at him like she knew he wasn't, those bright lips of hers skewed in a smirk.

"I don't think it matters."

"Why don't you let me be the judge?"

"She had a way of looking at people."

"Oh, yeah? Could you be more specific?"

"Like she thought she knew things."

"Knew things?"

"I imagine if she looked at the wrong person like that she might have made him angry."

"Is that right?"

"It's just a theory."

"Ok. So let me make sure I have this straight. Did she look at you like that? Like she knew things? About you?"

Quark felt uncomfortable. The office was too warm and he was very hungry.

"What things?" the sheriff asked.

"I'm not...what do you mean?"

"What things did she know?"

"I wouldn't...I have no idea."

"But you just said she looked at you like she knew things and I'm trying to understand what you thought she knew."

Quark had a bad feeling. His childhood had taught him about the traps of inquiry. All he had to do was take two steps, and he'd be out the door.

"What was this expression, then? Can you tell me that? This look on her face? Can you describe it?"

"Yes. Well. Her lips were very red. Like a wound."

"A wound?"

"Like Snow White," he hastened to add. "The first time I saw her I thought she looked like that girl in the fairy tale. That's what I mean."

The sheriff, busy writing, asked what she looked like, the last time Quark had seen her.

"I already said." He shifted uncomfortably. "I already told you."

Healy nodded as he scratched behind his ear. "Right. I'm just trying to understand. When you saw her last did she still remind you of Snow White? Or maybe some other storybook character?"

Quark did not know how to answer the odd question. He had assumed the sheriff knew what he was doing, but the conversation's course caused him to suspect the girl would never be found.

"Just Snow White."

"Her lips like a wound?"

Why did he keep repeating it? The man had no original thoughts. There had been so few moments in Quark's life when he'd felt superior—or at least not inadequate—he wasn't sure how to proceed. The conversation had become absurd. He decided it was best to leave without further comment. He had done all he could to help. He'd done his best. To show he harbored no ill feelings, he tipped his hat before stepping out of the stifling office onto a sidewalk uncharacteristically populated with people wearing bright orange vests, "Search Team" printed on the back. Quark thought most of them looked too confused to be of any use to the mission. A large dog, also wearing a vest, lunged at him. Not generally nimble, he nonetheless skirted away from the animal. The girl's smiling face was tacked to telephone poles and taped to storefront windows. It wasn't a good likeness. She looked friendly.

When he arrived at Sushi's, Quark was startled to discover the place packed.

"Can seat ya in at the counter," Dory said, squeezing past, a food-laden tray hoisted above her shoulder.

He hesitated. He wasn't next in line, but he was very hungry. "Pardon me," he muttered, working his way through the crowd.

A child gasped, "Look, a giant." Several people turned then looked away as if he were invisible.

He sidled onto the stool, and opened a menu, peering over the rim at the crowd reflected in the mirror. Dory rushed past with a plated doughnut. The other waitress—he never could remember her name—cleared a table while a small clan hovered nearby. All dressed in city flannel they carried an aura of authority no one in Bellfairie assumed, not even Healy. Thinking of the sheriff and the girl whose fate was tied to his incompetence, Quark sighed.

"Sorry," Dory said, suddenly standing before him. "Doing the best I can."

He tried to explain. He was not dissatisfied with the service. In fact, he appreciated how she'd directed him to the only available seat.

The cook rang the bell, and a man seated nearby said, "Can we get someone to take our order, here?" The other waitress rushed past. Dory leaned closer, almost resting on the counter to ask if Quark had heard the news.

He said he hadn't. When she repeated what he already knew about the missing girl, he didn't try to correct the impression he'd given of knowing nothing about it. Later, much was made of this, but it was an innocent misunderstanding.

"Why weren't all these people looking for Thayer?" he asked.

Dory scrunched up her face like one of those old dolls named after a cabbage. "Well, it isn't really the same thing, is it?" She pulled a pencil out from behind her ear as if from the air, which reminded Quark of that brief period in his childhood when he'd been a magician, believing he'd drawn a lightning bolt from the blue sky and made people disappear.

"The usual?" she asked.

He nodded then pointed at the empty cup. "When you get a chance."

Dory spun away, but quickly returned with the coffee pot she poured without spilling as she continued along the counter, filling cups with one hand, setting tabs down with the other. Quark didn't generally like crowds, but found it interesting to watch the strangers in huddled conference. So many rosy cheeks, so many shining eyes! *Why was it,* he wondered, *that people came most to life when reminded of its temporary state?* Not that he was judging. He felt it too. It wasn't excitement, exactly, more like wonder.

"Heya are. Number five. Not sweet." Dory announced the plate as Quark drew his elbows off the counter. "Didn't mean offense about Thayer. It's just no one ever believed he murdered anyone, or that he was in real danger. We all figured he'd turn up, eventually. That's all I was saying."

Quark nodded. He hated it when his food got cold. He wanted to eat in peace. "Yes. All right."

"She's just so young," Dory sighed, her voice cracked at the end.

"I'm sure she'll show up," Quark said.

"Oh, yeah? What makes you say so?"

He was surprised by the way she looked at him, as if he were the sort of person who could provide solace. "Hope, I guess."

"Hope?" Dory said the word like a curse, and without further comment, turned away.

He didn't even realize he was shaking his head until the other waitress, the one whose name he never could remember said, "Something the matter, Quark?"

In some ways she reminded him of the missing girl though she wasn't young, nor her lips so red, but her face—like the girl's—was pale and round as a plate.

"More coffee?"

"Actually, do you have chocolate soda?"

She looked at him as if he'd spoken an unknown language but before he could understand what he'd said wrong, she nodded.

"I would like to order one. Large. To go. With a straw, please."

Quark didn't know when he had forgotten about chocolate soda, but was quite pleased to have access to the refreshing drink, fondly recalled from his childhood. When the waitress returned to hand him the cold plastic cup, he unwrapped the straw and stabbed it through the lid, maneuvering through the crowd on his way to the cash register, startled by the grim man where the girl usually stood. He had just paid his bill when a siren sliced the air between them. Suddenly, as though cast under a spell, everyone stopped what they were doing to watch the squad car scream past, spinning red over their stunned faces.

"Move aside, please. Could you move so we can get out of here?"

Suddenly everyone was checking their phones, putting on coats, setting money beside plates.

"A body," someone said, pushing past.

When the waitress approached, Quark stepped boldly in her path. "What happened?"

"They found her."

"Who?"

"Phoebe," she said, shaking her head as she continued walking out the front door, still carrying the coffee pot like some kind of ghost, herself, trapped in the rituals of a life she'd left behind.

Rather than press through the sudden rush to exit, Quark remained drinking his chocolate soda, slurping through the straw. They were weeping, putting sweaters on inside-out, forgetting their hats beside abandoned meals, unfinished omelets with cheese melting from the cuts, coffee steaming in cups, and green melon balls perched beside strawberries that glistened like miniature hearts. As if death were an extraordinary event arrived in Bellfairie like a hundred-year curse they had forgotten.

"Oh, Quark, can you believe it?"

He had not noticed Dory come stand by his side to watch the mass of people stream past the diner. When had the day turned so bright? He looked away from the light, and discovered that she was staring up at him with tears in her eyes. When she inhaled deeply he did as well, sucking in the cold revival of the chocolate soda which was very good, he thought.

· 18 ·

A massive cloud expanded dark wings, like a doomed angel hovering above the mob, cordoned so far from the scene they might as well have remained in the diner with their coffee and eggs, their hope of being a part of something that mattered.

"Fell from the bluff," they said. "Or jumped," they murmured. "No, pushed."

Slurping his chocolate soda, Quark moved through the crowd, causing a bit of a sensation when they parted for him until he stood beside the yellow police tape. Nothing human could be seen of the mass that lay at a distance, neither wisp of hair, nor glimpse of flesh. She might have been a pile of clothes, or a garbage bag washed on shore instead of a dead girl marooned on the rocks.

Quark had watched enough crime shows to understand what tide and time could do to evidence, yet was still surprised at the urgency displayed by the officers who arrived from other municipalities (judging by the various insignia on their uniforms) and bossed their way through the throng.

Have they no sense of futility, he wondered as they breached the divide, lumbering across the beach towards the sheriff who stood beside the body, watching the waves, as if only he understood that reinforcement had come too late to matter.

It was then Quark noticed the woman hobbling across the sand in high heels, twisting and floundering in her narrow skirt, a beaded necklace flailing over her sweater and whipping her chin. When someone called from the crowd she turned, her mouth agape.

It was almost imperceptible—perhaps imagined—but Quark thought she leaned slightly forward to lock eyes on him. As if, through some magical element, he had reached across space to dangle his finger above her mouth, it closed with the gentle defiance of a sea urchin, their connection fully severed by a policeman she tried to beat away, and another, and another. The crowd was hushed, the only sound the waves until she let out a piercing cry.

Quark lifted his face to the winged cloud pressed across the sun. *Like the work of a celestial lepidopterist,* he thought, regretting he had not pursued the boneless art.

Lately, so much of life was about regret. He regretted the time he hadn't spent with Thayer as much as the time he had. He regretted that he had returned to Bellfairie. He regretted the girl. He regretted not insisting she get into the truck as much as he regretted stopping for her at all, and he regretted joining the curious horde. He should have realized how dangerous it was to stand amongst them.

His reverie was broken by the dull rhythmic click of stones. They had begun stacking the cairn that marked where a body was found, even though it was at some distance. *Because of the tide,* he thought. It was difficult to bend while keeping both hat and soda from succumbing to gravity. He grabbed the nearest pebble, gray and unremarkable.

Once again they gave him a wide berth as he made his way, hushed except for the child who exclaimed, "Look, mom. See. I told you. A giant!"

Quark did not feel so grand, however. He was just a man, after all, another one like the rest. After placing his pebble on top of the stack, he paused for a moment, but couldn't think why he had and, when a woman came to wait behind him, left.

It snowed on his way back, a flurry of salty flakes entirely

melted by the time he walked up the long drive to the house, so
squat and ordinary it was hard to believe a ship stood behind
it. He almost thought he imagined her, but there she was, her
masts piercing the cirrus remnants of wings.

There was only so much he could do. Quark's customers
might initially confuse his skill with mad science, but eventually the limitation of his craft became apparent. While it was
true he could give the appearance of animation to the dead,
he could not give them life. Even Mocha developed a dull,
dry film over her eyes Quark periodically wiped with a damp
cloth, confronted by the glassy stare.

He wanted. He wanted so much. He wanted to heal everything between the boy he'd been and the man who raised
him. He wanted to save the girl, remember his mother, defend
himself, refuse the albatross, and forgive everyone. He wanted
to do the right thing at the right time in the real world, and
not just in his imagination. He wanted to be a hero, or at least
good.

He wondered if the girl's grieving parents hoped for her
return. Maybe their love was so strong they wouldn't mind the
flies, the disturbed sleep, the puddles and smoke or whatever
elements her spirit left in her wake: a baby's cry, a red smear of
lipstick, a mocking laugh. Maybe they wouldn't mind any of
it, if only she would come back. Quark sighed at his own inadequacy. What he wanted most from the Old Man's ghost was
nothing more than the impenetrable distance that had separated them when he was alive.

· 19 ·

Quark worried, the next morning, on his walk into town, that his lack of distress about the girl might be a sign of some corrupt element in his nature. He understood her death was a sad circumstance but could not grieve for her. *People die every day,* he reasoned. Every hour, every minute, every second. Dead, dead, dead. There. Another person dead. What was he supposed to do, live in a state of perpetual mourning? He, still alive, had tasks to complete, errands to run, responsibilities to execute.

The girl still smiled from posters tacked to light-posts and affixed to storefront windows though, occasionally, all that remained were four squares of tape on the glass, marking the border of her absence. Many pedestrians wore black, and a few wiped away tears. Yet, life continued, even as the rules of this new reality were unclear. A stranger held the door to the post office open, but when Quark tipped his hat in appreciation, the man turned glum, apparently remembering the solemn situation.

"Quark," the postmaster shouted as though through a gale. "How you doing, son?"

"I am here to pick up Thayer's mail. I would also like to close his post office box."

Without comment, the postmaster slipped through the curtain behind him, exposing bins of envelopes, and packages wrapped in brown paper. Quark listened to the voices in murmured conversation before a hand parted the drape, and a different man stepped out, smiling broadly beneath an impressively curled moustache.

"Quark? I thought you left weeks ago. Don't you recognize me?"

"I am sorry, I do not."

"It's Hank. Hank Pauly, your old classmate."

He had such a friendly face. Even back when he'd been one of the tormentors, he'd sported deceptive dimples.

"Yeah? You're remembering now, ain't you? I woulda recognized you anywhere. You ain't changed at all, excepting maybe got even taller."

He might have been the worst of the bunch, relentless, really.

"I heard about your Old Man. Sorry."

Quark nodded.

"Wanted to help with the ship-build, but I never got over there. Sick kids. Shit like that."

It hadn't occurred to Quark that any of his old tormenters would have had something to do with the ship. It was disturbing to think of them so near when he was unaware.

"Here you go." The postmaster stepped through the curtain with a small bundle. "This was in the box. You don't gotta check now. I already looked. This is all of it."

Quark was shocked to see a half-naked woman on the magazine cover.

"Yeah, that might cheer you up some, son." Both the postmaster and Hank laughed.

"Thank you for your assistance."

"Aw, come on, don't be like that. Most folks enjoy a friendly exchange. Don't mean any harm by it. Anyway, that's the reason Thayer never wanted mail delivered."

"What reason?"

"Excuse me?"

"The reason. You said that's the reason he didn't want mail delivered."

"Yeah?"

"'That's the reason,' you said. What's the reason? I would like to know why he had mail sent here when he could have had it delivered to the house. I am trying to understand why he did the things he did."

"Hey now, calm down. You ain't gonna have one of your fits, are ya?"

Quark felt over heated. It was impossible to know how to dress. One hour held the chill and dread of late November, while the next was all blue sky and summer.

"I merely want to inquire what you meant by the reason. You said my...Thayer had a reason for not having mail delivered to the house, and I am curious what that reason was."

The postmaster and Hank exchanged a look. "Well, 'cause of me, I guess. He got sorta lonely the last few years and could make me laugh, you know. Your Old Man used to like a good joke, didn't he?"

Quark felt appalled by the notion that Thayer not only had a sense of humor, but shared it with the dopey postmaster.

"From now on, please just deliver mail to the house." Though Quark directed his comment to the postmaster, both men nodded solemnly. He held the magazine firmly tucked under his arm. The only thing that would have made the entire enterprise worse would have been dropping the naked woman on the floor.

He did not drop her, however, not then or on the long, hot walk home, even when crossed by a small gang of boys who said something he couldn't hear, followed by a very audible, "Oh that's just Frankenquark. My dad says he's nothing to worry about."

Exhausted, Quark collapsed into the bed to peruse the magazine, hoping to discover the mysterious element that motivated others. While he looked at the naked women in disturbing poses, he thought about how seldom he'd been touched, unsure if all those clawed-hands on his shoulders offered as recent consolation counted. He felt relieved not to have ever been confronted by the spectacle displayed on the pages he turned with increasing horror. Finally, having only incited confusion and shame, he closed the magazine and watched the ship instead. What kind of man was he? None of the definitions seemed to apply. It was a distressing thought, but he felt calmed by the ship's presence just as—all those years ago—he'd found solace in the trees from which she was made.

· 20 ·

Quark initially mistook the ringing for the bells tolling in their watery grave. But no, it was the telephone. Who would call, he wondered as he hurried into the kitchen, worried he wouldn't get to it in time, stumbling as he picked up the receiver. He didn't mean to shout.

"Hello?"

"Quark?"

"Yes?"

"This is Maude. From the funeral home?"

"I mailed the check last week."

"This is about something else."

The flies had returned. He felt both discouraged by their tenacity and mesmerized by their dance as they darted in and out of the late afternoon light.

"Quark? Can you hear me?"

"Yes."

"I understand you've been looking for a captain. Not sure you know, but I have experience with a ship like yours. Summer work, when I was young. I've been in all kinds of seas, going out since I was a girl. What I'm trying to say is I'd like the position. I can't think, and I bet you can't either, of another person better prepared for shepherding the dead. I hope you don't mind me saying, but I heard you ain't much of a sailor."

"That is correct."

"Well, let me take care of her and you can concentrate on your grief. I'll navigate while you focus on the remains."

"I am not planning to go on the trip."

"Oh. Well, all right. It would be an honor for me to take her out. You got no idea how many shitheads around here wanna do it but are afraid of a corpse and a curse. I can put together a crew too, if you like. I got friends in the business, and none of 'em are afraid of ghosts. A ship like yours...well, I never thought I'd get another chance, and back then I didn't fully appreciate it. The way a ship like yours moves is as close to being a part of the sea as a person can get. Without getting swallowed by it, I mean."

"Are you crying?"

"You know, fuck it. I suppose you want someone who never cries, right? I spose—"

"I am pleased to learn of your interest."

"You want someone more like your old man. Well, good luck with that, 'cause I heard...wait. What? What did you say?"

"Your tears are of no significance."

"Excuse me?"

"I mean as pertains to the position."

"You mean...right. All right."

"I do have one question."

"Yeah?"

"What happens if someone dies?"

"If someone dies?"

"Will that impede your availability?"

"You mean, like if someone needs an undertaker?"

"Yes. That is what I am referring to."

"We're only talking a day trip, right? Sunrise departure, back before dark?"

"Yes. That's correct."

"My assistant is new, but she can handle things for a day. If she can't, I fuckin need a new assistant."

"All right."

"You saying we've got a deal?"

"Yes."

"All right, then. All right. Good. You won't regret it. I'll take care of her, and him too. Just tell me when and we'll be there."

"I must secure a way to transport her to the dock. Once that's confirmed, I will notify you of the chosen date of departure."

"You won't regret it, Quark."

"I won't?"

"I promise. And you know what they say about an undertaker's promise, right?"

"Actually, I—"

"Thank you for making this shitty time so much better."

It was then Quark understood. Why hadn't he realized sooner? She was the undertaker. She must have attended to the girl's remains. Of course she was upset!

"Sorry."

"For what?"

"Sorry about the girl."

He waited for a response but all he heard was a vague whispered noise, like the sound inside a seashell. He wondered if there was something wrong with his ears. How would he know? What if people had been saying important things to him all his life that he never heard?

"I will notify you of the day of departure once it is arranged," he shouted.

The only response was a dial tone, which was puzzling. On another day, he might have taken offense, but Quark decided to focus on the pleasant feeling of accomplishment. He had a captain and a crew, his difficult mission almost complete.

It won't be long before the Old Man is returned to the sea where his corpse will sink and the ghost can roam his drowned kingdom, he thought, pleased.

Emboldened, Quark retrieved the slim phone book with the incongruous picture of palm trees on its cover, using his finger to track columns made complex by oversized ads placed without deference to alphabetization. When he located the number for Riddle's Tow and Plow Company he was so disoriented by optimism that he failed to consider the implications of the name until his request had been laid out: the ship in the backyard, the need for a way to get her to the dock.

"Frankenquark? It's me, Brian! Don't you remember?"

"Yes, yes, of course." Quark tried to sound amiable. "How could I forget?"

"Yah, Tony said he saw you at the diner."

Quark had to hold himself very still. There was only one tow company in Bellfairie. He had to make it work.

"Yes, I saw him too."

"Right. And Gooseneck? You seen him? I suppose you heard about what happened to his girl?"

"His girl?"

"Yah. Right. That one that gone missing."

"Was she his girlfriend?"

"What? Fuck Quark, you got a sick sense of humor. Talking that way 'bout his daughter."

To think that Gooseneck had grown up to be a man with a daughter was shocking. Gooseneck! Out of all of them!

"I didn't realize. I'm sorry. She's dead."

"Sick bastard is all I'm saying. Doing that to a fifteen-year-old girl."

"It is my understanding she was trying to fly away."

"Yah? Well I don't know what you...hey, hold on a minute."

It sounded like he cupped his hand over the phone to shout something to someone named Roadkill. Quark was thinking about Brian Riddle's unpleasant habit of assigning nicknames when he came back on the line and asked what day had been chosen for the launch. Distracted, Quark said the first thing that came to his mind, Thursday.

"What? Why you gonna do that? No one sails on Thursday if they got a choice. Don't you remember?"

Quark was unable to recall why Thursday was a problem, but there was no use arguing about it. Friday was out too because that was the day of the crucifixion. It didn't matter your religion, either. The sea (and much of Bellfairie) was ruled by an odd confluence of Christian paganism. He might have suggested Saturday—there was nothing wrong with Saturday, exactly—but rather than prolong the conversation, he said she'd go out on Sunday.

"Okay. Sunday it is. We'll come by Saturday afternoon, and get her to the dock so ya got a early start. I ain't gonna lie, it's gonna cost ya."

"Yes, all right."

"I should stop by. See what it is we're dealing with."

"All right."

"You don't gotta be there. Jesus. It's been a hell of a long time since we had a launch."

In spite of its proximity to the sea, ship building was not a part of the local economy. Most Bellfairians had neither the money nor leisure necessary for such an endeavor. Quark had only one memory of a boat launch when he was quite young. Had the dead girl ever experienced a party? It made him feel sad to think she had not. He wondered if this sorrow redeemed him. Deep in rumination, he realized Riddle had asked a question.

"I'm afraid I did not hear you."

"Her name. What's her name?"

"Oh. Phoebe."

"Fuck it is. I ain't gonna have nothing to do with that. You can't name her after a dead girl. She'll go down for sure. Jesus Christ Quark, you ain't changed at all, have you?"

He had changed quite a bit, however. He knew he didn't have to stand there and be insulted, for instance, the way he

believed he had to when he was a boy. "I'm afraid there has
been a misunderstanding. I thought you were enquiring about
the girl's name. The ship does not yet have a name."

"Yah? Well, you better get 'er one. A nameless ship is a
coffin."

"Yes, all right."

"Might wanna sleep on her a few nights, you know? Some
say that's the best way to get to know her."

"Hmmmmm." Quark hoped to convey interest without
outright lying. Why would he abandon his comfortable bed
for hard wood on a cold night?

"Don't worry about making a big fancy feast or nothin."

"I appreciate that, I—"

"Me and my boys are perfectly happy with a good ol' fish
boil or a pig roast. Nothing fancy."

"Yes. Well. All right."

After hanging up, Quark wondered if he was actually
expected to feed his old tormentor. It seemed like more than
he could do. A cruel joke. Would Thayer have sacrificed so
much on Quark's behalf?

Determined to make all the arrangements in one fortunate
hour Quark searched again through the phone book, finally
locating the number for Sushi's, but got a recording saying
it had been disconnected, which he found upsetting until he
remembered it wasn't really Sushi's any longer, though that
was the name on the sign and what everyone called it. Even if
he could find the correct number, Quark realized, it probably
wasn't the best time to call. Everyone who worked there
seemed so upset about the girl. He wondered if she had been
nicer to them than she had been to him.

His hope of settling all his business in one fortunate
hour—or day—dashed, Quark decided to use his good spirits
to help him cross more tasks off his to-do list. It was irritating
how much useless stuff Thayer had saved, stashed in closets,
cupboards and drawers, junk Quark had no attachment to

until confronted with the choice between bin for saving or bin for resale. He found a small roll of flowered wallpaper tucked in a back corner of the bedroom closet, which he guessed belonged to his grandmother or mother. The print was pretty. Tiny yellow blossoms with white centers on a pale blue background. What would his life have been like if he'd lived in a home of walls camouflaged with flowers, rather than the weathered boards of a doomed ship? There was barely enough of it to cover a book, Quark thought, remembering how he'd folded paper bags for his school texts when he was young and, just like that, he smelled the waxy scent of crayons, as if he'd fallen through time and space the way the Old Man had—trapped between life and death—though Quark was just trapped. He tossed the wallpaper in the bin for resale.

He did not need stubby pencils, rolls of string, old plastic bags, or sheets of wrinkled aluminum foil. He did keep the small piece of scrimshaw however, a whale's tooth delicately engraved with roses twined around its circumference. He wondered who had carved it. A man of the sea, that was certain, yet someone with whom he shared some affinity.

It was a shock to find the mask of the horned beast that used to terrorize him every Christmas, the old tradition preserved in Bellfairie even as surrounding counties were visited by a kindly Santa Claus. Of course, Quark knew there was no such creature. He had forgotten about it for decades, he thought, standing in the closet, holding its monstrous face in his hands.

How he used to tremble, spying over the edge of his blanket as the thing shuffled into the dark room to hang a stocking from the bedpost; not daring to move until he heard the back door slam shut then rushing to his window to watch the beast—hunched beneath its cape and the tattered sack it carried over its shoulder—stop in the yard to face the house, its paw raised. For years, Quark ducked, and scampered back to bed, shivering in cold excitement, measuring terror against anticipation until the latter won out, only then raiding his stocking filled with peppermint sticks, gingerbread men, acorns, chocolate swans, an apple, once a small knife and, later, bones.

Eventually the time came when he no longer cowered at the creature paused beneath the winter moon and, when it waved, Quark raised his own hand in response, surprised that the terrifying thing lifted one bent knee high, and then the other, in a little beastly dance.

Quark stared at the mask with the unoccupied holes for eyes, feeling the same sense of dislocation he'd felt all those years ago, trying to understand the correlation between beast, and dancer.

What would have happened to me, Quark wondered, *if not for the Old Man who had given the last decades of his life to raise a child not his own?*

Quark set the mask in the bin for saving, moving the small roll of wallpaper to cover the eye sockets along with some rope from those long afternoons of knot-tying lessons. He was not blind to the folly of his choice, but tried to be kind to himself. After all, he was in mourning, doing the best he could with the greatest loss of his life. What was it everyone kept saying? Grief is a ship without a captain? Yes, that was right.

He didn't generally enjoy cooking, and mostly considered it a necessary task best performed with efficiency: a can of beans, rice or yams, toast smeared with peanut butter, but that evening Quark diced six russet potatoes tossed in oil until they glistened, and the salt and pepper stuck, then spread them across the least objectionable looking pan to roast beside tofu cut in slabs and seasoned.

After dinner he sat in the old chair with the library book he'd set aside for far too long, reading with great sympathy for the poor, nameless creature until his eyes drooped and— though he revived himself to continue—became heavy again.

He dressed in the Old Man's flannel pajamas which were

too small, though Quark appreciated that the material was soft against his dry skin. Brushing his teeth, he caught his reflection in the mirror, his long arms stuck out from the sleeves like the creature who had pilloried Frankenstein's wardrobe, so unloved no one had bothered to clothe him, or even give him a name. He rinsed the toothbrush, placed it on the medicine cabinet shelf and turned off the light, his lips pursed, returned to the childhood pursuit of whistling, though only able to produce a small sound like a leak, abruptly abandoned as he stepped out of the bathroom into a room of floating color.

He knew immediately what it was. How could he have ever forgotten the bloom of the Aurora borealis? It couldn't have happened often, but he thought it happened more than once, watching the show with the Old Man then pretending to fall asleep so he could savor the sensation of being held close to Thayer's beating heart as he carried Quark back into the house, up the stairs to tuck into bed.

He laced on his shoes, pulled the blanket into a ball beneath his arm, grabbed the limp feather pillow, hurrying, worried it would be over before he got outside.

It wasn't. He climbed the ship's ladder beneath arcs of green and pink, so cold when he lay down he didn't think he'd stay long. Soon enough, mesmerized by the streamers and rippled curtains of light, he found himself thrusting his arm up, as though to pluck lights from the sky. *This was his father's country. Not the one who raised him, but the one who named him; overhead all that time.* My sky, Quark thought. *Not sea, but sky.*

Bellfairians said the Aurora borealis was the spirits of the dead so far removed from human form all that remained was luminescence. Quark knew the color was not benevolence, merely a collision of electrically charged particles, and yet, when he heard the noise, felt like that boy again, the one who believed in a world beyond the material. They said sometimes you could hear the lights. He never had, not before that night when the crackling sound—like the first sparks of a campfire—

grew into applause. Was it true? Was it possible all those years when he'd felt so alone, they had been there, watching over him, rooting for him, and waiting for his return?

· 21 ·

Quark couldn't remember when he'd slept so well. He lay, staring at the clouds. He could have been anywhere; even the sea with her reported charms intact though, just thinking about it made him feel a little nauseous right there, in the landlocked safety of the ship.

"Time to steer my own passage," he whispered, in case anyone was listening. The words did not bring the relief he expected. Yes, he was eager to be rid of the Old Man, but that didn't mean he wanted to be alone. He had not expected that the promise of freedom would leave him feeling so unmoored.

Maybe he was doing it all wrong. Perhaps he should have a traditional funeral, bury Thayer and order a headstone engraved with a loving phrase.

Yet, as soon as the notion was formed, Quark rejected it. How angry the Old Man would be if anchored to the ground for all eternity. Just the thought of such a betrayal incited a violent shiver.

Quark decided to have a box built. Not a casket, but a ditty box, the kind sailors made to carry small things that were precious to them. Inside of it he would place mementos of Thayer's life: a knotted rope, a whiskey tumbler or coffee mug, a sprinkling of the shards of glass he'd found in an old pickle jar on the kitchen counter beside a note scratched in pencil. "In case you need it." He could bury the box, and visit the Old Man without fear of retribution. Quark knew others considered cemeteries bleak, but he fondly recalled playing amongst the tombstones, the sense he'd enjoyed then of the sky as both vast and close. The more he thought about it, the more he liked the idea.

He went inside to prepare his coffee, which he drank in the comfort of the old chair, watching the morning light change from diaphanous to bright. Perhaps he would not sell the house, after all. He couldn't stay, of course. He had obligations and a life for himself away from there, but for the first time it occurred to him that Bellfairie might be a place he'd like to return to. Maybe it had been a child's logic to believe good and bad memories must be sorted, as though one contaminated the other. Maybe he could live with both.

Since he had errands to do anyway, he decided to stop at Sushi's. *Killing two birds with one stone,* he thought then winced. Why did such phrases persist? Why wasn't there a saying like "plucking two flowers with one hand" or "calling two birds with a single song?" He shook his head at the inscrutable cruelty of the world, only drawn to stop when he heard someone whisper his name which, upon further consideration, he decided had merely been his stomach growling.

Won't be long now, Quark thought as he walked into town, his hat tilted jauntily on his head, once more in pursuit of whistling, his lips fixed in the shape of a kiss, undeterred by the stares of others who—he assumed—were fascinated by his good spirits, the way he had always been enchanted by signs of happiness in others.

He noticed the usual group of teenage boys congregated in front of "Fran's Bait and Floral." They had taunted Quark with the old nickname for weeks, but he would no longer be shamed. Whether they knew it or not, the moniker was a compliment. What could be more admirable than to be called a creator? Thinking about their folly caused Quark to chuckle as he passed them and the glaring boys said nothing, though their silence, and the way they turned in eerie unison, reminded him of requiem sharks.

"I'll become a shark," the Old Man used to say. "When my time comes, throw me overboard. Why are you making that face? Shows what you know. We are not Barbarians, wasting our dead by putting them in the ground. When I go, take me home."

"Not long now," Quark whispered to the Old Man, wherever he might be, lodged in the past or hovering overhead. "Soon you will go to your watery grave."

Unfortunately, the harmless rejoinder landed on Mrs. Neller's ancient ears. Not usually disposed to acute hearing, something in that day—the course of wind, or the wicked remains of some spirit—caused her to catch every syllable Quark muttered as he passed on the narrow sidewalk. She brought her hands, still clutching the bouquet of baby's breath she'd purchased for the dead girl, over her heart. Later, she reported that when he tipped his ridiculous hat in her direction she felt as though she was being mocked by death, himself.

Quark continued, arms swinging and lips pursed until he encountered the weeping girls huddled in front of Sushi's, which struck him as problematic. His chief concern was not with the location of their grief, but the delicate matter of making his way to the door. When they saw him, however, they broke apart as if gunshot. He was still pondering their confusing behavior as he stepped into the diner. Had it been his ineffective whistling that disturbed them? Did they think he was drinking again, like the Old Man, never able to fully recover sobriety?

Quark quickly found a seat at the counter, picked up a menu, and peeked over the ketchup-stained rim to observe. Dory passed by several times without comment before pausing long enough to pour his coffee, the pot held at a listless tilt she didn't appear aware of until, just as he thought to warn against a spill, she righted it and continued on her shuffling way, returning shortly after to slide a plate against the menu until he set it aside. Pleased to discover his usual number five, which he had no memory of ordering, Quark tried to convince himself the sauce was not bitter, the oysters not gritty, the waffle not undercooked, but it was all a lie.

When Dory placed the tab beside his plate—for an order of eggs with potatoes and toast—it took Quark several minutes to get her attention. He explained the problem, but she appeared to be staring into the deep as he segued into an inquiry about catering options.

"You having a party?"

"Yes, yes," he said, nodding vigorously. *Who knows*, he thought, *maybe this would be just the first of many such celebratory occasions.*

"When? When is this party?"

"You're invited, of course. Saturday. Saturday evening."

Dory suddenly possessed the same cold eyes within an immobile countenance that signified a violent change in Thayer's temper, though when she spoke her voice was so soft Quark had to tilt his head to hear. She scolded him for being callous and clueless, which confused him so thoroughly he began to suspect she was right. When she called him hulking, he sat back. *What did his posture have to do with anything?*

"Don't you ever think about anyone but yourself? What would ever possess you to throw a party on the same day as Phoebe's funeral? Are you nuts or just stupid, anyway?"

Quark slammed his hands on the counter, so hard his palms burned. He observed, as if outside himself and not in any way responsible, Dory's eyes widen as she stepped back, but he could not stop.

"I am not stupid! I am not stupid! I am not stupid!"

He became dimly aware of children with faces buried into protective sleeves and tucked against parental chests, forks stopped mid-air, salt shakers held like lanterns against a storm, everyone paused. He wished to be equally paralyzed, yet found himself tapping his chest, stuck in replay. "I am not stupid. I am not stupid. I am not stupid," until his voice lost vigor, and Chef, who had come out of the kitchen with a meat cleaver, gently ushered him towards the exit.

Aware he was being watched, Quark whispered, "I cannot leave. I have not yet paid my bill."

"We'll put it on your tab. You can take care of it next time."

"I also have to make arrangements for Saturday evening. Nothing extravagant. Some fish, some potatoes. Coleslaw might be nice."

"You having a party?"

He stared into Chef's dark eyes, *like two currants in a hot cross bun*, Quark thought, and felt ashamed for the meanness of his mind. "It is not a party. It is a funeral. For my...for Thayer. Will you please tell her?"

"What's that?"

"Will you explain to Dory? It's not a party."

Chef nodded then guided Quark out the door where he stood alone and embarrassed, replaying everything until he arrived at the point of his distress and, once again, tapped his chest. Turning to go back to explain, he almost stumbled into Henry Yarly. The elderly man stepped nimbly aside as was later reported by several patrons who observed the exchange through the large window while they drank their coffee and buttered their biscuits.

"I am very sorry," Quark said. "I did not notice your approach."

"That's all right, son. Nothing to be upset about. I'm surprised to see you. Heard you'd left a while ago."

Quark, who did not enjoy small talk, even on a good day, would have liked to tip his hat and go on his way but didn't want to be unkind to Yarly who had been a friend to the Old Man.

"I want to thank you. For everything you did for...for Thayer."

"You don't have to thank me, son. I enjoyed his company.

I'm going to miss him and his stories. No one could tell one like he could, I suppose I don't have to say. No one could make me laugh like him! Now, you just take it easy. Don't get worked up. It's just the natural course. You remember what he said about your name?"

Quark didn't think it was necessary to respond, but Yarly waited as if the question were sincere.

"I do not."

"We were sitting on the porch. Do you remember how we used to do that?"

Quark had pleasant memories of evenings spent at Yarly's cabin on the shore. As an adult he understood what the boy had not. How the two men were joined in a confederacy of grief after Yarly's wife—speeding, they said—plummeted into the cove, killing both her and their baby girl. The two men would sit in the porch rockers, saying little, while Quark built sand castles and pebble graveyards, sometimes falling asleep on the stairs like an old dog.

"Well, you know how he would get with his sorrows. He was talking about you the way he did."

"He did? He was?"

"He said it was a good name for you, though he didn't like it at first."

Well, that makes two of us, Quark thought. How often he'd imagined being called something ordinary like Todd, or Chad, or Lincoln.

"He said, now listen to this, he said, it was the perfect name because you turned out to be like a strange star, not the movie ones, you know, but the ones in the sky."

Quark thought there must be more, but Yarly looked up expectantly, a beatific smile on his worn face.

"Yes, well."

"Oh, now, I didn't mean to upset you. I heard you're taking it hard. Listen, son. Don't let it drown you. You know what they say?"

Quark nodded. "With grief," he sighed. For the first time wondering if everyone was right. Had he been so overcome that he didn't even know it? Was it possible that others knew his own heart better than he did? "I have made plans for his funeral. You are invited."

"Oh?"

"Saturday night before the launch. Maude is going to take the ship out. Burial at sea. It's what he wanted."

"He always did say he wanted to go back to the sea so he—"

"Could turn into a shark."

"What? Ha! See, you do take after him, don't ya, with that humor? So he could turn into a shark! Ha!"

"You are invited. To the funeral. Saturday night. We're having fish and coleslaw. The launch is Sunday. You are invited to both."

"Well, I appreciate it, I really do, but I ain't gone to a funeral since.... I just came from Whitman's. You remember Seamus Whitman? Wayne's father? He's building that girl's coffin."

"Phoebe?"

"Yah, that's right. Hell's bells, son. Getting forgetful in my old age. I don't mean to be disrespectful. I understand you knew her and all."

"I didn't really. I—"

"Saw you stop and give her a ride that evening in the rain."

"I didn't. I stopped but—"

"Nothing to be ashamed of, son. That was real decent of you. Well, we do what we can, don't we? To ease the mortal coil?"

Unsure how to respond, Quark nodded.

"Tell you what, why don't you come for a visit? We can say our goodbyes in private. Would you like that? Would that work? Remember how we used to do? Remember those castles you used to make with little stone forests around them?"

Quark felt suddenly seasick as he peered at the face smiling up at him. He said he was glad they ran into each other, and maybe he was. His gratitude wasn't completely fraudulent, only complicated. "Thank you." He tipped his hat at Yarly and, after a moment's pause to recall the way, headed towards Whitmans.

Unfortunately, the most direct route was blocked by police tape. An assortment of the curious—some Quark recognized and some he didn't—stood near the cairn, watching the rolling waves, as though her spirit might rise from the sea to tell the tale of the last moments of her life. A few children, oblivious to the gravity of the location, searched gleefully through shells for beach glass Quark remembered from his childhood. One little girl ran to add her find to the stack.

"Look, Mummy," she said. "A mermaid's tear for the dead girl!"

Quark took the detour, finally making his awkward ascent up the side of a hill he recalled as the mountain he and Wayne climbed all those years ago during that period when they were friends and conquerors. At the summit he scratched his dirty palms, still burning from when he'd slammed them on the counter, an embarrassing display he did not like to remember.

The crooked house, alone on the bluff, had the best view in all of Bellfairie. He had found it frightening when he was young and thought the jagged rocks below looked like the unkempt teeth of a monster. The sea that day was calm, the sky clear. Standing at a safe distance from the edge, Quark felt like he was looking at the end of the world. It didn't seem so difficult to understand how people once believed they would fall off the horizon though, obviously, he knew that was impossible.

The ghost ship appeared out of nowhere, the water untroubled by the vessel's course. So near, he could see the

sun through its ribs, the skeleton figurehead, and the shades
of men on board raising their arms even as they disappeared,
leaving only the echo of their cries until that, too, was gone.

Quark remained rooted for a while; to be sure what was
true. It would be a terrible thing to abandon men on the rocks
simply because his mind could not contain their suffering but,
no, it was the suffering that was imagined. The sea was clear,
the sky too, and the only sound was the waves, the distant
squawk of seagulls, and a motorized screech of some kind
of power tool emanating from the workshop he was headed
towards when Mrs. Whitman rounded the side of the house
with a basket of laundry. She greeted him by saying his name
with a gasp of exclamation. He felt bad he hadn't visited sooner.
He had not realized she felt so warmly towards him.

"I heard you'd come back," she said.

Deeply aware of the awkwardness of condolence, Quark
tipped his hat and bowed. He had no idea what inspired the
archaic gesture but, once committed, there was nothing left to
do but unbend himself and say how very sorry he was to learn
of Wayne's decapitation.

She looked so shocked he worried she'd forgotten the
tragic event of her own son's death and wondered how to
proceed as she turned to walk up the steps, the basket against
her hip, not even bothering to look back when she asked if he
was coming.

The foyer was cloyingly dark. Quark blinked away the
shadows until he could safely make his way to the kitchen,
painted picket fence white, the mullioned windows, wavy
with old glass, curtained in lace. It smelled damp; cut by a
sharply sweet perfume he guessed was detergent. A washing
machine and dryer fit snugly into the small mud room, the
basket of laundry set on top.

"Couldn't keep going into the basement. My knees
wouldn't take it. Seamus and some of the men brung 'em up
here. I don't mind the door being blocked. You know what they

say about trouble coming through the back door, right?"

Quark, who had no idea what they said about most things, studied her face for clues while she peered at him as if on a similar excavation. Pretending not to mind the uncomfortable atmosphere, he pulled out a chair to sit at the table, momentarily distracted by gouge marks in the wood. Did everyone have a life of slipped knives and secret cuts?

"Seamus will be along any minute," Mrs. Whitman said, setting a cup and saucer before him. "Maybe you should just tell me why you're here?"

He explained how he'd come to ask Mr. Whitman to build a ditty box. "Not a coffin," he hastened to clarify. "Just a little box, you know. That's all I'm asking."

"Is that right?"

He didn't understand why she was frowning or why she crossed her arms over her chest, the kettle untouched, all the burners cold. He explained his plans for the ship launch and Thayer's burial, backing into Saturday's feast in order to make clear it was not a party, but a funeral. "You're invited, of course."

"I don't think so."

He stared at the table.

"I don't think you should expect any more from Seamus. He was at your place for almost a month, you know, finishing Thayer's folly. That's all right. Lots of folks helped us after what happened to Wayne. That's just what we do 'round here. But now there's this dead girl and you know, maybe it's time you start thinking about what you can do for yourself."

"It's not what I do best," Quark said.

"What's that?"

"My specialty is bones." What had he been thinking, anyway? She was right. Everyone had already done so much while he had been wandering about like a fool falling asleep all over town. When he stood to leave she startled back, so quickly she fairly jumped, which he found surprising; up to that point he had taken her for someone whose girth made all movement languid.

"Seamus will be here any second."

"Could you thank him for me? I should have done so sooner. For all he did for Aurora?"

"Aurora?"

"The ship. That's her name. I'd appreciate it if you could tell him how grateful I am. For everything. I'm afraid I've been, well, you know what they say."

"Naming a ship that ends in a vowel is unlucky. Don't you remember?"

"I don't remember much."

"Nothing to be done for it now."

"I might change it to something else. Catfish, maybe."

"Nope. Can't change a ship's name once it's decided. Doesn't work like that. Don't you remember anything?"

Quark considered confiding his concern about the great gaps in his memory but quickly rejected the idea. He tipped his hat—embarrassed that he'd neglected to take it off—thanked her, then walked down the dark hallway and out the front door.

Standing on the top step, trying to decide what to do next, he heard a noise he thought might be the drawing of the lock. Bellfairie had changed more than he'd realized if folks had begun locking their doors.

Hunched against the wind, he continued on his way, stopping to inspect a glint of gold in his path; a tiny heart, the sort that would hang on a chain. He considered bringing it to Mrs. Whitman. Perhaps it was something she'd been looking for, precious for sentimental reasons (because it certainly wasn't an expensive piece) he pocketed it instead, feeling bold and guilty, a confluence of emotion he found disturbing. He did not alleviate his burden by returning the heart to its resting place, however. He wanted the cheap thing. It was pretty and he wanted it.

· 22 ·

Quark could fashion a lovely container from a femur but where would he get one without a lot of trouble? Besides, it seemed a fitting tribute to make a ditty box from ship remnants. He collected a small pile in the backyard then sat on the cold ground to work, soon remembering the comfort he'd taken, all those years ago, in carving, when his knife had helped him discover a brand of mastery different from brute power. How mystifying to learn that the enigma he'd always thought his terrible father was actually his generous grandfather, a man who'd sacrificed the last decades of life to raise an orphaned child. Quark could not dismiss that fact, or the memories that arose from the wood shavings as though released by the blade. The Christmas lobsters, purchased at the market every December twenty-fourth (even the year of the big storm when Thayer snow-shoed into town and returned with ice chips in his beard and eyebrows) the time a teacher began calling Quark "Frank," and Thayer roared into the classroom (both embarrassing and thrilling) to tell the woman "his" boy's name. "Like in the sky" he'd said which, at the time, had made no sense. To think, such a force reduced to a whiff of tobacco, suspicious puddles, weeping figments, clouds of flies.

And a ship! Quark admonished himself not to forget that accomplishment, even if created from his loss.

"I know they meant nothing to you," he'd said when he visited and found the trees gone. "But they were my friends."

"Your friends? Your friends!" the Old Man mocked. "Listen to you. A grown man who thinks trees are his friends!"

Nothing had prepared Quark for the cavern that opened within, as though his ribs were torn apart to reveal a labyrinth of loss: the tyrant who raised him, who fed him, who defended him, who left both the magnificent legacy of a ship and the hideous waste of their alliance.

Yet, when his fascination turned from wood to vertebrae, which even as a child Quark suspected was weird, didn't Thayer come from town with that corpse?

"Come here, son. This is what I've been trying to tell you. Never mind that nonsense. You are not of the air, but the sea. Don't listen to that witch. Birds are not your kin. Your people are sailors and shipmen. Your great-great grandfather was a whaler. Long nights on the sea with nothing to do but carve bones and teeth. See this? Right here? This wing is filled with song. Gonna carve 'er up for ya, son. Come on, now, don't be a pansy. I want you to watch me cut her up. Learn how it's done."

Later, the Old Man made albatross stew he served with a prune sauce Quark pretended to enjoy. Afterwards, he made it all the way to the end of the drive, but only part way down the road before throwing up. Yet, when he finished the flute, carved from Albatross bone, hadn't the Old Man held it tenderly and called it a fine piece of scrimshaw, and Quark a fine Scrimshander?

What had become of that odd instrument? Had it truly possessed the right geometry for music? Quark remembered playing it, but maybe that was just fancy, the same state that caused him to believe Mrs. Winter had made it snow in his classroom, or that once he had a magic wand so powerful it made people disappear.

He paused to brush away the wood shavings and a sliver burrowed beneath his skin causing a sharp point of pain, its tiny edge, like a fibrous eyelash, protruding just enough to be drawn out. Finished with the delicate excavation he raised his face to find an old seagull, landed nearby, watching as if it knew Quark's worst impulse.

It was a terrible thing the way she had died too young, and too soon. He wished he could change it back, return to that watercolor night and the girl walking in the rain. "Get in," he would say, and she would open the door, and be saved, and her child, and the generations to follow. But what was the use of pretending?

He returned to the task, fitting the box in the old way, without nails, a puzzle of sorts. One section was off kilter. He shaved the edge and tried again. Just as it fit, he thought of the bedside table in his old room. *Is the mind a ditty box all its own,* he wondered, *filled with an assortment of scraps tucked in the dark until some strange force opens it to retrieve forgotten things?*

After storing the tools (he would never forget the Old Man's temper incited by a hammer left in the rain) Quark brought the box into the house and set it on the plank table, cautioning himself against optimism as he walked up the stairs to the little crooked room. Pretending it didn't matter, he sauntered across the creaking floor to pull and jiggle the stubborn drawer until it released its hold, revealing a stack of paper he had used for folding into birds, a pencil with broken lead, and the slender flute made of bone.

Like sighting a firefly, a monarch, a shooting star, or a moment from my own childhood, he thought. He sat on the side of the bed, eyeing the instrument as though it might flicker and disappear, surprised at how small it was.

Upon close inspection, it appeared clumsily executed, but when he brought it to his lips he found—after some effort and adjustment—he was able to produce an unpleasant noise through which he persisted until it became a melody created a long time ago, a gift from the boy he'd been to the man he became.

He played the tune over and over again, in spite of

Thayer's complaints, thundering at "that ghastly sound," which incited a few terrifying squawks. With furrowed brow and trembling fingers, Quark vanquished the ghost only to have it replaced by another. She came into the room and said, "Will you come with me to walk the bluffs?"

Startled, he squinted into the shadows. "Will you come with me to walk the bluffs?" she asked again, and for a moment he was a boy who loved that voice, who happily abandoned everything to run to her.

What kind of person am I, Quark wondered as he returned the instrument to the drawer. *What kind of person forgets his own mother?* He curled in the fetal position on his old bed, closed his eyes and listened to the dark, daring to hope someone would tell him he was not unforgivable.

Did he sleep? He didn't think so but then again, he must have. It must have been a nightmare, the Old Man sitting by the side of the bed, a phantom of dejection. Quark feared the revealed face, as it turned, would be something horrible—a monster of decay—but it was only Thayer.

"Your wait is almost over," Quark said, surprised to hear the scratched sorrow of his voice. "I found someone to take you out to sea. You remember Maude? She owns the funeral home? She's very well suited for the position."

The Old Man shook his head.

"It won't be long," Quark whispered. "Just what you want. Burial at sea," and his focus broadened to a room filled with the dead. He wondered if the confused looking young man with binoculars draped around his neck was his father, the woman beside him, who did look vaguely familiar, his mother. Wayne was there, his head, thankfully, still attached, and Cheryl, her yellow tail erect as she ran across the covers. Quark's happiness at finding his lost pet was quickly dissipated by the girl, her cape blowing in a phantom wind, dark hair lashing her face into a mask of blood red lips, gone before he could ask why she'd said no. The animals arrived on stealthy paws, bounding over his bed, landing without a sound, and scurrying across the coverlet yet leaving no imprint: squirrels, and gophers, and mice, and rabbits. The albatross swooped down from the ceiling, its wings cutting the air with the ghostly music of its bones. When the seagulls arrived, they filled the room with flap of wings and sharp beaks, squawking his name, and accusing him of murder.

Overcome, all Quark could do was cry, not the rare somber silent tears of a grown man, but the humiliating chirps of a wren, his hands cupped over his eyes. When at last he looked up, all that was left were flies settled in their various locations, crawling up the windowpane, resting on the pillow, perched on the bedpost. He escaped the room, briefly considering another night on the ship, he chose the couch instead.

· 23 ·

The next morning, Quark's hands shook as he lifted the mug of bitter coffee to his trembling lips. Why, he wondered. Why had he not found, within his spectral visitors, a spiritual sense, the sort of mystical experience others considered a resource? Instead, he felt depleted. What did they want from him? He knew the people who brought him animals had killed them. What could he to do about all the dead? He could not heal the past. The gunshot and arrow, driven by human hands, had more power than he ever would. All he could do was restore an appearance of animation to each corpse. He could spend the rest of his days seeking absolution for the albatross murdered in his name, but it would never be enough. His life was an act of contrition.

Quark almost spilled his coffee when he saw the sheriff's car come up the drive. He had often heard about an invisible thread between friends—the way one sensed when the other was in trouble—but did not know how to process the unfamiliar tremor of affection that coursed through his body.

"I'm very pleased to see you," he said when he opened the door.

"I'm here on official business."

"Welcome, welcome!" Quark waved his hand as though ushering in a recalcitrant traveler, though Healy stepped inside without hesitation. "Would you like some coffee?"

The sheriff half-shook his head no then shrugged. He would have a cup, he said. "Been a long coupla days."

Quark was relieved that Healy didn't accompany him into the kitchen. Friendship was one thing, invasion another. Apparently the previous night's dream had been a portent of good. After all, didn't he have a visitor who'd come to offer the sort of companionship one seeks when weary? Quark never had another friend after Wayne, and hadn't ever understood what happened between them. One minute they were playing war with plastic soldiers (their green faces in rigor mortis of concentration, weapons forever held in fighting position, shot dead with a flick of finger and thumb) and the next he was watching through the wavy glass of an old window, Thayer's grim approach. And that was the end of that. They never played together again.

Quark was pleased that he'd continued with the habit of preparing coffee for two. Perhaps he had actually anticipated, through some psychic element, this surprise visit of a friend. Once again, he wondered if he'd misunderstood his place in Bellfairie, his focus impeded by the stye known as Thayer. So entertained was Quark by his own wit, that he was chuckling when he handed the mug of steaming brew to the sheriff.

"Something funny?" Healy asked, stepping away from the large window.

"Probably not," Quark said, reminded of the man's lack of humor. "I am sorry I don't have cream or sugar. I hope it's all right."

Healy brought the mug to his lips which, Quark noted, were surprisingly pretty, rosy pink and pleasantly shaped.

"I hope it isn't too strong. We...that is, I have always enjoyed a bitter cup."

Healy pointed at Thayer's chair. "You mind?"

The thought of the sheriff sitting in the Old Man's place disturbed Quark, but he couldn't decide how to communicate so without offense. Healy set the mug on the cluttered table then, stronger than he looked, turned the chair with a flick of his wrist, frowning at Quark who stepped forward to help.

"Why don't you take a seat? So we can talk?"

Quark sat on the couch. He didn't mind, really. It didn't smell that bad. He was embarrassed however, when Healy frowned at the chair as though it, too, emitted a sour odor, then leaned over to pluck a white feather he held up like an accusation.

"I wonder where that came from," Quark said.

"I have a few questions. If that's all right."

Probably brought in on a breeze, or stuck to clothing, a natural occurrence and not in any way evidence of a breach between the living and the dead, proof of nothing more than the existence of birds.

"Anything I can do to be of assistance."

"Heard about your trouble at Sushi's yesterday."

Had that only been yesterday? Quark sighed.

"Wanna tell me about it?"

Quark looked past Healy's shoulder, out the large window, remembering, all those years ago, having his first coffee with the man who had beaten him so thoroughly his skin blossomed into a bruise garden. He didn't go to school for a week. Or was it longer? He recalled the time as almost idyllic, marred only by pain and the oppression of long sleeves and pants Thayer insisted Quark wear in the bright heat of tree climbing, eating wild blueberries, learning to feed a fire. Every morning, during that period, he had sat beside the Old Man drinking coffee, staring out the window, waiting to be rescued by the bird folk. Unlike Mrs. Winter, who had declined their offer, Quark planned to join them. They never came, however, and when he finally returned to school, he'd found himself behind in everything.

"I'm not stupid," he mumbled.

"What's that?"

"I'm not stupid.'"

The sheriff nodded.

"Dory, said I was stupid and I'm not."

"Why would she say that?"

Quark had no idea. His whole life people had been describing him in ways he knew to be untrue.

"Were you having a fight?"

"It was a misunderstanding. She thought I was having a party but it's a funeral. That's all. For my…for Thayer."

"Well, why would she think that was stupid? I feel like I'm missing something here."

"Perhaps you should talk to her." Quark eyed the abandoned coffee. He never had a cup he liked better than his own homemade. He was disappointed Healy didn't appear to agree.

"Quark?"

"Yes?"

"I want to ask a few questions about the girl. Phoebe?"

"All right."

"What happened between you two?"

"Nothing. That is…I offered her a ride. She declined."

"Right. But can we back up a moment?"

"Yes."

"No. I don't mean literally. Just stay seated the way you are. Let me say it a different way. The other day, at Sushi's, do you remember that? When I came and spoke to you?"

"Yes. Of course."

"Well, as you know, Phoebe was upset. She said you waved a knife at her."

"Yes."

"I wonder if I made a mistake not taking that more seriously. Cause if I did—"

"I wasn't waving it at her. It was in my hand. I was pointing out the window."

"I will get to the bottom of this, Quark."

"She said there were no oysters!"

"This isn't one of those things I can pretend I didn't see. I hope you know that."

"There are plenty of oysters. That's all I meant."

Healy stared at Quark, who stared back until the sheriff abruptly nodded.

"It was good you told me about seeing her that night."

"Well, I thought you should know." Quark wasn't being fully honest. It was doubtful he would have ever reported the sighting had Mrs. Winter not insisted on it but, at that moment, he felt proud of himself for having done so. He enjoyed the feeling of being appreciated.

"You're the last person we know of who saw her alive. That was a big help. It tells us where she was after she had the fight with her boyfriend. He said she left alone, but until you came along, we weren't sure we believed him."

Quark nodded.

"Yep. You seeing her made a big difference. It makes a big difference for everyone, but it especially makes a big difference for Chicky."

"Chicky?"

"The boyfriend."

"Chicky?"

Healy shrugged.

What kind of name is that? Quark wondered.

"The thing is, I can't say much about an active investigation, but seeing as how you have already been such a help, I thought I'd stop by to find out if there's anything else you wanna tell me."

Relieved to have moved on from the disturbing subject, Quark perked up. "Yes. You're invited."

"Excuse me?"

"Nothing formal. Just a little gathering before Aurora's launch."

"Aurora?"

"That's her name."

"Who's name?"

"The ship."

"Oh yeah? You know it's not a good idea to name a ship with a word that ends in a vowel."

"I'm thinking of changing it."

"Can't change it now. What's set is set."

Quark decided to forge on. "We're having a little get together on Saturday."

"Oh, yeah? Gonna be a long day with Phoebe's funeral."

Did no one care about the Old Man, after all?

"I'll try. I can't promise, cause of this being an active investigation, but I'll try, all right? The thing is, and I'm only asking since you already been so helpful, are you sure you really saw her? Are you sure it was Phoebe, and not just, you know, something you imagined?"

Quark sat back, stunned.

"I have to ask, did you start drinking again? Nothing to be ashamed of, if you did. Everyone knows you were devastated by your loss. Is it possible—"

"It is not."

"All right. Did you touch her?"

"What?"

"You said she never entered your truck, right? Did you touch her, or anything?"

"Why would I do such a thing?"

"Well, see, that's my point. How do you even know she was really there?"

Quark puzzled through the odd question, disturbingly similar to Mrs. Winter's concern. He wondered if he had been wrong to trust the old woman. "She was dripping wet and... she was there."

"Mind if I have a look?"

"What?"

"I'd like to take your truck for a few hours. Maybe a day. Two at the most. Have a look on the inside. See if there are any signs of her."

"She never entered the vehicle."

"Right. But Chicky, well, he says he watched her get into your truck."

"What?"

"Says he followed her to try to work things out, and saw her get into your truck."

"That did not occur."

"Yarly saw too."

"But it never happened."

"Yeah? Well, you can see how it might be a good idea for us to check the vehicle, right? If we can say there are no signs of her, like a hair, or something—"

"She said no."

"I'm just saying. We take a look at the truck and don't find any evidence of her presence, we'll move on."

"I'm not in trouble, am I?"

Healy stared at Quark as if studying an odd artifact, turning at the sound of a tow truck rumbling up the drive. "Seeing as how you've already been such a help, I took the liberty of asking Riddle to meet me here. Of course, at this point I can't take the vehicle without your permission. I am hoping you'll allow it."

Of course he agreed. He had nothing to hide, after all, and if it would aid in solving the mystery of what happened to the girl, he was happy to be of some assistance. The last thing Healy said, before stepping into the squad car, was how some people found it easier to write things down. "You know if you think of anything you want to say. You'd be surprised how one little bit can jog your memory."

Quark stood on the front step to wave farewell, pondering the idea. He didn't think there was much more to add to what he'd already shared but he couldn't get the notion of writing it all down out of his head. A confession, of sorts.

He never meant to hurt anyone. That was the point.

But when it came time to set pen to page he found himself unsure how to express himself. Mrs. Winter had reminded him about that period of time when he'd been a boy obsessed with the secrets hidden in rocks. He tried to write about that. How something can look one way on the outside but be entirely different on the inside. How sorry he was for the lies he told. How he should have behaved differently with the girl and how, all those years ago, he should have closed his eyes and not spied on Dory. But most of all, he wrote, he was very sorry for the tragic murder of that beautiful bird. "I was just a boy," he wrote, "though I fully understood the implications." He suffered from a strange paralysis in times of crisis. At first it was a relief to write it, but after a while he felt mortified and exposed. It was too much.

He almost gave up, but when he set aside the pen and sat back in his chair, it came to him what he really meant. He wrote the word over and over again. Initially it seemed too small, but after he'd written it a hundred times, it became larger than his personal grief, a lamentation for the world though, by the time he was finished, it had returned to its humble roots.

"Sorry. Sorry. Sorry," he wrote. "Sorry."

And he was.

✦

The phone calls started that evening. They accused Quark of doing things to Phoebe he never even had the capacity to imagine. He tried to explain, but the callers—who sounded young and gleeful—had no interest in negotiation.

"Everything that happened to her, is gonna happen to you, only worse. You ain't just gonna die, you're gonna wanna die."

When one caller began to launch into a detailed account of torture ("First, we're gonna tear out your fingernails...") Quark hung up. He was still standing with his hand on the receiver, when it rang again. He got on the floor to crawl in search of the outlet, finally located inside a cupboard behind the pots and pans. The phone had rung, stopped, and rang again by the time he pulled the plug, restoring the room to the resonant silence of a bell tower. Curled in a fetal position in the midst of pans and pot lids, he observed crumbs scattered along the floorboard and beneath the corners of the stove and refrigerator. It seemed only recently someone had cleaned the house in preparation for the anticipated funeral, but how long had it been? He'd lost track of time.

Although certain he had cleared the place of rum, Quark felt such a strong urge for a drink he considered searching anyway, just as the Old Man used to weave through the house trying to find bottles he, himself, had hidden. Instead of annoying Quark—the way such memories usually did—he felt an unfamiliar tug of sympathy for anyone possessed of such decency and debacle in dispute.

He kicked aside the pots and pans to stumble out the back door. Standing in Aurora's shadow, being near her, calmed his raging heart, but it began to rain and, with his truck gone, he was trapped. Suffering the familiar beginning beats of a headache, he went inside to sit in the old chair and contemplate his plight as he watched the enveloping dark broken by spears of light, his reflection in the rain-lashed window ghostly.

What was he so frightened of, anyway?

Back in the life he had made for himself, Quark enjoyed watching storms from the safety of his work table, the corpses revealed in brief moments of luminescence as though the dark, itself, had vertebrae, femur and eyes. He knew people found his vocation bizarre—even those who brought him their dead shuddered at the details of his work—but when he held bones, or sewed flesh, or saw a pelvic arch in a blaze of lightning, he felt electrified by the fragile radiance of life.

He tried to convince himself he could enjoy a Bellfairie storm, but the pain made doing so, difficult. He was cradling his aching head when he glanced up and saw a face beyond the glass, and then another, and another snaking up the drive;

each countenance lit for a moment, black eye sockets, mouths darkly slashed in grievance or resolve.

Quark sprang to lock the doors, first the front, then the back, surprised to find his hand shaking as he closed the drapes.

Collapsed into the chair again, he noticed the scent of pipe tobacco. How he used to judge the Old Man when he weaved through rooms as though everything substantial—even the floor beneath him—was an illusion that might be broken by the next step!

"Is it you?" Quark whispered. "Are you inside me?"

The muffled response was punctured by a searing flash and thunder clap, and the next thing he knew, Quark was standing in the middle of the room, shaking his head so hard his neck hurt while someone outside rattled the doorknob.

"Quark? Let me in. Can you hear me? Quark?"

"No, no, no."

"Aunt Charlotte asked me to come. She's worried about you."

He leapt to open the door for Coral who was wearing a yellow slicker with a matching hat that flopped over much of her face, though enough remained visible to reveal her annoyed expression. She reminded him of a picture book from his childhood. It was about a bear named—

"Quark? Can you hear me?"

"Yes. Your voice is very loud."

She took her hat off with a flourish, creating a little storm of raindrops. "Aunt Charlotte asked me to come. She can't drive in this kind of weather. Really, she shouldn't drive at all but…. Oh, I didn't know you smoked," she sniffed. "I'm allergic."

Quark went into the bathroom to unspool a wad of toilet paper he handed her in the middle of an impressive run of sneezes. She had taken off her coat by then, holding it out with one hand while she pressed the toilet paper over her nose with the other. By the time he returned from hanging the wet garment in the shower she had made herself comfortable on the couch, peering up at him as if he were the surprise visitor.

"She tried to call, but your phone's out."

"Oh." Quark glanced at the kitchen, embarrassed that his fear of teenagers had caused so much trouble.

"She said I should stay until the storm passes."

Normally he would object but, relieved to have the company, he decided to do whatever necessary to keep her.

"Would you like coffee? Tea?" he asked. "I am glad you arrived safely. There are hoodlums outside. Did you see them?"

"Yes," she said. "I mean yes to the tea, if you have decaf. No, I didn't see anyone. No one's out there. Aunt Charlotte said you might say something like that."

"Why?"

"Excuse me?"

"Why would she say such a thing?"

Frowning at the drawn curtains, Coral shrugged. "Well, you know. I guess cause of your hallucinations."

She spoke with such nonchalance, Quark felt hesitant to admit he didn't know what she was referring to. What hallucinations? Was this something he was supposed to know about?

"I'm not sure I have decaf."

"It's all right. Forget it. Seems like the storm might be passing."

"I'll look."

There was one box of tea in the cupboard and it wasn't decaf. Nonetheless, Quark set the kettle on the burner. Though the thunder and lightning had subsided he was disturbed by the thought of being left alone with the rain. He dropped the fully caffeinated teabag into a mug and carefully tucked the incriminating box to the back of the cupboard.

Hallucinations? What hallucinations? He tapped the box

just to be sure it did, in fact, exist.

Determined to ask Coral what she meant, he found her perched at the end of the couch, finger jabbing at her phone, a scowl on her face. He decided not to interrupt. He needed to organize his thoughts, always difficult to do during one of his headaches. He returned to the kitchen, and stared out the round window—so lashed with rain he couldn't see anything but the wet dark—until the kettle whistled.

"I'm sorry," he would say. "I'm not sure what you are referring to. I do not have hallucinations."

He was taken aback, however, to find her no longer sitting on the couch but standing by the plank table, frowning at the stack of letters.

"Oh! I thought maybe you were writing a novel, or something. I didn't mean—"

"Here's your tea." After catching her so obviously transgressing his privacy, Quark no longer felt bad about the caffeine. He gave her the mug, which she cupped with both hands. "Just some letters to the good citizens of Bellfairie."

She nodded. He wondered if she suspected what he had done. Though how could she? Had she even taken a sip? He neatened the pages, tapping the stack against the table. When, after a good deal of time, she said nothing, he raised his face, surprised to find her watching.

"Sit," he said. "You should sit."

He pulled a chair away from the table. She looked from it, to the front door then sat. He started to sit across from her, but she said, "I would be more comfortable if you were on the couch."

He thought it was an odd request, but what did he know about women? He did as she asked, folding his hands neatly in his lap. "I regret I don't have any cake to offer."

Frowning at the stack of letters—caught again—she turned to look at him. "No. Thank you." She sipped her tea, peering over the mug's rim at Quark, which made him uncomfortable. He pretended sudden interest in the corner where the figurehead once stood.

"I hope you aren't giving up the ship, Quark. You can't blame yourself for something that happened so long ago. I'm sure it's been difficult. Everyone, that is almost everyone, understands. What happened to you was.... Well, obviously I don't know what it was like. What it's been like. I don't know all your symptoms. I shouldn't assume that I do."

"My symptoms?"

"People who are struck by lightning have all kinds of symptoms, actually."

"Yes, yes," Quark said, confused by the change in topic. "They talk to ghosts."

"What?"

"My...Thayer always said someone struck by lightning can talk to the dead."

"Well, I wouldn't know anything about that."

It was almost imperceptible, but Quark had much experience observing small alterations of expression in people, and he thought her eyes narrowed with suspicion.

"Aunt Charlotte doesn't think you remember. She thinks you've forgotten all about it."

"All about what?"

"Being struck by lightning. I told her that's not possible. I mean you have the scars to remind you."

Quark remained with his hands in his lap, the expression on his face, he hoped, nonplussed. He'd had years of practice with such duplicity, after all, not wanting to invite the Old Man's wrath by revealing confusion or uncertainty.

"Then again," she said, "memory loss is one of the affects."

"It is?"

"Yes. Memory loss, hearing loss, hallucinations, seizures, headaches, all of it."

Quark suddenly felt as though the storm had relocated

to his own head. "I'm sorry. Are you saying I was struck by lightning?"

"You don't have to apologize. Everyone knows it wasn't your fault. Are you all right?"

"I don't remember."

"What don't you remember?"

What an impossible question. How was he supposed to answer? How could he know what he couldn't remember? Once he had a cat, and then he didn't. He used to build small graveyards out of stones, carved a flute from bone, folded paper into birds he tossed from his bedroom window; he remembered all that. But he had a mother—or so he was told—and all he recalled of her was a vague, uncertain recollection of a woman waiting by the door, a voice asking him to walk on the bluffs.

Suddenly the room was so bright Quark thought the house must have been struck, though Coral sat sipping her tea as if nothing had changed. He couldn't figure out how to proceed. The rain made a sound like stones against the glass, and he felt as though pebbles pelted his head.

"Quark? Quark? Please stop shaking your head."

"No, no, no, no."

"Do I need to call someone? Should I call a doctor?"

With great resolve, he was finally able to make it stop, but the effort left him exhausted. "That is not necessary. I am fine. Everything is perfectly fine. I just need to lay down now."

"What about soup?"

"Soup?"

"I could make you some chicken noodle—"

"Chicken?" Quark barked, frightening both of them. "Thank you," he amended. "I'm Pescatarian."

"Pescatarian?"

"I don't eat birds. No one in Bellfairie eats birds. Is that some kind of trick?"

"Whoa, hold on there. You're starting to sound a little

paranoid. Plenty of people eat birds, Quark. What do you think happens on Thanksgiving? I'm just saying don't put your dietary restrictions on everyone else, okay? This is America. Why don't you go to bed? I'll make you some soup. Don't worry about it. It hardly takes anything to make good soup. Whatever you have will be enough. By the time it's done, the storm will be over. I'll leave it in the refrigerator, and you can heat it up when you're hungry."

He walked away right in the middle of her saying something about potatoes. In the dark shelter of the bedroom he sat on the edge of the bed to struggle through the torment of unlacing his shoes then kicked them off, and laid back, so thoroughly racked with pain he dared not move further, not even to locate the pillow.

He didn't know how long he slept before he was awoken by the tinny melody of a cell phone. He wondered if Mrs. Winter had called to inquire about his well-being. Though his head still hurt he found that, by moving slowly, he could turn on his side to relax into the comfort of the worn indentation of the old mattress. A narrow strip of light emanated from beneath the closed door, but he was overwhelmed by the aroma of onions. He closed his eyes, hoping he could will himself to leave the taunt of nausea, even if accompanied by the unfamiliar solace of someone in the kitchen making his supper.

He was awoken again when the door popped open just enough to reveal a slice of silhouette.

"Are you awake?" she whispered. "Would you like some soup?"

"No. Not at this moment. Thank you."

"Are you going to be all right?"

Honestly, he wasn't sure he would be, but guessed she didn't mean the question broadly. "I'm quite adequate."

"The storm stopped a while ago. I'm going to leave. Did you say something? Do you need anything?"

"Of course not."

He decided to pretend he'd fallen back asleep, altering the volume of his breath until he heard the sound of her footsteps cross the wooden floor, the front door opened then closed. He counted to ten before stumbling to draw the lock and return to bed, no longer made seasick by the aroma that permeated the house.

He positioned the pillow under his head and stared into the dark. "What am I?" he whispered, daring to hope the spirits would reassure him he was good but all he heard was the cawing of gulls.

"Quawk. Quawk. Quawk," the jury said, as if his name was synonymous with guilty. He folded the pillow up to cover his ears but, still, heard them calling his name.

· 24 ·

Quark awoke to a bright sky and a sun dart that lit a singular point on the dresser, causing something there to sparkle. It took a few seconds before he remembered the gold heart he'd found on the Whitman property, glittering like a fallen star, extinguished while he watched.

He slowly turned his head to gaze at the ship framed perfectly in the window. Was it just an illusion, he wondered then quickly reminded himself of all the people who had commented on her presence. If she was an apparition then much of Bellfairie suffered the same malady of perception.

As often happened after one of his headaches, Quark felt taxed by the weight of his own body. He eased carefully out of his bed, meandered to the bathroom and then to the kitchen where he inspected the soup Coral left in the refrigerator, popping the old Tupperware lid to confront an unpleasant sludge of potato and carrots, dipping his finger into the glop to prove it was there and not simply a dream created out of his sad hope for affection.

Quark had a lot of questions he was unable to answer without assistance. When he walked out into the rain-washed day, his hat tilted back so he could enjoy the sunshine on his face, he wondered why the previous night's revelations made him feel in danger of floating away. Was the sensation just an effect of skipping breakfast? Or was his existence so composed of illusion that, as he stripped himself of everything false, he would find only absence where a life should have been?

When he arrived at the small park it was deserted but for a distressed gull pacing beside another collapsed in the rocks, its neck at a disjointed angle, wings spread uselessly beneath its body. He steadied himself against the uneven terrain to investigate, squatting for a closer look. When he heard the guttural cry, he thought it came from the surviving bird before realizing that it came from him. What was he so upset about?

"Quark? Quark? Is that you?"

Mrs. Winter stood in front of her house. He hoped she hadn't witnessed his display of anguish. It was embarrassing how easily he was overcome. The Old Man would have been irate if he had lived to see it.

"Are you all right?"

Quark wasn't sure he was. He abandoned the gull and its pacing mate, walking slowly as a child in trouble.

"What a lovely surprise," she said, looking like she meant it. "Come in, come in." She left the door open for him to follow. The room was dark and overheated from the small fire in the hearth, though the open windows created a pleasant confluence of ocean air and wood smoke.

"I didn't realize the day was so lovely," she laughed. "Woke up with winter in my bones. You don't know this yet, but old age is a cold season."

Had Thayer suffered a similar chill, Quark wondered. Should he have done more to help? Had he been as bad of a son as the Old Man was a father?

"Are you all right?"

"I was just thinking about my...Thayer."

"Yes, well," Mrs. Winter peered up at him. "He was your captain, wasn't he?"

Quark, who had never thought it was a wholly accurate description, had to admit he felt adrift.

"I know!" she said, as if they had been in discourse. "Why don't we have tea in the garden? This might be the last beautiful day. Will you help?"

He assumed she was trying to make him feel like he mattered but after the tray was loaded with teapot, saucers and cups, silver spoons, sugar cubes, lemon slices, paper napkins and scones, he discovered how challenging it was to maneuver down the back steps, across the yard to the table beneath a leafy arbor. When he finally sat on the hard chair (it was made out of iron, a bewildering choice for comfort) Quark found his view encompassed both the garden and the cemetery he'd played in as a child. He had no memory of enjoying the park, but recalled several instances of weaving through headstones reading names and dates, words of faith and sorrow, pointing his wand at each grave, trying to raise the dead.

"How nice to sit and watch you drink strawberry tea again. I remember how you liked it sweet."

He added a sugar cube and, after stirring it with a silver spoon that had metal roses twined up its stem, took a sip. It tasted all right, though he was amazed to think it had ever been a favorite.

"My niece says you aren't feeling well."

He felt disturbed to consider others talking about his personal business. The scone was quite delicious, however, and he reached for another.

"You seem fine now."

"I am not used to people knowing more about my life than I do."

"Oh, well. No one knows their whole story. It's impossible. We, most of us, have felt some responsibility to carry yours ever since your accident."

"I don't remember an accident," Quark said, feeling as though he'd just made a shameful confession.

"Oh? Not even that?"

He resisted the temptation to shake his head, uncertain he'd be able to stop.

"Surely you must have wondered about the scars?"

He hadn't. He just bore the marks—a pattern similar to

winter trees across his arms and chest—the same way he bore his hair, his fingernails, his great height, his unfortunate face, his skin. He learned a long time ago that any taxonomy of his own body quickly became a distressing meditation on amputation, and a somber reflection on beauty and its opposite.

She peered at him beneath a glowering brow. "I think it's best you hear it from me, don't you agree?"

He suspected she was right. Eyeing the distant headstones that had provided so much entertainment when he was young, he nodded.

"Many people don't realize lightning can strike on a clear day like this, but it can and does. A single bolt contains up to one billion volts of electricity. Can you imagine? One hundred lightning bolts strike the earth every second. Did you know that?"

"Oh, yes. I know this story."

"What story, Quark?"

"How the ship of bells went down. How the men, women and children drowned. How survivors said that rescuers held up lanterns on the shore to guide them to safety, but it was actually the reflective glare of sun on quartz. It was a sunny day only a mile away from the stormy one, and they were rescued by the rocks."

Quark found Mrs. Winter's expressions difficult to read. He thought she looked disapproving, but her voice was kind.

"That is all true, Quark, though it is not what we are talking about. You were always...when you were young, you were quite creative. Other boys your age were playing with boats and baseballs while you were walking all over Bellfairie in your father's old Stovepipe hat, waving that fishing pole at everyone and everything."

"I was a magician."

"Yes. That's right. See, you remember some things. A magician, and a mere boy. You had no way to know. It could have happened to anyone. It was a beautiful afternoon. The

storm came later. That's when Thayer went to look for you. I'm
sure you realize what an effort that was for him. Ever since his
wreck he did not go out in storms. But he went out for you,
and carried you back into town. You were still unconscious.
Only later did he learn that you'd gone to walk with her. That's
when he realized she was missing."

"Who?" Quark asked, though he had a bad feeling.

"Do you want me to say it?"

He nodded.

"Your mother. You were with her on the bluff, dear, when
you raised that fishing rod—"

"My magic wand."

"Everyone knows you meant it as something good. You
were always turning people into birds and whatnot—"

"I'm not sure I—"

"Like I said. Such an imagination!"

"I still don't—"

"Lightning. Right out of the bluest sky. Many of us saw the
flash. Before we found out what had happened, we thought it
was a sign of something good."

"Are you saying…"

"It struck that wand of yours, just as you pointed it at her.
Quark? Can you hear me?"

"I killed my own mother?"

"It wasn't you. It was the lightning. A tragedy."

"But I—"

"You were a child. You were playing."

"Did anyone see me do it?" Quark asked, hoping he'd discovered a dispensation.

"Oh, no one saw it occur. Thayer searched everywhere
for you, right in the middle of that storm, which had turned
quite violent by that time. He was the one who found you,
naked as a little bird and unconscious. He picked you up and
carried you home. You were the one who told everyone how
you raised your wand and pointed it at her. I can't remember

why, exactly, only that it was for something good, which no one has ever doubted. You were always a sweet boy."

"I was?"

"Yes, I know folks like to say that the lightning changed you, made you well...the way you are."

"The way I am?"

"It didn't though. I mean, naturally the scars were new, and your distress in a storm but those fits of yours and the rest of your particular ways has been your nature since you were a small boy."

"My fits?"

"That head shaking and whatnot. In case you ever wondered. I know it's made things hard for you, but not all people are the same. I explained this to Healy though I'm not sure he understands. Don't you worry now, just ignore what everyone's saying."

What was everyone saying? Later, Quark wondered if things might have been different had he investigated, but she'd advised him to ignore the scuttlebutt, so he decided to begin immediately. *A man can only hold so much*, he thought, watching an errant gold leaf swirl down from the sky, surprising himself by standing to reach for it, though when it fluttered past his fingers he was left clasping air.

"Ha," he heard the Old Man bark. "What are yah? Some kind of fag?"

What am I, Quark wondered, aware of the shaking only as it slowed to a stop.

It took a great deal of courage to ask the question. He whispered at first, so softly even he barely heard it then, after a deep breath, raised his voice to ask again.

"Am I a monster?"

She was silent for so long Quark began to despair, but when he finally found the strength to face his old friend, discovered her head thrown back, eyes closed, mouth agape. *How easily she sleeps*, he thought, carrying the tray back to the house where he carefully washed the cups and saucers patterned with violets, the little plates, spoons and teapot. From the window over the sink he could see her silver hair, and the slope of shoulders beneath the shawl flittering in a breeze. He leaned closer, almost touching the glass with his nose, to watch a swarm of tiny white butterflies flit around her as though she were a giant flower, or a globe of light.

He felt aware in a way he never had before, as if he died out there under the arbor and joined the spectral plane, which was nonsense, of course. Yet, he observed the killer go about the ordinary tasks of placing dishes in the cupboard, check that the burners were turned off, walk down the long hallway to the parlor to ascertain that the fire was properly contained. When he stepped out the front door Quark was surprised and saddened to find the gull still cawing and pacing in distress over its dead mate. He wished he could think of some way to alleviate the pain. To be in mourning was a solitary state. *Maybe by dawn,* he thought, *she'll have forgotten. Maybe by sunrise she'll have flown away.* Maybe forgetting wasn't the worst thing, after all.

· 25 ·

Quark tried to believe people weren't looking at him funny, but then he'd catch someone eyeing him with revulsion. When he paid for envelopes at the Emporium and slid a ten dollar bill across the counter, the cashier (not Felix, a man Quark had never seen before) waited for him to lift his fingers before taking the money as if contaminated. Relieved he was able to buy stamps there and avoid the post office entirely, Quark barely minded being treated like a leper; it reminded him of his childhood. When had he ever been able to count on the kindness of others?

Inhaling the sweet aroma that emanated from the candy store, he decided to treat himself well even if others did not. He selected an assortment of salt water taffy, and was feeling better about his state in life but, while perusing the caramel apples in the window, discovered he was being followed by those boys again. They were huddled across the street, pretending to play a game on their phones until one of them saw him watching through the forest of apple sticks and said something that made the others look up then run, expletives trailing in their wake. When Quark turned to pay for the small assortment of taffy, he was surprised to find a woman holding two children pressed to her side like shields against some dire element.

"Pardon me," he said as he passed, tipping his hat in her direction.

"Murderer," she hissed.

Time stops so rarely, but Quark had a clear memory of how once, as a boy running down a hill, he took flight—both feet hovered above the earth—a brief experience of transcendence he longed to replicate. And once, when they lay beneath the Aurora Borealis, the Old Man had reached across the gulf that separated them to pat Quark's hand, which caused the whole world to hold its breath, even the lights paused their undulations to hang, momentarily suspended, across the sky. It happened again that day. The sun shone through the glass jars of peppermint sticks and lemon drops, causing candy colored rainbows to rest like confectionary butterflies pinned to the air, the girl behind the counter stuck too, her mouth agape.

"Murderer," the woman said again, louder.

It was a horrible accusation, one that Quark had recently leveled against himself, but hearing it spoken by the stranger made something rise within him. He had been an innocent boy. It was a tragedy. He didn't kill his mother, the lightning did. "It was an accident," he said.

When the young cashier looked at the pastel colored discs of salt water taffy Quark placed on the counter as though they were radioactive, he was reminded of how, one day when he worked at the diner, he had been asked to attend the register, which he'd done successfully until a man who looked remarkably like Thayer stepped up. Even as it was happening, Quark knew it wasn't real. The stranger's hands never formed into fists and he never said an unkind word. But, as the doppelganger's gaze turned into a sneer, Quark began to shake his head. The next thing he knew, he was back in the kitchen scrubbing pots and pans.

The cashier stared at Quark, her mouth agape. It saddened him to realize how universal pain was. Clearly, he reminded her of her own tormentor.

"I won't hurt you," he said, softly.

"What did you say?"

He glanced back at the woman, still pressing the children against her side, but chose not to respond. He did not have to share his private conversation with the nosy stranger.

"Three twenty-eight," the cashier said, pulling the five dollar bill from his fingers as though plucking a dirty feather. She counted and recounted the change, then dumped it on the counter. Quark had to pick each coin up with his long fingers.

When he tipped his hat at the poor girl, she took a step back. What could he do about her unreasonable fear? How could he help her, or any of them? For the first time in his life Quark suspected everyone suffered both personal and broad maladies of illusion. Seeking to offer some small repair to the damaged world, he tipped his hat on his way out of the store. Her eyes widened then slit, in as quick a reversal from astonishment to anger as he'd ever seen, though Thayer had often done it adroitly. Quark wished he could do something for her and the children who tried to wiggle out from beneath the long blue fingernails pressed against their arms, but the best he could manage was an awkward wink which, once executed, caused the boy to cry.

Quark paused on the sidewalk—envelopes held in one hand, the small white bag of salt water taffy clutched in the other—closing his eyes to inhale the Bellfairie scent of ocean infused with the familiar stench of decay, all wrapped in a sweet swirl of sugar and chocolate. When he opened his eyes he had to blink away spinning sunspots before he could continue walking. Had he always been too self-absorbed to realize the world was populated by people so afraid to make eye contact they turned away as if threatened? Had he crossed to the other side of the road to avoid personal exchange so often he never noticed how others did so as well? Even the young hoodlums scattered when he turned in their direction. What they were so frightened of, he had no idea. What everyone was so afraid of, he couldn't guess.

All he knew was that finally understanding the

composition of his own fear made him less afraid. It was a terrible thing that happened a long time ago. A little boy raised a wand and destroyed his world, but he was neither magician nor monster. Sometimes, he knew, the best intentions cause great harm.

"Look up, look up," he wanted to say, and maybe would have, had anyone paused in their fearful course to acknowledge his presence. *A perfect sky, devoid of clouds, a beautiful day,* he thought as he leaned back, one hand pressed against the back of his hat to prevent it from falling.

✦

The Old Man used to say Quark's mother had become sea foam. Nonsense, of course. Yet, that night, he indulged the fantasy of her existence as vast and continual. Was that the gift Thayer had tried to give all along, a story a son could feel good about? He liked to think of her undiminished by death, expanded beyond the borders of life, and he, a conduit for her transformation.

When he awoke that next morning, after having slept deeply and without interruption, Quark remembered the vague whispers of a dream. Mrs. Winter stood beneath the arbor, dressed in bridal attire, holding a bouquet of feathers, hundreds of seagulls silently swooping through the blue sky. Though she was smiling, it gave him a bad feeling.

· 26 ·

"Found beneath the arbor," Healy said.

Coral, who checked on her aunt every evening, phoned, then drove to Wintercairn, already fearful of what she might discover; steeling herself against the sight of her aunt fallen to the floor, blood pooling from a gash in her head, or clutching her chest and gasping. Only after all the rooms were inspected, left with the horror of a mystifying absence, did Coral look out the kitchen window and see, in the moonlight, the familiar slope of shoulders beneath that silver aura of hair.

"The boys tell me they saw you over there yesterday." Healy, perched at the edge of the saggy couch, appeared to expect a response but Quark could barely find the strength to nod.

"You wanna tell me about it?"

He shook his head no, which went on for a while. Stopped at last, he realized Healy had spoken. "Excuse me. What did you say?"

"Riddle's gonna bring the truck back. We didn't find any signs of Phoebe."

The sheriff's comment was baffling. Why was he talking about the girl and the truck? Was the man incapable of understanding grief? Quark wondered if solitude was, after all, preferable to the loneliness of being misunderstood.

"Got a call from Angela Kalin. You know Angela? Her daughter, Heather, works at the candy store?"

Quark nodded. "I don't actually know her," he clarified. "I

180

was there yesterday."

"Yep. That's what she told me."

"Would you like a piece of salt water taffy?"

Healy shook his head no. It was so quick and abrupt Quark felt envious.

"Also got a call from Betty Sheveally. She was there with her two kids."

"Oh, yes. She has blue fingernails," Quark immediately felt embarrassed. What difference did the color of her nails make?

"She was very upset."

He hadn't expected to find a companion of concern in the woman who had been so unkind, but of course she, too, had been witness to the cashier's distress. "Then you know what happened."

"Why don't you tell me about it?"

Quark took a deep breath, unsure where to begin. "I'm very worried about her."

"Oh, yeah? Who are we talking about now?"

It was distressing to realize that the man in charge of investigations couldn't even keep track of a simple conversation. "We are talking about the girl at the candy store."

"All right. Let's talk about Heather."

"There is something wrong with her," Quark said, too loudly.

"Oh, yeah?"

"I don't mean like that."

"Like what?"

"I think she's in trouble. That's what I'm trying to say."

"Oh, yeah?"

"I wasn't sure what to do."

"I'm here to help. You know that, right?"

Quark nodded, though he wasn't being entirely truthful. He had come to understand that the sheriff was inept. "She was nervous," he said.

"Who?"

"We are talking about the cashier at the candy store. Remember?" Quark had often experienced mean interrogation, and did not wish to cause Healy similar distress.

"Okay. Go on."

"She appeared quite frightened."

"Yes."

"I thought you should know."

The sheriff nodded a few times, his brow furrowed. "Well, why do you think that is? That she was frightened?"

"I suspect I reminded her of someone. I wonder if I look like her father."

Healy leaned back slightly to asses. "You don't. You have a very unique appearance."

Quark didn't know what to say next. After all, he had no experience with the law, he was a taxidermist. Besides, Mrs. Winter was dead! He had almost forgotten the bitter news but, once recalled, had to fight back tears.

"Mrs. Sheveally confirmed what Heather told her mother."

"Who?"

"Mrs. Sheveally. Blue fingernails?"

"Oh." Quark had to concentrate very hard not to shake his head at the memory of that woman. How was his life her business, anyway? It was bad enough he had to deal with the boys taunting him. "That reminds me," he said. "I would like to report some prank calls I received."

"Oh, yeah?"

"I can't be sure, but I think it might have been those boys. Those teenagers. They also came to my house during the storm. They follow me, actually."

"Is that right?"

"I would like them to leave me alone."

"So you say the boys were here?"

"Yes."

"Was this before or after Coral's visit?"

Quark was startled to learn Healy knew about that. What else did he know?

"Did they do anything? Harm you?"

"Harm me?"

"What, exactly, are you reporting?"

"I don't know why they came."

"Let's take one thing at a time, all right?"

He nodded.

"I'm not gonna beat around the bush. Mrs. Sheveally was very upset. They both were."

"Both?"

"Heather's mom was upset too. As was Heather, of course."

"Yes. That's what I noticed."

"What's that?"

"She was very frightened."

"Oh, yeah? How could you tell?"

"She was trembling. She wouldn't look at me. She had trouble counting change."

"Why was she acting that way, Quark? Can you think of anything you said that might have made her uncomfortable?"

"Anything I said?"

"You said you wouldn't hurt her, didn't you?"

"I, that is…"

"Go on."

Healy's dark gaze was suddenly reminiscent of the way the Old Man used to look at Quark as if he were hideous.

"I only just remembered."

"Remembered what?"

"I thought I was doing something good."

"What did you do?"

"I was just a kid."

"You're a grown man."

Quark's pleasure at being so described was quickly

vanquished by the memory of all the other things he had been called throughout his life. Boy, Monster, Freak, Frankenquark, Murderer.

"Help me out, here. What am I not understanding?"

"I'm a grown man now, but I was a boy when I killed her."

"How's that?"

"It was an accident. I think that is significant."

"Who? Who are you talking about now, Quark?"

"I thought you knew. She told me everyone did."

"Who told you that?"

"Mrs. Winter."

"Who did you kill?"

Quark looked down at the floor, searching for the screaming face in the whorl of wood. "My mother."

"So let's just back up here a minute. Mrs. Winter told you everyone knew you killed your own mother?"

"Yes."

"When was that?"

"When I was a child."

"Right. But I'm asking when did she, when did she tell you?"

"She?"

"Charlotte. Mrs. Winter."

"Oh. Yesterday."

"Are you saying you only just remembered this about your mother?"

"I still don't remember it, actually."

"Huh. You forgot it for all these years?"

"Yes."

"Must have been pretty upsetting to learn about what you did."

"Yes. Yes it was."

"Did you have one of your fits? After she told you?"

"I. No. I don't think so."

"You don't know?"

"I did not."

"You have a problem with memory, don't you, Quark?"

"No one remembers everything."

"Is it possible you don't remember having one of your fits yesterday? With Charlotte?"

"How would I know?"

Quark felt pained by the searing truth of his own question. What if he was forgetting things all the time? What if nothing in his life was what he thought it had been?

"I appreciated you stopping by the other day. To tell me about Phoebe."

Quark, rarely complimented outside his work, enjoyed the small swell of pleasure that fluttered from his chest even in the midst of such an unpleasant exchange.

"Mrs. Winter dropped you off that day, right? At my office?"

"Yes."

"How'd that come about? She see you out walking and offer a ride?"

"Well, actually, she came here and said I needed to see you. She insisted."

"You don't mind if I take notes, do you Quark?"

"Oh. It's just…"

"Yes?"

"Am I in some kind of trouble?"

Healy leaned back into the couch. "I won't lie to ya. I have some concerns."

"You do?"

"For instance, you were the last person who saw Phoebe alive."

Quark nodded.

"And you were the last person with Charlotte."

Quark sighed. Mrs. Winter! Dead!

"Then, of course, there was Thayer."

"What about him?"

"People seem to die in your company, Quark. That's what I'm saying."

He hadn't realized he'd been holding his breath until he exhaled with a surprising lip blurt. "Yes. It keeps happening. It's terribly upsetting."

"I talked to Charlotte."

Quark was confused. Was this a confession of sorts? Did the sheriff see ghosts too?

"She reminded me about your special name for Phoebe."

"What?"

"Snow White. Isn't that right?"

If there was anyone Quark considered a real friend it had been Mrs. Winter. He was disappointed to discover her spirit was gossiping with the sheriff.

"When you came to my office you said…"

Healy flipped through his little notebook. Quark looked out the window at the sky, so grey it reminded him of a giant net.

"Here it is. You said her lips were 'red like a wound.' And then you said, 'like Snow White.'"

He thought he saw a glimmer on the horizon, a figure of light, but perhaps it was just a break in the clouds.

"I'm not an expert on fairy tales, but I decided to look into it and I have to ask, were you the prince?"

"What?"

"You told me she crossed the street to get away from you."

"I was not threatening her."

"That's what you said."

Quark appreciated the lull that fell between them at that point. It gave him space to concentrate on not shaking his head. It would be most unfortunate to have one of his fits at that moment.

"So, when exactly, did you last see Charlotte?"

"Yesterday."

"What time?"

"I am not certain. I believe I slept later than usual. It must have been very late in the morning, or very early in the afternoon."

"And where was she when you left?"

"Under the arbor. We drank tea and ate scones. They were delicious."

"Oh? There wasn't any sign of that."

"We ate all of them."

"There wasn't any sign of a picnic, is what I'm saying."

"We sat in chairs. It wasn't a blanket picnic."

"There weren't any dishes out there."

"I washed them and dried them and put them away before I left."

"Why?"

"Why?"

"Yes. Why would you clean everything like that?"

"I…. To help. I wanted to help."

"But you left Charlotte under the arbor?"

"She looked so peaceful. I didn't want to disturb her. I was trying to do something good."

"Was she breathing when you left?"

"Yes," Quark said, though even to his own ears he sounded uncertain.

"Right. I got some other folks I need to talk to."

Hoping he didn't appear over-eager, Quark opened the door for Healy who, cap in hand, took a step forward, then stopped abruptly. "They saw you break her neck."

"What? Who?"

"The gull. At the park. They saw you kill it, Quark. The boys. You were right about them following you. They saw what you did."

"I never…that is…. Those boys."

"What about 'em?"

"They are liars."

"I found the bird." Healy leaned closer. "Just something to keep in mind; we didn't locate any signs of Phoebe in your truck, but there were quite a few traces of animal blood."

"I think…"

"What?" Healy's eyes narrowed. "I'll tell you what I think. Your time is running out. You got anything you wanna tell me? This might be your last chance."

Quark wanted to say what he was feeling, but it was all mixed up, an aurora borealis of emotion. The sorrow of Mrs. Winter's passing, the regret that, while she'd been alive, he neglected to thank her for all she'd given him, the touch of wonder in his childhood, the strawberry tea, the kindness.

Not everyone knows when they save a life, he thought, as the sheriff donned his cap and, with an abrupt nod, walked out the door. Quark stood with his back against it, waiting until he heard the car drive away. "Are you here?" he asked, and asked again.

When no one answered, he stumbled to the couch, and wept.

He wept for Mrs. Winter, found so close to the cemetery her spirit might have arrived there on the last gasp of her final exhalation. He wept for Thayer, trapped in some way Quark was incapable of penetrating—much like a mirror world, he guessed—bearing great resemblance to reality without containing any of its consequences. He wept for the gull that mourned its mate with no capacity to understand life's course. He wept for the mortal loss he'd known as inevitable, yet never embraced, as though the truth of it was another Bellfairian fiction, death as a ghost ship leaving only absence in her wake. So much absence! He wept for the mother he barely remembered, the touch he could not recall, the smile he could not conjure, her stories lost, too, with Mrs. Winter's passing. Gone. Mrs. Winter gone and, with her, anyone who would shelter him in a storm.

Gone was the girl with bright red lips. Gone, forever, Quark's—or anyone's—opportunity to save her and, because of his inadequacy, gone too, her chance for love. Love! He wept for the mystery everyone else seemed to understand, reminded of how the Old Man used to say he was saved— all those years ago after the wreck—by a sweet scent he first thought was a sign of doom. "Hell's perfume," Thayer called it, which he followed "like a starving dog after a poisonous bone," through the roiling sea, on the back of a horse. ("I don't know where she came from, and I don't know where she went" he used to weep) to that small island where red flowers bloomed beneath the moon.

"And I was saved," he'd add with so much anger in his voice Quark was never sure if it was a happy ending or not. "Saved so I could raise you, I guess."

· 27 ·

He felt lost at sea—the way he'd always feared—lying on the tattered vessel of that stinky couch. How long did he roil in despair before the Old Man arrived, signaling with a crook of his finger for Quark to follow? By the time he sat up, he was alone.

How to proceed? So many had fed him, those early days of his mourning and, while some of the food had spoiled under his poor management, Quark greatly appreciated all of it. He decided to make a cake for Coral. Doing so necessitated a trip to the grocery store and, since he would be out anyway, it seemed a good a time to visit Henry Yarly.

Before any of that, however, Quark sat at the plank table folding each letter into a neat rectangle he tucked inside an envelope and addressed using the phone book as a resource. His tongue soon felt so unpleasant from licking the glue that he briefly considered abandoning the project. Instead, he reminded himself of the kind of person he wanted to be which was not the sort of man who never apologized simply because it left a bad taste in his mouth.

Finished, at last, he turned his attention to the ditty box. He soon felt overwhelmed by the choices, peering into the chipped and stained coffee mug many times, as if it would reveal the secrets that had been whispered over its rim. If he had been successful in finding the Old Man's ship building book, it might have been easier to part with such detritus but, when Quark brought the shot glass to his nose, he inhaled—

beneath the vague scent of dish soap—the notes of cinnamon and clove and that particular Bellfairie aroma of water, stone, and something sour. It was no longer a simple glass but a portal to their last night together.

Why hoard such meager material as if the memories were good? Nonetheless, he set aside a box of small things to keep. Inside it went one mug, both shot glasses, a belt made of knotted rope, and the tie he puzzled over. It looked new. Quark wondered if it had ever been worn and why it was purchased. He asked the shadows but got no answer. Eventually, struck by either inspiration or desperation, he scoured the backyard for cedar shavings. Staring up at the figurehead leaning into the sky, he wondered if Aurora would actually float. It was no small thing to create something buoyant enough to ride waves, yet strong enough to resist gale force winds.

Back inside, he pressed one of Thayer's old socks into the ditty box, topped with a combination of wood shavings and driveway glass. He regretted his decision as he prepared to leave, searching for his own socks which he vaguely recalled taking off after stepping into one of the many puddles that kept appearing throughout the house. Where were they? Why did everything keep disappearing?

He didn't like wearing shoes without socks but had no other choice, unless he ransacked the ditty box, which felt like grave robbing. He decided, instead, that he would stop at the Emporium to purchase another pair. On his way out of the bedroom, he spied that little gold heart on the dresser and decided to set it on the shards; he liked the way it looked in the nest of glass and cedar. He grabbed the letters, and dropped them off at the mailbox, flipping the flag to signal for pick up.

Grief is a man without his truck, Quark thought, trudging towards the shore.

He had accompanied the Old Man to Yarly's house many times, stacking pebbles and collecting seashells while the two men sat on the porch with their whiskey and tobacco.

Sometimes their visits lasted so late both men fell asleep in the rocking chairs while Quark watched the waves lick nearer until the cairns he'd built were destroyed. Remembering those long ago nights perfumed with acrid smoke and the briny scent of the sea filled him with longing, as if he would choose to go back to that time he had been so eager to leave.

It was true he had no interest in being out on the Old Man's ship, or any other, but Quark did appreciate being near water, imagining a world that flourished below the waves where bells still rang and the dead danced in Fiddler's Green. He had not anticipated that he would find the way to Yarly's uncertain but he turned into a rock-strewn cove, then rounded another bend and came upon a large, modern home he stared at in confusion until he saw a face looking down at him from an upstairs window. Finally, after a few more such false arrivals, he found the place, much as he remembered it, in need of paint, two rocking chairs on the sagging porch. For a moment he thought he saw someone sitting there but it was just the way light shimmered near water, rippling the air like a curtain.

He surveyed the beloved shoreline of his childhood, surprised to find Yarly facing the ocean, as if stopped in midstride, knees slightly bent, hands cupped towards the horizon, pushing away the waves, though that was obviously an illusion.

"Ahoy! It is I!"

Yarly turned at the salutation but stood immobile for so long Quark worried he was not welcome, unprepared for the confluence of emotion that arose within the embrace.

"What brings you, here, son?"

"You said I should come. So we could say goodbye to Thayer in private."

"That's right. I'm getting old. Memory dies, you know. Time ships away. Well, you don't want to hear all that. You're still young. In your prime."

Quark held out the ditty box in both hands, presenting it

as though it were made of glass.

"Is this...is he?"

"Just some of his things. Nothing else. I am going to bury it. Like a grave. So we have a place to visit."

Yarly nodded, though he continued to stare at the box as if worried Thayer might arise from its shallow depth. "It's good you did this. After all, you know what they say."

Bothered by the sand in his shoes, Quark shifted from foot to foot. "Grief is a ship without a captain."

"That's right, son. Come on, now. Let's go inside."

He followed Yarly up the crooked stairs, pausing to ask himself if he had ever been more at peace than on the rickety porch he'd nearly forgotten.

"Son? You coming?"

The last time Quark had been there he was young and not interested in the stone mantel above the hearth cluttered with framed photographs—a smiling woman in a white dress, a baby on a blanket—seashells, stones, feathers, a wisp of hair tied with pink ribbon.

"Did you make this?" Sitting in a chair across from the couch, Yarly held up the ditty box as if Quark might have forgotten about it.

"Yes."

"Mind if I take a look?"

"What?"

"I don't have to, if you don't want."

Quark hadn't anticipated the question. He wasn't sure how he felt about it.

"Never mind. I shouldn't have asked."

"Go ahead. It isn't much." He sat on the sagging couch to watch.

Yarly lifted the lid with such reverence that Quark found himself leaning forward as if he had no idea what he, himself, had placed there.

"I know it's not much. Just a few old things."

Yarly held the sock aloft.

"I just...." Quark started, then stopped. He just what, after all? What had he been thinking?

Yarly let the sock fall, moved to close the lid, stopped, reached in and pulled out the small gold heart, staring at it as if mesmerized.

Quark wasn't sure if he was expected to explain. He was uncertain what he had meant by putting it there. Something about love, he thought.

"You still drink tea?" Yarly asked, closing the lid.

"Yes, I do."

"I keep the kettle going all day. It'll be just a minute."

Quark peered at the window, watching waves roll over his reflection. He shouldn't have come. He never should have returned to Bellfairie. Or he did the right thing by coming but should have left as soon as Thayer was found.

"I wasn't sure what to do," he said, surprised to hear himself share his private thoughts. "I was hoping to find his book."

"What book would that be, son?" Yarly asked as he pulled cups and saucers down from the shelf.

"His ship building book. The one he was writing. That's what he said it was. He carried it with him everywhere when I was young. It was bound in leather. He told me I could have it after he died. You don't know where it might be, do you?"

"Sorry, I never heard nothing about it. But that makes sense, right? You two knew each other best. I ain't got any of that strawberry tea you used to like. Hope you are okay with black." Yarly set the tray on the old sailor chest that served as a coffee table and pointed at a little plate of star shaped cookies dusted with yellow sugar. "Saved some of these Thayer made."

"He made cookies?"

"Yah."

When Yarly lifted the teapot, his hands trembled so much,

the lid rattled in its perch. *He's old,* Quark thought. *Not much time left for him, now.* Something flashed from Yarly's eyes—too quickly to be examined—before he looked down to set the teapot on the tray.

"Don't think I didn't know how he put you under pressure, son. I should of done better by you. After what happened to your mother he just had no more in him to give. Don't think you ever knew the man, really. He was hard on you. Too hard, and I'm sorry. I should have done more. We all should have. Still, there comes a time when you are no longer a child, and must take responsibility for your own actions."

Quark reached for a cookie, his hand hovering above the plate as if the choice had deep implications.

"Go on," Yarly said. "They're a little stale, but good. They have that smoky flavor you don't get in store bought."

Quark selected a star he held up to catch the light, surprised he felt something like reverence, disappointed when, seeking a neat break, it crumbled in his hands.

Yarly handed him a cloth napkin from the stack neatly folded on the tray. "You always have underestimated your strength," he said softly.

Rather than debate the topic, Quark brushed crumbs into the napkin then set it aside and picked up his tea cup, careful of the delicate handle.

"I think it would be best if you leave all this with me." Yarly said, tapping the ditty box with his finger.

Quark shook his head no.

"Now, don't be angry, son."

But once begun, he could not stop, trapped within a necessary rhythm of his own body, no easier to terminate—through will alone—than the beating of his heart. When it was all over, he saw the shattered cup and Yarly's eyes locked wide in horror. It was more than Quark could bear, this creature he'd become. He knew he should stay to clean up the mess, but he grabbed the box and ran.

· 28 ·

Quark was standing at Felix's Emporium, a bag of groceries held against his chest and a new pair of socks dangling from his hand, when he noticed the picture of the girl tacked to the bulletin board, "Missing" printed in bold letters over her head. Once again he thought how he had never actually seen her smile, and was struck by the difference it made. He knew the flyer was one of many distributed before the body was discovered, yet found himself pondering the implication of her happy face. Leaning forward for a closer look, he startled back as if electrocuted by the little gold heart that dangled from a chain around her neck.

It took all of his strength not to run out of the store, even as he plodded to the register.

"You all right there, Quark?"

He blinked to focus on Felix.

"I heard you're in trouble."

Unsure how to respond, Quark stared straight ahead.

"Yeah, well don't give much mind to what people say. That'll be two fifty-six."

"What?

"Two fifty-six. For the socks."

"Oh, yes. They're for my feet." Quark set the bag on the counter to search his pockets for cash.

"You baking a cake?"

"Yes. For Mrs. Winter." He handed Felix a five dollar bill. "I mean for Coral. Mrs. Winter is dead."

"See. That's what I mean."

"Yes, well."

"She used to come in here, and she wasn't all innocent like they're making her out to be."

"Mrs. Winter?"

"No. The girl. I saw you looking at her poster. She wasn't no saint is what I'm saying."

"Well."

"Not that she deserved what happened. I ain't saying that."

Quark extended his hand, palm up, for the change.

"Hey, I been meaning to ask."

"Yes?"

"You ever get rid of that dybbuk? You know, the one was bothering you?"

"I need to go."

Quark didn't mean to be rude, merely direct, but Felix's eyebrows shot up like buckshot crows. "Don't gotta get that way with me," he said. "I might be your only friend, don't you know?"

Quark pocketed the change, tucked the socks in the bag next to the cake mix and, with a tip of his hat, exited the Emporium. Though he saw several people on his way back to the house, they were on the other side of the street, and he was relieved not to have to engage with them.

Was the heart a coincidence or a clue? He pictured, as if his life had turned into a movie, his own fingers reach through the shrub grass for that glint of gold, and the next thing he knew he was shaking his head slowly enough to glimpse a woman across the street glaring at him as if he were disagreeing with a point she held dear.

What if everyone has a piece of the truth, he wondered, once he had continued on his way, *that we are all afraid to share?*

His pondering was interrupted, however, by the welcome sight of his truck returned. He set the bag down to peer inside at the keys left on the driver's seat. When he heard the noise, he turned in time to see the hoodlums (five or six of them) emerge from behind the house. Later, he would ponder the animal sound that came from his mouth, a guttural scream perfectly calibrated to be mocked, but the boys screamed too, squealing in their boyish tenor as they escaped down the long drive.

He walked to the backyard to see what they had done; reassured to perceive no damage, though he did discover footprints in the dirt all around Aurora. It was upsetting to think of them so near her.

"Won't be long now. Soon you'll be free," he whispered, not knowing it was a lie, as he brushed his fingers across her hull.

· 29 ·

Quark realized he should have allowed the cake to cool when the frosting melted into a drippy, anemic glaze, but didn't let that minor issue discourage him. He considered and rejected several ideas about how to improve the appearance, from a sprinkle of shredded carrot to trashing the thing and starting over. Judging by what he'd sampled of the batter, the final product would be delicious, even if it did look vaguely like a giant bird dropping. It wasn't perfect, but it had to be enough. After all, he was in the midst of preparations for Thayer's burial at sea and ship launch. Had it been anyone else, anyone at all, Quark would not have bothered. But Mrs. Winter had been exceedingly kind to him, and Coral had tried to be as well.

He needed to get the cake out of the house before it was ruined; a lesson learned recently when he'd set aside a peanut butter and radish sandwich one afternoon while playing his flute, peering out the window as if he really believed the old song might conjure his mother. Finally tired of the repeated melody (and the despair of hope) he turned to his sandwich, appalled to find it buried beneath black writhing wings, set upon like a corpse.

He carried the cake, perched on the best plate (only one crack, near the rim) to his truck. Keeping a watchful eye on the culinary passenger, and his foot light on the gas, he drove without incident all the way to Wintercairn beneath a darkening sky, as if all of Bellfairie was draped in funeral cloth. Finding no spaces available in front of the house, he

regrettably had to park near the cemetery. He gave himself
a good talking-to about proceeding with focus. Certainly he
could carry a cake further than anticipated without fear of
ghosts or a spill.

Quark took careful, measured steps, the plate grasped
tightly in both hands, his hat at a jaunty tilt. Yet, when he
finally arrived at the stairs to Wintercairn, he paused. How
horrible to think she would never again be waiting on the
other side of the door! By the time he made it up the steps
without incident (the trickiest maneuver of all) Quark was so
sad about his reason for being there he considered abandoning the cake on the stoop where someone would surely find it
and bring it into the house. Who knows what he might have
done had not the front door opened just then, and a couple he
had never seen before stepped out?

"Here, let me hold the door for you, hun," the woman
said.

He wanted to object but, worried any negative response
might incite the uncontrollable head shaking that would surely
prove disastrous, he mumbled thank you and stepped inside.
Expecting to face a roomful of mourners, he was surprised to
find himself alone in the parlor.

The thing Quark was beginning to understand, at
that rather late point in life, was how every death felt like a
drowning; as if he could reach through the present to rescue
what sank just beneath the surface, if only he knew how. There
she was looking up at him beneath her hat with birds trembling on the brim, there she was walking down the hallway,
and there she was asleep in the chair beside the dying fire.

"Quark."

He hadn't noticed Coral enter the room, but there she
was, her usually neat hair a hive around her pale face, her lips
parted with the gasp of his name.

"I brought you a cake."

"How could you?"

"It wasn't difficult. I just followed the directions on the box." She glanced over her shoulder. Quark heard voices coming from the back of the house. Afraid she would insist he join the others, he tried to settle the dispute before it started. "I can't stay."

"No. Go."

"Here." He extended the plate. "It's a carrot cake."

She took it as though under confused enchantment.

He understood. He remembered the period after Thayer's death as infused with absurdity. "I am very sorry. I..." Quark lost track of what he was saying. Coral's eyes slit, her lips so firm, he was reminded of a cloth doll he'd seen at the Emporium, its mouth sewn shut with black cross stitches.

"I can't believe you had the gall to do this."

He shifted awkwardly from foot to foot. In all the excitement he'd forgotten to put on his new socks, and the sand felt gritty against his skin.

"Yes, well," he said, confused.

"Do you have no shame?"

"Well, I—"

"She trusted you."

"Yes."

"You need to leave."

She sounded so bossy Quark didn't even consider disobeying. He turned quickly, plummeting towards the doorknob, just grasping it when he heard a man's voice.

"What's he doing here? Are you all right? Should I get the sheriff?"

Quark stumbled outside—distressed when he didn't immediately see his truck before remembering he'd parked further down the road—running in his awkward manner, as if chased by a mob, though no one followed. When he finally sat behind the steering wheel, his breathing labored, he squinted through the dirty windshield at the serene graveyard, leaning forward at an uncomfortable angle to look up at the sky, already graced with an early star. What was it Mrs. Winter said? "No one even knows if a Quark exists."

Did he? Had Mrs. Winter made it snow in his classroom? Or had he imagined that? Were there ever, really, bird folk? Was he one of them, or born for the sea he despised? Had he been raised by a man who loved him as much as hated him? Had he ever really lived? Or was he a figment? Did he leave a trail of good and bad in his wake? Or nothing at all?

It was too much to figure out after the mystifying exchange with Coral. She had gone a little nuts, he decided as he turned the key in the ignition. But hadn't he once awoken in Mrs. Neller's garden? Hadn't he been in a fugue the whole time others had come in and out of his house completing the work on Aurora? Hadn't he thought they were intruders when actually they had been friends? Who knows what terrible thing he said, or did, in his own grief! Maybe he could forgive Coral the way everyone had forgiven him. He drove slowly, as if the cake still rested beside him. Would she eat it, or shove it to the back of the refrigerator until it turned stale and moldy? He hoped she would give it a try. The cream cheese frosting was a mess but the batter was flavored with pineapple, pecans and cinnamon. He worried about its uncertain fate.

Back at the house, he flicked on the lights, which set the room abuzz. He hoped it meant he merely needed to change a bulb, but flies came out, darting at him with the rumored intensity of sharks. He had a plastic cup and sympathy card set aside for times like this. Cup in one hand, card in the other, he scanned the room until settling on a fly that rested on the plank table. He slammed the cup over the little creature then slid the card beneath the cup's rim and hard surface, carefully executed so as not to sever leg or wing as sometimes happened, much to his horror. Once that was done, Quark carried card and cup outside where he released the fly, capturing and freeing several more before it occurred to him to wonder if he was making everything worse by sending them into the cold night. What trouble were they, really?

Perhaps, he thought, if he donned his hat, the buzzing would not be so bothersome. But where was it? He had no memory of taking it off, though clearly he must have for it wasn't on his head. He looked behind the chair and under the couch. He opened the cupboards to search even as he chastised himself for being ridiculous, and then proved the self-recrimination true by going upstairs to the little bedroom as if the hat might have flown there. Finally, he looked outside, scouring the yard and long drive for any hat-shaped blob in the dark. He stood for quite awhile, unable to process this loss amongst all the rest until it occurred to him that it must have fallen off when he ran from Wintercairn.

He drove back the same way he came, cruising up and down the road several times before accepting the tragic truth. He reserved a fragment of hope that he would see the beloved stovepipe hat on his drive back but, instead, glancing in the rearview mirror, saw only Phoebe. Not her, of course, her spirit scowling at his receding truck and only for a moment before she was gone, absorbed by the dark.

He thought he heard a noise—something out of order in the natural world—as he slogged across the muddy drive to the front door. Another time he might have made an investigation of the property, but he was exhausted by that day's turmoil. After all, Mrs. Winter had died, he'd made a mess of things with Yarly, discovered the gold heart belonged to Phoebe, given a cake to Coral that was so ugly she was insulted, and lost his hat. His dear, dear hat! Quark sank into the old chair, cradling his head to muffle the first beats of pain, the flies buzzing around his head like a dark halo as though he'd gone through some kind of transfiguration; either lit from within like a saint or infected with decay. They meant no harm, he knew, but even for all the lives he'd saved they could never be other than what they were, just as he could never be some other man, some acceptable creature.

· 30 ·

*A*woken by a flash he thought was a falling star, Quark sat up slowly, disoriented to find himself watching flakes drift past the window. Was it snowing? The room flickered with luminescence, and there was a sound—a vague hiss and crack—like breaking ice. Once, the Old Man made Quark walk barefoot in the snow; the crackling reminded him of that starlit pain. He tiptoed to the kitchen. Like a somnambulist half in the woken world and half in slumber, he opened the back door with an expectation of wonder.

He told himself she was not on fire even as he knew she was then spun into the kitchen to pick up the phone, but it was dead. *Idiot*, he thought, as he crouched to the floor, pulling out pots and pans to plug in the cord, hitting his head on the shelf when he moved to stand but, still, no dial tone. He set the lobster pot in the sink and, as he watched the water's unhurried flow, felt a sear in his chest as if he had caught a spark, patting his shirt provided assurance he had not. Scolding himself not to be distracted by his own pain, he opened the door wide, hoping he had made false assumptions from fragments but there she was, her skeletal core revealed by the flames that consumed her.

The yard, filled with shadows and winged light, might have been beautiful had not the effect been created by something so terrible, and he might have remained transfixed, had he not heard the voice, exhorting him to act.

"Hello? Who's there?" he asked, trying to sound like the

204

menace people sometimes believed he was, though he could not control the tremor in his voice.

Struggling to find purchase on the pot's wet rim, he stumbled then righted himself with hardly a spill. When he got so close he couldn't tolerate more heat, he heaved the water towards the flames, but might as well have tried squelching it with his tears.

He picked up the phone again. Still no dial tone. What was wrong with him that he had even hoped? He wanted to shake his head at his foolish heart, but clenched his jaw against the risk. Once more, he rushed out with the pot full of water, though it was obviously futile. He turned his face upward— like a man who believed in God—and watched smoke lick the stars from the sky. When he lowered his gaze, he saw the Old Man standing in the flames. A trick of light? A shadow? A figment of guilt? He imagined he heard a siren even as reason scolded no one was coming to help.

But he was wrong. The fire engine and sheriff's car screamed, their red lights spinning a bloody kaleidoscope over the yard, the house, the sparkling shards on the side of the long drive, and him.

He tried to watch from the shelter of the kitchen but someone—her face obscured by a helmet—insisted he wait outside where, she said, he would be safe. They turned one hose on the back of the house, and another on what was left of Aurora, working in a flurry, able to understand each other with an economical use of language and gesture Quark found impossible to decipher. Watching them behave as if the ship could be saved (clearly she was lost) he shook his head at the persistence of hope.

When that was done, he blinked to an awareness of the grand flame diminished into a series of small ones, each answered by an overwhelming force of water. It didn't seem long before they were coiling hoses, and picking up tools, their movements languid.

"Wouldn't of come if it wann't for Thayer," one of them said.

"Saved the house, I guess."

"Might a been better to let it burn."

"What? That's no way to talk."

"You know what folks are saying. Might of been better to let it burn. With him in it too."

"Don't. You sound like the devil. Leave it to Healy."

"I would like to express my appreciation," Quark began, but it was as if he hadn't spoken. *Was this what it felt like to be a ghost?* Was it possible he had died in the fire? Maybe it wouldn't be so terrible to watch the world without any expectation of being tended by it.

"What about it? Is it safe?" one of the fireman asked another who shrugged and said something low, then laughed, a shocking sound within the burnt stillness.

The seared house reminded Quark of the time he'd covered an entire page with bright colored crayon he was instructed to blight with black before using a pin to scratch a little rainbow dwelling out of the dark. He thought he didn't care about the place he grew up in, but seeing it in such a state made him realize he had. Hoping to be reassured by the side that had not been exposed to flames, he walked to the front yard where he found Healy standing as if guarding the place.

"You wanna tell me what happened?"

Quark shrugged, a particularly complicated gesture he never learned to properly execute.

"You all right?"

He had to concentrate and stand very still in order not to shake his head.

"Chief says it's arson. You know anything about that?"

A fireman, walking past, brushed into Quark's shoulder, continuing on without apology. He knew he shouldn't judge, they had just saved the house, but Quark found the behavior upsetting. Did no one care about his grief?

"What did you say?"

"Looks like arson."

Quark nodded. Well, of course. "Those boys."

Healy leaned back slightly.

"They have been following me and taunting me. They were here. I saw them."

"When was that?"

"The night of the storm. When Coral arrived she scared them off."

"That was days ago, Quark."

"They came back. Obviously. I heard them. I should have made an inspection but I had a bad day."

"What did you hear? Exactly?"

"A noise."

"Did you say, 'a noise'?"

"Yes. An unnatural noise."

"Okay. So you heard an unnatural noise. Could you be more specific?"

"It wasn't the wind, or anything like that. It was them." He watched a lone seagull dive from the sky to peck at the ground near his feet. "I know they are young, but they did a lot of damage."

"Who?"

"The boys."

"We're back to them, are we?"

He didn't know what to say.

"I gotta tell you. Things aren't looking good."

The gull stopped searching for grubs to watch Quark with a cold gaze.

"I think you know what I'm saying."

He had a whole box of eyes made of glass in his office. Sometimes he rolled them in the palm of his hand, enjoying the way they caught the light.

"There's only so far you can take this. It's just a matter of time. Things might go easier for you if you confess."

"Confess?"

"Tell me what you did."

"What I did?"

"That's right."

He kept forgetting nothing made sense. There were brief moments of clarity but, just as insight flamed, it flickered out.

"I..."

"Yeah?"

"I did nothing at all."

Healy lowered his gaze, scratched his brow. "Don't try to leave town. It'll just make things worse."

He nodded. It wasn't meant as an indication of agreeing to the order, but as acknowledgment of having heard it. The sheriff and firemen drove away, their sirens mute, the red lights as immobile as clots. He was still standing there when the hearse came slowly up the long drive.

✦

"What do you mean?"

"I'm sorry, Quark. This has never happened before."

"But, how?"

"I wish I could give you a good explanation. I don't have one. It was a terrible mistake. My new assistant. Former. Assistant. She...well, she fucked up, is the only way to say it."

"I don't understand."

"I am so sorry."

"Sorry?"

"Maybe I should of waited. I felt I should tell you as soon as I found out, but maybe I should of waited."

"You say you're sorry?"

"I know it's not enough."

Quark considered that for a moment.

"We're not going to charge you, of course. For any of it. The storage, or the urn, or.... Obviously."

"Well."

"It's the least I can do. Also, if you don't like this one, we have others. You can choose whatever you want. No limit. This is one of the nicest. Just so you know."

He eyed the urn in his hands, and nodded.

"I chose it cause of the ships. But, like I said, you can have whatever you want."

It was bronze, and etched around the perimeter. He was surprised by its weight.

"I'm very sorry. Thayer deserved better."

She looked like she was hoping for some kind of response but he couldn't figure out what that might be and, after a moment, she began walking towards the hearse.

"Wait."

She turned but continued taking small backwards steps.

"Yes? Is there something else?"

"I hope you will come to the funeral."

"Are you kidding?"

"I am serious," Quark said, only then remembering he hadn't confirmed any of it.

"I just thought with what happened..."

"Bring a friend. If you like."

She tilted her head, as if trying to make sense of something crooked. "I'm sorry about everything that's happened, Quark. I really am. But you can't expect me to just forget what you said."

He was confused. What was she referring to? Rather than get bogged down in conversation, he lifted the urn, to remind her of what she had done. She didn't say anything, only pivoted to step into the hearse.

Quark watched the vehicle make the difficult maneuver in the muddy drive. The fancy car would need to be washed so it would look nice for the girl's funeral.

He stood for a while, thinking about the introduction he'd read in his library book about the author's husband's heart plucked from the ash, and fought over.

Who would ever want even such a small part of me, he wondered and, though he tried to resist, shook his head against the answer.

✦

Clutching the urn against his chest, Quark slogged through the house. The whole place was a mess, but the kitchen was the worst. The window shattered, glass littered the sink and shards glinted from the mire of a mud-splattered floor made treacherous by pots and pans. He stepped carefully across the room to close the door, but it hung from a broken hinge and would not budge. He stared at the blackened earth and seared wood where the ship once stood, before turning back inside.

It was cold, the air redolent with the scent of smoke. There was so much to take care of, but Quark needed a few minutes to come to terms with the state of his life. Weary with grief and a long night without sleep, he stumbled towards the couch, closing his eyes as he sank into it, opening them wide upon absorbing an unpleasant dampness, shocked to discover the old chair occupied.

"Hello?"

He assumed one of the firemen had been left behind. What other explanation could there be for the soot-covered figure sitting with bowed head? Yet, when he raised his face, familiar eyes peered out, two cobalt lights in the dark.

"Is it you?"

The Old Man or, more accurately, what remained of him, nodded, unleashing black flakes that fell with a lazy drift.

"What happened? Are you all right?" Quark asked and immediately steeled himself against the derision soon to follow. But, other than the eyes, it was impossible to find any familiar features or expression in the specter.

"What happened? Why are you like this?"

More dark flakes fell from the thing, diminished, Quark realized, by movement—subtle as the shadow of a quivering leaf—where a mouth should have been.

"Wait. Don't try to speak. I think you are falling apart."

The ghost emitted a low, buzzing sound, unleashing a shower of embers that flickered out as they fell.

"Please. I'm not sure you realize what is happening."

The spectre shook the dark, disintegrating orb that might once have been a head.

"Stop! You are making it worse."

Whether by force of intention or impetus, it did not stop, and Quark fell into its rhythm, shaking his own head, and moaning even while wondering, in the midst of that brutal union, if he, too, was falling apart.

When that was finished, all that remained of the Old Man was a blot of soot, which Quark stepped forward to inspect.

It wasn't the first time he walked into a puddle in the aftermath of a visitation, but it was the first time he bent down and dipped his hand in the water to lick the salt from his fingers in a desperate act of communion.

Unable to decide if he should wash or preserve the stain, Quark lifted the cushion for a closer look, and gasped. The Old Man's shipbuilding book's cover and pages were bent in such a way it seemed reasonable to surmise it had been tucked into the crevice between arm rest and cushion, fallen into the forgotten space with three pennies, a crumpled tissue, several downy feathers, and strings of lint.

Quark turned the cushion over to sit. Holding the book in his lap, he worked to flatten the pages, staring out the window rather than risk a glimpse before he was ready. Finally composed, he tried to think of something to say, like a prayer, but nothing came to him. He took a deep breath and opened the book, brushing his fingers across the pages filled with drawings—the Old Man's sketching hand was a heavy one—tracing little ships, infinitesimal suns, and crude whales, like

Braille touched by someone who had never learned to read it. He did this page-after-page until arriving at the only one marked with words. The sight of Thayer's sharp, square print seemed almost a visitation, more personal than the spirit of the man—or the man—had ever been.

Place your acorn with its cap on the side two inches deep in the ground. Cover it with dirt. That's how you build a ship.

· 31 ·

When someone knocked at the front door, Quark worried the boys had returned with tricks like the one he'd fallen for as a teenager, a small bag of dog shit set on fire that he heroically stamped out. The Old Man had been so furious when Quark tracked it into the house he had to wash the floor with a toothbrush. He opened the door (only a crack, ready to bear his full weight if it needed to be closed in a hurry) but it was only Dory.

"I just heard. I am sick about what happened. Just sick."

He waved her in, then quickly shut the door.

"Jesus, Quark. You all right?"

"Yes. I'm fine. Thank you for asking."

"I came as soon as I heard. Mind if I sit?"

Neither the damp couch nor sooty chair seemed suitable. He pulled one of the straight-back chairs away from the plank table. She seemed to think there was something amusing about that, but didn't comment as she unbuttoned her coat and set her purse on the floor beside her white shoes.

"I can't stay long. It's very busy at the diner today."

"Yes. Well."

"Folks coming into town for Phoebe's funeral, and all. Well, you can imagine, I'm sure."

"Is today Saturday?"

"Yes, it is, you poor thing. You sure you're all right? You look a little peaked."

"I've made a terrible mistake."

"Oh?"

"I haven't been myself lately. I lost track of time. I lost track of everything."

"Well, I'll keep this short. Before you say anything, I want to apologize for going off on you the other day the way I did. I was under distress, you know. Cause of Phoebe."

"I hope it's not too late."

"Excuse me?"

"I need it tonight."

"Need what?" she asked, her voice sharp.

"I want to keep it simple. Fish, coleslaw."

"Quark, what are you talking about?"

"The catering arrangements. For Thayer's launch."

"What? I heard there's no ship left."

"He is still dead."

"Well, yes but—"

"And I have this." Quark indicated, with a sweep of his hand, the urn, just then noticing how the lid was set crooked.

"Is that...him?"

"Yes, it is."

"But I thought..."

"They made a mistake."

"Jesus."

"Yes. Well."

"The thing is Quark, with Phoebe's funeral and all, I'm not sure anyone will come."

"I'll be here."

"Why don't you take a load off?"

"Excuse me?"

"Sit."

He was eager for her to leave but, rather than incite a confrontation, pulled out another chair he placed directly across from her only realizing, after he sat, that he'd created an uncomfortable atmosphere; so near, their knees almost touched. He considered making an adjustment but worried doing so would be awkward.

"How many folks you expecting?"

"Oh. I don't know. Five? Six?"

"Well, maybe. Cause of Phoebe's funeral, you know. But let's just round it up to a even ten. If you have extra, you can freeze it. Always nice to have a fish dinner, don't you think?"

Quark nodded, though he would have much preferred a stash of vegetarian lasagna. Actually he would have appreciated a big plate of lasagna right at that moment, even cold. He hadn't eaten yet, and was quite hungry.

"So, we're talking potato salad, coleslaw, cod, rolls and cake, right? I think we should throw in a few slices of pie. Some people are cake people, and some are pie people, you know. Coffee, water. Tea, I suppose. You always get the odd tea drinker. Just a general fish dinner, sound about right?"

He nodded.

"You feeling okay? This would be a shock for anyone. I remember how bad those headaches of yours used to get."

"You do?"

"Sure. All through school you had them. I had a little crush on you, you know. Oh, don't look so afraid. I'm over it, obviously. But you and me back then, I thought we were kind of alike, both being outsiders and all. You should hang fly strips, Quark."

"I don't like to kill them."

"See, that's what I've been saying."

"Do I pay now?"

"That's why I'm telling you, as your friend, sort of. I know you wouldn't harm even a mosquito, but there's been a lot of gossip. I want you to understand I know it's nonsense. Do you have any idea what I'm talking about?"

He considered shaking his head but, worried where that might lead, held very still. "I do not. Sorry."

"I'm not sure you realize how people misjudge you, cause of your size and, well, you know. You do have your defenders, though. Me. And Charlotte. Before she died, of course. Yarly.

Though he isn't a talker, in general. The folks who really know
you, is what I'm saying. I don't wanna upset you more on top
of everything you already been through, but I think you have
a right to know."

"All right."

"People. Some people. Well a lot of people to be honest,
think you killed Phoebe. They say you killed Thayer too. And
your mother. Now they're saying you killed Charlotte. Where's
it going to end? Suddenly you're like the angel of death, or
something. Some say you were the cat killer all along. There's
even a rumor going around that you strangle birds with your
bare hands."

"Who said that? Was it Tony?"

"What?" Dory's head twitched, as if someone had just
snapped fingers against her nape. "No. Why would you think
that? Kids saw you at the park."

"I would never."

"Well, of course you wouldn't. That's my point. I just think
you should be aware, is what I'm saying. You're having one of
your headaches right now, aren't you? I can tell cause of the
way your skin color goes kind of green, and you start breathing funny. You want aspirin? I got some."

"Thank you. They don't work on me."

"Tylenol?"

"Nothing helps. Sometimes I just need to eat." As if for
emphasis Quark's stomach growled. He might have considered it divine intervention had he believed in such things.

"You wanna ride? To the diner? I can have you set up
with a number five in no time. Wouldn't that be nice? On the
house?"

"I don't need charity."

"Who said anything about charity? It's called solace." She
leaned over to pick up her purse. "There's a big draft in here,
by the way. It's coming from the kitchen."

"Thank you," he said. "I can drive myself."

Trying to be polite, he thanked her again for stopping by to tell him what was on people's minds as he walked her to the door, relieved to close it after she stepped outside.

Then began a search for his keys during which he felt increasing despair he suspected was not commiserate with the situation. After all, they had to be somewhere, didn't they? Or was all the material of his life slowly disappearing?

In the truck! Of course! The keys must be in his truck.

Surprised to discover Dory's small car remained parked in the drive, he was standing beside it, proving to himself that it was not an illusion, when she came from the back of house, her shoes covered in soot.

"Oh, I just had to look! It's horrible, horrible," she said.

"Yes. Well."

"I heard it was arson. How could anyone destroy something so beautiful? I don't know what has become of Bellfairie. I really don't."

He nodded and again said how much he appreciated her telling him of her concern then got into his truck, but the keys weren't there, either. Embarrassed, he decided to wait until she departed, but she stood with her arms crossed over her chest, watching. He rolled down the window to ask if she needed something.

She pointed at the truck's tires. "You wanna ride?"

Quark slammed the door much harder than he intended. It was not always easy to control himself. All four tires were deflated and, upon inspection, he saw they were slashed.

"You ready?" she asked. "You got everything?"

Quark didn't want to explain about his hat. He said he had everything he needed, surprised when she didn't comment on its absence. Scrunched uncomfortably in the passenger seat, feeling like the giant some people thought he was, he startled back at the blast of music she quickly muted with a jab of her finger.

"What a shitty thing for someone to do," she sighed, the

usually easy maneuver of turning the car around made difficult by muddy ruts left behind by the fire truck. "Legwart and Charlie said it was bad, but I figured they were exaggerating."

"Who?"

"Leg—coupla the guys. Firemen. They came to the diner afterwards."

"Do you mind if I roll down the window?" he asked.

"Great idea. I'm gonna roll down mine too. Might as well enjoy this before it gets too cold, right? Take a whiff of that sea air. I know things look bad now Quark, but whenever I feel terrible I just close my eyes and take a deep breath. First Phoebe, then Charlotte, and yeah, she was old, all right, but she was the kind of person who you'd think would live to be a hundred at least, you know? And now your beautiful ship, burned to the ground."

Quark leaned his head towards the open window, closed his eyes, and imagined he was flying.

"Also, Thayer."

"Excuse me?"

"You were just listing everyone who died."

"Oh. Right. Of course. Thayer."

He drew his head back to look at Dory. Years ago her lips had reminded him of strawberries. Maybe they still would, if she hadn't applied that orange lipstick which, smeared past the borders, created a sad-clown look.

"Jesus, whyn't you take a picture?"

"Sorry." He turned to watch the road. "Do you really think Bellfairie has changed?"

"You're joking, right? Remember how it was? Remember that time Charlotte made it snow in our classroom? I always wondered how she did it. She made me believe in magic. For a while."

"You remember that too? Do you remember the other things?"

"Like that time the guys were making fun of you, calling you some silly name and your Old Man killed that albatross?"

"What?"

"He shot it out of the sky to show them how good his aim was. Said he was gonna do that to them if they didn't stop teasing you."

"He never told me that part."

"Yeah, he dragged that bird right through town, trailing blood, and singing at the top of his voice, like he wanted everyone to see what he'd done."

"He was drunk."

"But still."

They drove the rest of the way in silence. Quark didn't even realize his head was shaking until Dory parked, and explained that she really had to get back to work. She was sorry, but she couldn't wait for him to stop.

How insubstantial everything is, Quark thought. For so long he believed the Old Man had cut down the oaks out of spite, only to learn there had been a plan all along, a plan for something larger than both of them, a ship dreamt of before Quark was even born. One minute he thought the Old Man had never loved anyone, and the next thought maybe he had. Once there had been an Albatross, its wingspan twelve feet across, soaring across the sky, shot down as a warning to cruel boys. From that corpse, Quark had learned to make song, even as he feared the brutality of its cost.

Sitting in the car, growing cold with the windows closed, he stared at the Birdman statue with its great wings and talons raised to the sky where a gull came to rest, and then another, and one more.

When Quark got out of the car, the gulls squawked his name. *Who is dying now,* he wondered, following Dory's trail of ashy footprints into the diner.

✦

Quark hoped to discreetly slide into a booth, but the only available space was at the counter, and he wasn't going to make a scene about it. Besides, with the help of the large mirror, he could spy on the patrons dressed in mourning clothes, so much black he felt like he was dining with crows. The strangers seated nearby paused in their egg yolks to impart sideways looks, which made him wonder if he had been talking to himself, a bad habit he thought he'd vanquished years ago. When he covered his mouth with his hand, he was startled by the scent of smoke.

"Quark? Can you hear me?"

The waitress, the one whose name he never could remember, slid a number five he didn't recall ordering across the counter. "Sorry. I heard about what happened," she said, patting his hand, one quick tap, before ambling away.

It was almost too much. He could not lift that hand—though it was the one he usually ate with—for fear of shedding what remained of her touch. He sliced clumsily into the waffle with the side of his fork, concentrating not to make a mess.

After the man on the right departed, the waitress pocketed the tip then topped off Quark's coffee, bitter-black just how he liked it. A new patron slid onto the stool, cleared his throat and asked if something was burning. The waitress leaned over to whisper to the stranger who said, "How sad to lose your home." Quark wasn't sure if the comment was directed at him. After all, he hadn't lost his home. He wasn't even sure he'd ever found it. Before he could figure it out, the man picked up his cup and followed the waitress to a recently vacated table. No one came to fill the unoccupied space. When the woman seated on Quark's left departed, he found himself quite isolated in the midst of the busy diner.

He wished he'd stayed at the house. He never imagined he'd miss it, or the flies which settled momentarily on his skin before darting off again, leaving him with flickers of irritation that made him feel alive. It didn't make sense to miss such annoyance, but he did. He suddenly longed for Thayer's ghost and the old chair where he used to sit to stare out the window just as Quark had come to do, himself, waiting for something he had not yet been able to define. The chair was ruined of course, suitable only for the dead: the mother he barely remembered, and Wayne who had been kind to him for a while, his beloved pet, Cheryl, Mrs. Winter with her secret formula for making snow, Phoebe with her unborn child, and Mocha who Quark had never known alive (though he sometimes dreamt about the little dog running through sunny fields) and all the animals. Suddenly, Quark began to weep, quietly at first, and then with abandon; cupping his hands over his eyes, not caring if he disturbed anyone.

For a while the diner noise continued—the conversations, the cash register clicks and bells, chairs scraped across the floor, the metallic clang of utensils, a crack of laughter, a baby's yelp—but it wasn't long before a hush landed on his shoulders like an invisible shawl, followed by a low buzz.

At first he thought it came from flies—as if his longing had called them to him—until he realized it was the murmur of Sushi's patrons: the dead girl's relatives, the curious, the lost, the waitress with the forgotten name, everyone whispering. Only the baby, swaddled in black, cooed pleasantly, staring at the ceiling as though something fascinating floated there.

"Why don't you just admit it and apologize? Why not just get it over with? Hey! Stop acting like you can't hear me."

Initially, Quark was confused, but it soon became clear the woman was talking to him. He didn't understand why she thought he was acting like he couldn't hear, and had no idea why she was so angry, or how to improve the situation. "I'm sorry," he said, cringing at the whine in his voice.

"Did you catch that? Everyone heard him, right?"

He recognized many of the scowling faces, though not all

of them. A man dressed in a well-fitted black suit, his dark hair cut with precision, glared at Quark as if they'd always been enemies.

"Leave it, Betty. Angela went to get Healy."

"I will not leave it. I told you, didn't I? I heard him say he did it! But no, Dolly said, not Frankenquark. He wouldn't hurt a fly. I told you. I told you he confessed."

He scanned the crowd, hoping to locate a friendly face as Tony Kindall, cleaver in hand, emerged from the kitchen followed by Chef. Quark felt hesitant to turn his back on them but what did he think would happen? This was where he'd grown up! He'd worked in this very diner! These were his people. His gaze landed on a boy whose expression fluttered from freckled innocence to scorn.

"We seen him strangle a seagull with his bare hands. He was going to drink its blood, and when he saw us he hollered, so we got out of there but then he was staring through the candy store window like, well, you know, staring."

"Tommy, I told you—"

"It's the truth, Mom. Why won't you believe me? Everyone else does."

Quark turned to the woman, certain she saw his innocence even as he saw something of her own, quickly smote by a resigned expression. Of course. She was the boy's mother. Her loyalties rightly resided with her son.

"Yeah," another voice chimed in. "We saw him sitting in his house, all hunched over and holding his head like he felt really guilty about something."

"When did you…" a woman asked, but her voice trailed off. In the gap between accusations Quark was surprised to discover Mrs. Whitman, sitting in a booth, scowling at him.

"I always knew you were trouble," she said.

He bowed his head.

"I was relieved when Wayne stopped playing with you and started spending his time with regular kids like Hank

and Brian. Then you moved away and hardly came around
even to visit Thayer which, well the nut don't fall far from the
tree, is what I always say.

"And that was that. I didn't give you any more thought until
Wayne passed and I received condolences from every person
in his class. Every. Single. One. Except you, and I thought well,
it just goes to show, don't it? It just goes to show."

"But, Mrs. Whitman, I didn't even know—"

"Goes to show what?" a stranger asked, raising his finger
over his coffee cup to signal Dory for a refill, which she delivered with one eye on Quark as if afraid what he might do
next.

"He said his specialty was bones."

"What?"

"I was out doing laundry and all of a sudden there he was
lurking around my yard, and I don't know why I did it, I guess
cause I felt sorry for him but I invited him into the house, and
that's when he said his specialty was bones."

"There's been a misunderstanding. I never—"

But no one was listening. Everyone was murmuring, and
staring at him. Even the black-swaddled baby looked at Quark
with wide eyes. The small bell above the door rang, signaling
the arrival of a woman who appeared oblivious to the atmosphere until she raised her face. "Oh," she said. "I guess you
already heard. Henry Yarly. Who would of believed it?"

"What about Henry?" Dory asked.

"Dead."

The bearer of this bad news turned at Quark's anguished
cry.

"Oh! I'm sorry," she said. "You're his friend, aren't you?
You're the one I saw, right? You were down that way, headed
towards his house. Sheriff's looking for you."

"I had nothing to do with his death."

"No one's saying anything like that. He just wants to ask
some questions. Normal business when someone dies. They

always want to talk to the last person who saw 'em alive."

How can anyone be so clueless, Quark wondered, watching her walk across the diner as though it were just an ordinary day. She had almost made it all the way to the counter, apparently with the intention of sitting on one of the unoccupied stools when she slowed to a stop. "Wait," she said. "Did I interrupt something?"

Tony used the cleaver to wave her back. "You don't wanna get too close to him," he said. "Looks like we have a serial killer in our mitts. I knew something was up when he was in here, threatening Phoebe."

"I never—"

"Everyone heard you."

"What are you talking about?" Dory asked.

"I told you—"

"No. You never—"

"He came in here 'n pointed a knife at her."

"I didn't. I mean. Not like that. I wanted my breakfast. It was a misunderstanding."

"Why didn't you do something?"

"Why are you getting on me? He's the one. Besides, I called Healy. He came and talked to him."

"And Phoebe? What about Phoebe?"

"You know how she was. Kind of bitchy. I don't mean no disrespect. Whoa. Hold on there, Quark. Where do you think you're going?"

"I would like to pay my bill now."

"I don't think so."

"I won't accept charity."

"Charity?" Dory spun away from her husband. "Who said anything about charity? Not everything is about you, Quark. Why do you always think everything is about you? Like when Phoebe went missing and you got angry cause I couldn't wait on you right away!"

"I have never—"

"Soon you will go to your watery grave."

Mrs. Neller sat at a table, wearing her coat and hat. Quark couldn't tell if she had just arrived or was on her way out, though he decided it probably didn't matter. "That's what he said to me. I was minding my own business, trying to keep my spirit up even though I'd just purchased flowers for a dead girl and her baby too, when he walks by and goes, 'soon you will go to your watery grave' and I felt like I was being mocked by death, himself. I've been locking my door and sleeping with a fishhook tucked under my pillow ever since."

"Mrs. Neller I—"

"Then I come in and see him here this morning like he's got nothing to be ashamed of."

"I never—"

"Haven't you done enough?" Dory spoke so softly that several diners leaned forward to hear.

"I told you. I told you, didn't I?"

"Shut up, Betty."

"I saw you talking to Yarly," a man said.

"I don't even know you."

"Yeah, well what's that got to do with it? I saw you. Where's Chef? There you are. Right? Right? You walked him outta here cause he was having one of his fits and I was sittin' over there and I saw him almost walk right into Yarly like no one else in the whole world matters but him, you know how he is."

"Henry Yarly is my friend."

"And now he's dead."

"I am not dead," Quark said, which had a quieting affect on the room. Those who had been leaning forward sat back in their chairs, shoulders slumped. A few people picked up their forks and poked at their eggs.

"No one thinks you're dead," Dory said. "Do you even understand anything that's happening?"

Before he could stop himself, Quark was shaking his head no, which went on even after the sheriff arrived, giving everyone a cold look as he walked across the diner, pausing to tell Tony to take the cleaver back into the kitchen.

"I got my rights," Tony said.

"Yeah, well I got my badge."

Tony kicked the swinging kitchen doors open, which was impressive until they swung back as he stepped through, momentarily trapping him like a small fish in the bite of a larger one, rescued by Chef who pushed him into the kitchen and did not return when Tony did, wearing his gun, glaring at Healy.

Quark finally wound down. "There's been an awful misunderstanding."

Healy opened his mouth, but before he could speak, the bell announced another arrival. She, too, was dressed all in black but of course she, more than anyone, had earned the terrible right. Even so, she scanned the establishment as if daring anyone to challenge her. When she saw Quark she made a guttural noise like an animal stuck in a trap, and lunged. Several people held her back long enough for Healy to step in front of Quark, blocking him.

"Hold on now, Shelia."

"He ain't worth it," someone said.

"Settle down! Everyone needs to calm down," an excited voice shouted.

"I've got kids here. Let me through. Coming through."

Quark watched a family weave through the tables, hats askew, coats unbuttoned. *What do they think is going to happen,* he wondered.

"I have a right. I have a right to speak."

"Of course you do, Shelia," the sheriff said. "But you sure this is what you want to be doing right now? Don't you wanna be home, preparing?"

"No. No, I don't want to be home 'preparing', as you say. For my daughter's funeral. I don't mean to be disrespectful. You have been real decent about all this, but now you need to be quiet. Angela told me what's going on here."

"Nothing's going on here, Shelia."

"Something's going on, and I think it's about time is all I have to say."

"Maybe you should—"

"Shut up, Dory. You been defending him all the while. It's my turn to talk."

"I—"

"He was there. I saw him."

"Where?" Healy asked.

"He was down there that day when you found my Phoebe."

"Well, a lot of people—" Healy began.

"No. My girl is dead. My grandchild too. And he was down there acting like he was at an amusement park or something."

"Now, Shelia—"

"Standing there, drinking your shake and watching everything like it was wonderful entertainment."

"I don't drink," Quark began, but was interrupted by Healy.

"It would be best for you not to speak."

Quark tried. He tried very hard not to say anything, but so many lies had been spoken, so many terrible things he could not simply ignore.

"I don't," he began, and again Healy interrupted.

"I'm warning you, Quark."

"But I don't drink shakes," he said. "I don't even like them."

Letty Andrews, who was passing by Sushi's at just that moment, later reported that the place erupted with a noise so terrifying, she hurried home, locked all her doors, and called the sheriff every ten minutes, feeling more distraught each time no one answered (she had always suspected some hideous fate to befall her) until, finally, after seven tries, Healy picked up and said, "Don't worry about it, Letty. It's all under control. Just a big misunderstanding."

"But it sounded like something violent was happening. And I heard there's a serial killer in Bellfairie."

"I was there," Healy said. "It's under control. I can assure you Bellfairie is perfectly safe. You are in no danger at all. There's no killer in Bellfairie any longer."

She asked him to explain but all he said was, "You are safe. I'll see you at the funeral."

· 32 ·

Had not Healy stepped in, Quark felt certain they would have attacked him with their butter knives and grease-smeared forks, or Tony with his gun.

"Go straight to your place," the sheriff said. "Don't talk to anyone."

"But I have not paid my bill, and this is the second time. I don't want people to think I'm a—"

"My treat. Go home. Stay there. Don't even think of showing up at Phoebe's funeral. I'll stop by later."

Quark saw the faces contorted with hate, and deemed the whole thing absurd. Why, after the terrible things they believed he'd done, had they arrived at their point of intolerance over his confessed aversion to shakes? It didn't make any sense.

Or did it? Maybe there was an explanation for everything wrong in his life that he'd been unwilling to consider. Perhaps he really was some kind of unacceptable creature. Maybe Thayer had seen that from the very start, and been right to treat Quark like something that needed to be tamed.

He walked the whole way home with his head bowed, careful of the bird scat and sea spiders that scuttled away from his large feet as he trampled over the old blue spine of a buried dragon, pondering how to make his way through the world without harm, only raising his face after he had made his way up the long drive to the back of the house, so distracted he'd lost track of all the reasons for his sorrow. Dismayed by the ruin, he stood at the edge of the blackened skeleton that had once been Aurora, wondering if something would occur to him, an epiphany that would create meaning out of his life, but that brief flutter of hope only left a crevice of despair.

The back door hung on its hinge, both difficult to open and vulnerable to breach. Struggling to lift its base from the ground it wedged against, Quark noticed an odd shape protruding from the earth, an acorn. Had he been possessed of any extra store of good humor, he might have laughed. Instead, he picked the nut up, rolling it in the palm of his hand.

The toolbox was missing. Luckily, a shovel remained abandoned on the ground like a worthless thing. He walked around the house a few times, as if surveying but, really, had an idea from the start that he would settle for a spot in front of the picture window to dig. The muddy remains of his yard— after the onslaught of fire hose—had already begun to harden. It felt good to press his foot into the blade's edge. He made the hole wider than necessary for the humble acorn he placed, on its side, and buried.

It took fifty years for a great oak to reach maturity. Maybe he would return, he thought. By then he would be an old man. Maybe he would come back to sit in the chair and stare out the window at the tree he'd planted. Maybe that little acorn contained hundreds of boxes for just as many secrets, or flocks of birds with coarse-grained wings, a small boat, ship boards, a monster's mask, or a table around which a family would tell the story of the felled tree and the man who planted it and, maybe by that time, he would be at peace.

✦

The rest of the day was spent preparing to leave: sweeping up glass, fixing the door, taping up the window. The rooms smelled like smoke, which Quark did not consider entirely unpleasant. Some of his best memories were of enjoying a fire in the midst of a cold night, and the light in the dark. Occasionally he paused to watch for Healy who had promised to stop by, but you couldn't always believe what people said. The day was almost over.

Quark donned one of Thayer's sweaters, dismayed to discover it riddled with holes. Apparently, the Old Man's entire wardrobe was in tatters. How hard would it have been to visit a few times a year to make sure he was eating and had warm clothes to wear?

"I never meant to be such a bad son," he said to the urn on the plank table.

He hoped Thayer would forgive him, but the opportunity for conversation had apparently passed. Now, when Quark wanted them most, the ghosts were gone, the flies too. All he had was a house full of memories and regret, stacked boxes of junk, an empty ditty box, embossed urn, an entire life gone like that.

Hungry again, he had just begun to inspect the refrigerator's meager pickings when he heard a car he thought was Healy, but when he went to look out the front window the entire drive was filled with headlights shutting off as if synchronized.

He recognized many of the people who stepped out of the vehicles, though he didn't know all their names. Most everyone wore black, which gave their heads a severed look in the inky light. He guessed they'd come from Phoebe's funeral where he imagined they had mingled throughout the grieving rooms eating salads, pickles and herring off little paper plates balanced in quivering hands, determined to neither laugh nor cry but be solemn avatars, proof that despair can be survived. After all, who had not lost someone? It was startling to think of all the grief assembled in his yard, all those people being swallowed by the dark, kicking at the earth with their best shoes.

It occurred to Quark to make an escape. He could slip out

back and return later for his things. Yet, he remained standing at the window, watching. He thought he should be afraid but what he most felt was curious.

What happens next, he wondered. *Will it hurt?*

They didn't move towards the house until Healy did. He wore his full uniform and, through some unexamined course of light, his sheriff's star blazed.

The knock was a surprise. It seemed so civil.

· 33 ·

"The community has asked me to relay their apology."

"Okay."

"It was a mistake."

Quark nodded and moved to close the door, only pausing to peer at a white van slowly maneuvering up the drive.

"Dory feels bad too," Healy said. "You gotta understand. It's been an emotional time. All the same, she is donating the food. You gotta appreciate that."

Quark just wanted to be alone. *Please go*, he thought. "Please."

"We want to have the launch for you," Healy said. "We know she can't sail obviously, but we want to do this right. We hope there's no hard feelings."

Quark felt as though he'd been suffering a long stupor, maybe his entire life, only just then blinking to awareness.

"What?"

"We've got food and drink. Folks want to share some of their stories. All we need is your go-ahead."

"Okay."

"What's that?"

"Yes, all right," Quark said.

The sheriff nodded at the assembled. A few cheered while the rest returned to their vehicles for folding tables and chairs, Tupperware and paper plates, napkins, and plastic utensils; moving in a flurry of activity that seemed oddly organized, as if they had set up picnics in Quark's yard many times before. A young girl set candles on every table, followed by a woman who lit the wicks with a long match that seemed perpetually in flame. Several people began stacking wood for a bonfire, which made Quark nervous though he did nothing to stop them. It was the way things were done in Bellfairie. Besides, it was a cold night.

It wasn't Dory in the van but Tony. He unloaded containers and buckets, and bossed everyone around, dictating where to place the coleslaw, how to position the coffee and hot water carafes. When that was finished he walked over to Quark.

"Can't stay. But I'm man enough to admit when I am wrong."

"Okay," Quark said. "Is Dory coming?"

Tony didn't give any indication he'd heard. He walked back to the van, got in, and drove away; the space he left quickly occupied by a truck loaded with beer kegs. Quark hadn't anticipated that there would be alcohol. What could he do about it? What could he do about anything?

He walked amongst them, careful to avoid the halos of light; once again thinking he might not mind being a ghost. He rather enjoyed the feeling of being amongst people eating, and talking, telling their stories about Thayer (a surprising number of which relayed humorous situations, judging by the laughter) without being expected to participate until, distracted, he wandered into the glowing aureole of bonfire blaze, and someone shouted his name. The single voice was soon joined by others, as if he had just thrown a winning touchdown. "Quark! Quark! Quark!"

He stood rapt, like someone who had stumbled upon something sacred, until Brian came up from behind, slapped him on the back and handed him a paper plate filled with food that was hard to identify in the smoky dark.

Quark was squinting at the mysterious blobs when someone with a talent for whistling cracked through the noise. He tamped down his irritation with those who continued talking. After all, it sometimes took a while to realize what was happening. The occasional shush and hush popped from various dark corners until finally everyone was quiet.

A man Quark didn't recognize stood on a folding chair, holding a red plastic cup aloft in a statue-of-liberty stance. "We've come to remember our friend and neighbor," he said. "Most of us came from one funeral to here for what was supposed to be a launch, but it seems like someone had other ideas. I ain't saying I know that for a fact, ok? I think we all learned our lesson about waiting to see the evidence, right?"

The crowd murmured in agreement and Quark, confused, nodded too. It had been unfair of him to assume the boys had set the fire though, honestly, he still believed they had. He didn't need to indulge his suspicions, however. Let the sheriff work things out.

"I just wanna say we should, you know, try to remember Thayer tonight and forget all the other shit. A man deserves his own funeral. Even if his ship is gone, right? Maybe especially if his ship is gone."

The crowd raised red cups and cheered.

"So here's to Thayer, the saltiest sea captain Bellfairie ever knew. He'd just as soon spit at small talk, but if you went lookin' for a man who settled his accounts with God, you never had to go nowhere else." Quark observed several arms bob in anticipation of the toast's conclusion but the speaker continued. "I remember once—"

"Heya go, son." Healy offered Quark a cup filled near to the brim. "Don't worry. It's soda."

The self-appointed toastmaster boomed, "And he says, I wouldn't touch her even if I was the wind!"

Quark suspected it was a cruel punch line, though everyone laughed. He raised his arm and drank, both relieved and disappointed by the sharp sweet flavor.

He turned to thank his friend, but Healy had moved into the crowd and, while Quark struggled with cup in one hand and plate in the other, an older man stepped onto the chair.

He looked vaguely familiar, but many of the older generation of Bellfairians sported handlebar moustaches and the squint-eyed expressions of folks who had stared too long at the sun.

"Thayer was a private person. I ain't gonna say too much about it but I think most of you know he stayed with me for a while. They say you can measure a man by who he is when he thinks no one is looking and I am here to tell you he came to our house with nothing but the clothes on his back and a bible."

"Amen," someone called from the buffet table.

"That's right. Amen. So here's a toast. To the saint of Bellfairie!"

"To the saint of Bellfairie!" the crowd roared.

Quark gulped the coke as though it were alcohol and, in fact, it did burn.

Healy was the next one to take the chair, both hands raised as if about to give a benediction.

"Before things get too far along, I wanna take care of some business. I will be collecting car keys."

A groan rolled through the crowd.

"If you aren't able to drive safely when it comes time to leave, and you don't have a person with you who can, I'll take you home. Stop by the station in the morning and I'll bring you back for your vehicle. Heck, bring the kids with you. Show them where you didn't drive off the bluff so you'll be around for their next birthday."

"Jesus, Healy," someone said, but Quark could hear the sound of keys rattling.

After studying the plate he'd been given (featuring something that looked like sausage on a bun) Quark made the difficult decision to toss it into the trash. He did not like to be wasteful but he could not eat meat, either. He walked beside the buffet, worried someone might slap him on the back again. Once his plate was filled with a few pickles and a huge helping of the lasagna he had heard someone complain about, saying it was all vegetables, he slid back into the shadows.

As others stepped to the chair, Quark recognized his old classmates—the occasional name, or something familiar in a face—though they all seemed to know a Thayer who did all sorts of things the man Quark knew never would have.

This Thayer helped plant a garden. "We just moved here and didn't understand how nothing hardly grows, but he helped just the same. He looked so old, but could dig into that dry ground like a knife in soft butter. It's a good garden now, and we remember him in our dinner blessing every night and thank him for our carrots."

Thayer had, shockingly, gone through a "bread baking period" the mention of which incited knowing chuckles and nods. "I don't know of anyone who didn't get at least one loaf, and the lucky ones got it warm."

Me, Quark thought. *I never got any bread.*

This Thayer waved at someone's child every morning. "Now she watches for him at the upstairs window, and just today she told me she saw him out there. I don't know what she saw. Maybe it was a angel."

When someone tapped Quark's arm he was so startled he almost dropped his plate but he braced the flimsy paper with both hands and saved his supper, his relief somewhat tarnished by the laughter that rose from the arm-tapper who turned out to be the waitress whose name he could never remember.

"Sorry. Didn't mean to scare you." She jutted her chin towards the orator on the chair. "You wanna hear this?"

"It isn't necessary," Quark said. "Most of it isn't true."

She laughed again. Unsure what to do, Quark took a bite out of a pickle.

"Listen. I don't mean to bother you, but I just wanted to tell you not to worry about the others."

"Ok."

"I think, we all do...well, not all of us, but anyway, it's very big of you to accept our apology like you did. Some people take a while, that's all."

"Yes. Well."

"And it's gonna take time to get our heads around it."

Quark looked longingly at his plate.

"I mean, to think it was Henry Yarly, all along."

Quark sighed. How could he have forgotten such an important matter? Henry. Dead.

"I know, right? He seemed like such a nice man."

"He was," Quark said. "He was a very nice man."

She peered up at him, her eyes slit. "See," she said. "That's what I'm talking about. It's very decent of you to say that, considering how he was just gonna let everyone think it was you."

"Me?"

"To think what might have happened if he hadn't died with that girl's heart."

"What?"

"Oh my gosh, don't you know? I can't believe no one told you. Well, it just goes to show, don't it? When Yarly died—they think it was a stroke or something like that—he had Phoebe's necklace. They didn't find it right away cause it was in his pocket. You must a seen it, it was on all the posters."

Quark licked his salty lips. "I'm sure many of those were made. There would be no way to be certain it was hers."

"Well, yeah. I guess. But, I mean, why else would he have it? He used to kill people's pets and sacrifice them in the cove, you know."

"But that...." Quark knew he should explain how it was just a rumor started when he was a boy. He knew he should confess how he had found the locket, but when he looked at her face she beamed up at him in a way he'd never been looked at in his entire life, as if love were possible.

"Excuse me," he said.

"No, no," she said. "You go. What am I doing? I didn't

mean to monopolease you."

The bonfire blazed an impressive flame around which revelers stood drinking from plastic cups, red dots of cigarettes marking exclamation points of tales shared about Thayer, the sea, whales and witches. Quark set his plate near the corner of a table, to make it look as if he planned to return shortly (in case anyone was watching) then escaped to the back yard which was dark and pleasingly quiet, the revelers' noise muffled.

Relieved he'd repaired the back door, Quark locked it then crawled, like a criminal in his own house, to the front window where he came to his knees to spy on his guests. Most of them were raising libations by some internal rhythm with the person who stood on the chair at that moment, a precariously teetering silhouette. He slowly drew the curtains shut so the movement would not cause attention, though everyone was likely already too drunk to notice much.

He couldn't risk turning on a light, but the rooms shimmered with bonfire glow. He searched the kitchen, stepping gingerly over the broken glass to open cupboards and drawers, sorry he'd done such a good job of clearing everything out. All that he had left was a cup, a plate, one set of utensils, a few sharp knives, the lobster pot and, neatly tucked in the side of a low cupboard, the baking sheet.

The urn's lid, never properly closed, was easy to pry off. He poured the contents into the pan, obscuring the shadowed imprints of stars leftover from cookie baking. He was not dismayed by the larger pieces of bone; but still. There he was. The Old Man. Quark cupped his palms over his eyes to gain his bearings. "Is this a life?" he asked.

Careful not to block the dim light, his long finger traced spirals in the ash until he stopped and spiraled back. No piece was too small, and many were larger than expected though, when he had finished sorting, he still needed something long and straight for the hull.

He unstacked the boxes he'd set aside, pawing through debris until, in frustration, dumping their contents onto the floor, finding glue and scraps of wood, buttons and string; good enough, but not what he was looking for. It came to him all of a sudden to use the flute. Once that was settled, he cupped the soft ash in his hands to pour back into the urn, thinking should anyone see what he was doing, whatever forgiveness he'd been granted would be rescinded.

It was difficult to execute such fine work in such poor light. Yet, thinking of what the Old Man had done, Quark persisted. He wished he had better supplies, and briefly considered rummaging through the backyard debris, but worried someone would discover him and drag him back to the party. It wasn't really supposed to be a party though by the sound of things—the hoots and screams of laughter, the shatter of broken glass—that's what it had become.

He hoped the tremble in his hands was just a result of weariness, not the warning sign of something he couldn't control. He needed to be steady. Several times he paused to rub his palms together and stretch his fingers, a few times he got up to pace, turning his back on his creation so he could surprise himself with it, cautioning against despair when the reveal proved disappointing. He'd learned, long ago, how beauty rose from monstrosity.

First, they were the bones of the human Quark knew as his father, moved by ligaments and desire into the gait of the man who—long after having left the sea—walked as though on a ship in unsteady water. Next, they were the fire, and the ash from the fire, pulverized to sandy grains and remnants of mortality, a life Quark struggled to reassemble. First, it was a macabre construction of bone and bits of wood like a puppet collapsed in its strings but, as the noise outside morphed into the deep silence of early morning before the birds sing, it became a ship; far too small for any person, but large enough for dreams.

· 34 ·

W alking through the yard that morning with the urn clutched against his chest, he was reminded of a fairy tale where everyone is suddenly made to slumber. Brian and Tony lay on the ground which, Quark knew from experience, was cold and hard. A woman had fallen asleep on the buffet table, her face cradled in the pillow of her arms, her long untidy braid dipped into the potato salad. Several children—stuffed into a single sleeping bag someone had the foresight to bring— slept near the bonfire where wisps of smoke rose into the gray sky like tattered ghosts.

A dog appeared, wagging his tail so hard his haunches wiggled too. Quark leaned down to pet him and scratch behind his ears. "Who's a good boy?" he whispered. "Here's a good boy. Oh, yes, you are." The dog followed for a while, but turned back before Quark reached the end of the drive where Healy's car was positioned at an angle, making it difficult for any vehicle to leave. The sheriff was asleep in the front seat, snoring loud enough to be heard through the closed windows, a pile of keys spilled across his lap.

Quark stepped carefully, his heart pounding against the urn. The worst thing he had ever done was to allow an entire night to pass with all of Bellfairie believing gentle Yarly had killed the girl. It was unforgivable. Perhaps he was a monster, after all. Maybe everyone had seen that dark element in him when he couldn't. Maybe it had always been there, ignited by his birth.

He walked past Sushi's empty parking lot. There were no lights on, the closed sign hung on the glass door, the tavern beside it also dark, the post office too—expected on a Sunday—though odd that the flag still hung there, uncharacteristically forgotten.

Even far from the bonfire, the air smelled of wood-smoke and, though the sun had risen above the roofline, the sky remained somber. Quark shivered in the damp chill. The whole enterprise might have been unbearable had not, just then, his hat tumbled in front of him. He carefully set the urn on the ground to make chase though, once landed, the hat remained still. He picked it up and, pleased to note it was not damaged, set it firmly atop his head.

The place where Phoebe's body had been found was returned to its natural state of broken shells and clumps of seaweed; the only reminder of the tragedy, a small, frayed section of police tape wedged between rocks. He watched the waves, comforted by their rhythm, and the gulls spiraling overhead, inhaling deeply the briny stinky scent of Bellfairie. In spite of everything, no place would ever compare.

He took the path up the bluff, the way that had been blocked to him so recently; relieved he didn't have to negotiate a climb, surprised to find himself whistling as he rounded the final switchback, like a happy man on a pleasant stroll which, maybe he was.

After all, look at it. Look at the great sea, and the sky dotted with seagulls. Look at the beautiful morning!

He approached the cliff's edge with care. He wanted to do this right. Satisfied, he opened the urn's lid. What should he say? What could he say? He almost panicked until struck by inspiration.

"Grief is a ship without a captain," he sighed. "Oh, my captain."

He turned the urn over to shake out the ash which fell, just as he had hoped, in a swirl, towards the sea. When a gull called his name, he looked up, stunned by the bright light, closed his eyes, inhaled the perfume of oranges and thought—for just a moment—how perfect it all was, but the breeze strengthened to a gust that blew his hat off and, forgetting where he stood, he reached for it.

· $\mathcal{A}$CKNOWLEDGEMENTS ·

I would like to say a few words about rejection. The writer's life is filled with it, and understanding this only makes things a little easier. What has helped me maneuver this spiky course has been the support of others.

I will always remember that post Michael Kelly wrote about having just finished reading something he loved and, later, discovering it was my manuscript. The experience of being published by Undertow Publications, from Michael's smart editorial comments to Carolyn Macdonell-Kelly's expertise as a proof-reader, has been wonderful, the way I imagined publishing would be when I was young.

Thank you, also, to Courtney Kelly for the interior design and typesetting, which is a pleasure to behold. You made my book beautiful.

I am also deeply grateful to Tithi Luadthong for the art and Vince Haig for the design. If it wasn't my own book, I would have bought it for the cover alone.

Thank you, also, to the people who work for Rapido Books in Montreal where the book is printed. You have helped make this writer's dream come true.

When it came time for me to seek feedback for the draft of this story, I was very fortunate to know three readers in possession of the not-always-easy-to-maintain skill for critique without destruction. Thank you to Bill Bauerband, Andrew Marshall, and Sofia Samatar for your smart insight. You helped make it better.

Although this book is not long, it did take years to write and that time was filled with friends and family who offered their support with tea and chocolate, long walks, talks, road trips, coffee shop chats, quilt shows and much appreciated patience when I spoke of "the novel I can't really talk about because if I tell the story, I won't write the story, but I think I figured out this issue that confused me and now it might work though of course that creates this other problem." You were all so kind.

Thank you, also, to Rietje Marie Angkuw for the wonderful (and kind of terrible) taxidermy details. You made Quark come alive.

Finally, I want to thank you, the readers. I know your time is dear, and many factors might have called you away from Quark's story. Thank you so much for choosing to stay.

You might have noticed that my "few words" about rejection have become a few paragraphs about acceptance. This transformation happened because of all of you mentioned here. You made a difference in my life, and because of you I have learned that, while rejection is fleeting, stories last forever. (Find the ones who love.) Thank you.

· ABOUT THE AUTHOR ·

Before earning her MFA from Vermont College of Fine Arts, Mary Rickert worked as kindergarten teacher, coffee shop barista, Disneyland balloon vendor, and personnel assistant in Sequoia National Park. She is the winner of the Locus Award, Crawford Award, World Fantasy Award, and Shirley Jackson Award. She is a frequent contributor to *The Magazine of Fantasy and Science Fiction*. Her short story, "Funeral Birds" is included in the anthology, *When Things Get Dark: Stories Inspired by Shirley Jackson*, published by Titan Books in the Fall of 2021. Her novella, *Lucky Girl, How I Became a Horror Writer: A Krampus Story* will be published by Tor.com in the Fall of 2022.

CPSIA information can be obtained
at www.ICGtesting.com
Printed in the USA
LVHW091810290821
696395LV00010B/79/J